1969

THE NARRATIVE OF ARTHUR GORDON PYM

THE NARRATIVE OF

American Century Series

 HILL AND WANG · NEW YORK

ARTHUR GORDON PYM

OF NANTUCKET · Comprising The Details of a Mutiny and Atrocious Butchery on Board of the American Brig Grampus, on Her Way to the South Seas—with an Account of the Recapture of the Vessel by the Survivors; Their Shipwreck, and Subsequent Horrible Sufferings, from Famine; Their Deliverance by Means of the British Schooner Jane Guy; The Brief Cruise of this Latter Vessel in the Antarctic Ocean; Her Capture, and of the Massacre of Her Crew, among a Group of Islands in the 84th Parallel of the Southern Latitude, together with the Incredible Adventures and Discoveries still further South, to which that Distressing Calamity gave Rise ·

EDGAR ALLAN POE

INTRODUCTION · SIDNEY KAPLAN

FIRST AMERICAN CENTURY SERIES EDITION MAY 1960
SECOND PRINTING JANUARY 1966
THIRD PRINTING DECEMBER 1966

CONTENTS

INTRODUCTION

"They who dream by day are cognizant of many things which escape those who dream only by night. In their grey visions they obtain glimpses of eternity, and thrill, in awaking, to find that they have been upon the verge of the great secret. In snatches, they learn something of the wisdom which is of good, and more of the mere knowledge which is of evil. They penetrate, however rudderless or compassless, into the vast ocean of the 'light ineffable' and again, like the adventurers of the Nubian geographer, *'agressi sunt mare tenebrarum, quid in eo esset exploraturi.'*" (Poe's "Eleanora," 1842).

The Narrative of Arthur Gordon Pym of Nantucket, published in New York during the summer of 1838, is in some ways Poe's plainest and most enigmatic story. It is the only long piece of fiction he ever wrote. As poet, critic, and teller of tales grotesque and arabesque, he had already made his mark as a "magazinist," when, in March 1836, James Kirke Paulding, who had just completed a weighty defense of American slavery, suggested that it might be worth his while to "undertake a Tale in a couple of volumes." In June Harper's turned down his *Tales of the Folio Club,* advising that American readers preferred "a single and connected story" of book length. Poe went quickly to work. Six months later the first three chapters of *Pym* appeared in the *Southern Literary Messenger.*

While in England *Pym* had a small success as hoax (the London editor deleted its terminal white god), in the United States, although Horace Greeley was taken in, the book fell flat as a narrative of real or imagined adventure.* To its final allegorical riddle, as far as the record shows, everyone was either blind or indifferent. Almost totally ignored by the reviewers, *Pym* was slashed in Philadelphia by Burton's *Gentleman's Magazine:* whereas "the voyages of Gulliver were politically

---

* Alfred Russel Wallace, the evolutionist, wrote to a friend: ". . . the Antarctic part completely spoils it, being so completely impossible, with its abundant vegetation, mild climate, fruits and land animals near the *South Pole!* Also the fantastic idea of *striped water* so utterly unnecessary . . . it was these absurdities that disgusted me with the story."

satirical," Gordon Pym's travels were an "impudent attempt at humbugging the public." A few years later Poe himself, in a letter to Burton, referred to *Pym* as "a very silly book." When in 1849, the year Poe died, Rufus Griswold, his literary executor —in a double sense—grumbled that the concocter of *Pym* had tried to give it *Robinson Crusoe*'s "air of truth," but had succeeded only in compiling "as liberal an array of paining and revolting horrors as ever was invented by Ann Radcliffe," he was probably echoing the popular view. As one Nathaniel Ames, who, a few years before *Pym*, had authored his own *Nautical Reminiscences*, put it, every barber's clerk who crossed the ocean favored the public with his memoirs.

A century has passed and *Pym*'s stock is steadily rising on the critical exchange; it may almost be said that a minor "*Pym* boom," stemming in part from Baudelaire's early worship of Poe, is now under way on both sides of the water.

For Baudelaire, Poe had many virtues, but "more important than anything else" was that in "a century infatuated with itself," this "child of a nation more infatuated with itself than all others" had "imperturbably affirmed the natural wickedness . . . the primordial perversity of man." Against all the "misguided equalitarians," Poe had proclaimed that "we are all born marked for evil." A year after *Les Fleurs du Mal*, Baudelaire embarked on a labor of love—a translation of *Pym*—about which he wrote to Sainte-Beuve: "You, who so love profundities, why not investigate the profundities of Edgar Poe?" A "purely realistic," "purely human book," in which the "genius of the author" reveled in "terrible scenes and in amazing descriptions of islands and tribes not shown on any map"—so Baudelaire assessed the "admirable novel" on which he planned to write some "Last Notes on Edgar Poe" to preface his translation of *Pym*.

Twenty years later, in his *French Poets and Novelists*, the early Henry James, who had no use for Baudelaire's "lurid landscape and unclean furniture," took occasion to demur. For Americans, James thought, Baudelaire was "compromised by his having made himself the apostle of our own Edgar Poe." Although Poe, "much the greater charlatan of the two," was the "greater genius," to take him with "more than a certain degree of seriousness" was to "lack seriousness one's self." Indeed, an enthusiasm for Poe was the "mark of a decidedly primitive stage of reflection. . . ." As for *Pym*, although the problematical Prince Amerigo of *The Golden Bowl* could remember the tale as showing "what imagination Americans *could* have," a few years later, speaking in his own voice in the preface to *The Altar of the Dead*, James would finally see *Pym* as without "intrinsic values," its "imaginative effort wasted."

Years before, in Baltimore, at the public reburial of Poe's bones, another American writer, feeling "a strong impulse" to be present "in memory of Poe," had hobbled to the platform, but refused a eulogy. In social talk after the ceremony was over, old Walt Whitman reminisced about Poe.

> For a long while, and until lately, I had a distaste for Poe's writings. I wanted, and still want for poetry, the clear sun shining, and fresh air blowing—the strength and power of health, not of delirium, even amid the stormiest passions—with always the background of the eternal moralities. Non-complying with these requirements, Poe's genius has yet conquer'd a special recognition for itself, and I too have come to fully admit it, and appreciate it and him.

In a dream he had once had, Whitman went on, he saw a vessel at midnight in a storm.

> It was no great full-rigg'd ship, nor majestic steamer, steering firmly through the gale, but seem'd one of those superb little schooner yachts . . . flying uncontroll'd with torn sails and broken spars through the wild sleet and winds and waves of the night. On the deck was a slender, slight, beautiful figure, a dim man, apparently enjoying all the terror, the murk and the dislocation of which he was the center and the victim. That figure of my lurid dream might stand for Edgar Poe, his spirit, his fortunes, and his poems—themselves all lurid dreams.

Was Whitman evoking the figure of Gordon Pym at the helm of the dismasted *Ariel* (Shelley's boat), flying through the stormy Atlantic night? There is sorrow and tenderness in this image of Poe, but five years later, as he approached the grave, in a New Year's memorandum on "Edgar Poe's Significance" (beginning with the un-Whitmanian words: "In diagnosing this disease called humanity"), while crediting Poe with an "intense faculty for technical and abstract beauty," Whitman spoke his last word on the subject: "Almost without the first sign of moral principle, or of the concrete or its heroisms, or the simpler affections of the heart," Poe had "an incorrigible propensity toward nocturnal themes, a demoniac undertone behind every page—and, by final judgment probably belongs among the electric lights of imaginative literature, brilliant and dazzling, but with no heat."

Pym's critics of the past quarter century have followed Baudelaire—and Freud—rather than James or Whitman. For Marie Bonaparte, psychoanalyzing Poe under the cautious imprimatur of the master, "all the depth of the tale . . . resembles the latent content of the dream" *—a lead picked up by W. H. Auden, who, appraising *Pym* as one of the finest stories of "pure adventure" ever written, "an object lesson in the art," describes its protagonist as a "hero" who is "as purely passive as the I in dreams." More recently, Patrick J. Quinn has also found *Pym* to be a "profoundly oneiric drama," a masterly integration of "the theme of deception with the pattern of revolt"—a criminally neglected classic from which Melville cribbed, without acknowledgment, in writing *Moby Dick*. It is "the intense death-wish," declares Quinn, which is the defining characteristic in the personality of Pym: "With his great imagination of disaster, Poe integrates the evil of men and the evil inherent in the nature of the material universe. . . ." Nor does another full-dress study of Poe lower this high value placed on *Pym*. A "minor but hitherto unacknowledged masterpiece"; a "symbolic enactment of man's search for logic and meaning"; an excursion into "a philosophy of knowledge"—thus does Edward H. Davidson laud the tale of a "curiously 'American hero,' uprooted, and yet determined to know himself." In a "mindless, chaotic world the only final reality is the single perceiving self."

> The search for the self is the loss of the self; the quest is the annihilation. To remain in ignorance is to maintain one's primal being; to be curious is to be suicidal. The world of reality constantly undergoes this cyclic metamorphosis, from life to death and back to life again; but man, though a creature submissive to the natural laws around him, can go only through death or perhaps to . . . the silence of total annihilation.

* In his introduction to her *Edgar Poe: Étude Psychanalytique* (1933) Freud wrote: "Investigations such as this do not claim to explain creative genius, but they do reveal the factors which awaken it and the sort of subject matter it is destined to choose."

Finally, in Harry Levin's recent study of *The Power of Blackness*
—which has so far spoken the most revealing words about the
tale—Pym's voyage is a part of "The American Nightmare," a
"Journey to the End of the Night."

Whether these critics have spoken rightly or wrongly of *Pym*
as a whole, each reader will, of course, decide for himself. For
three quarters of its pages, Poe's tale is perhaps plain—and
brilliant—enough, and this preface will not offer a disquisition on
the sources that Poe ransacked to give verisimilitude to Pym's
travels. Let the warning suffice, as Bryant once said, to be on
guard against "profound researches into things already sufficiently clear": the realism of Pym's trials in queer settings may
be a gambit to establish a "willing suspension of disbelief" in
the allegory to which they lead. Nor may it be bad policy to
hearken to Poe's answer given to an editor who, shortly before
Pym appeared, questioned the nature of his effects in the ghoulish
horrors of "Berenice": "You ask me in what this nature consists?
In the ludicrous heightened into the grotesque; the fearful
colored into the horrible; the witty exaggerated into the bur-
lesque; the singular wrought out into the strange and mystical."

*   *   *

It is the concluding portion of *Pym*—the "Incredible Adventures
and Discoveries Still Farther South," as Poe put it on his title
page—which, it might be argued, was conceived by itself and
tacked on at the end, that to the ordinary reader more than
a century later may not be sufficiently clear. "There have been
critics who object to what they are pleased to call an inconclu-
sive ending," wrote Arthur Hobson Quinn in his "critical"
biography of Poe twenty years ago. "But when the details of
the voyages have long been forgotten, the picture of the
mysterious figure remains, stimulating the imagination of those
readers who do not have to have everything explained to them
in words of one syllable." Regrettably, there have been other
readers, less knowing, who have been puzzled by the great
white image—and the black ones that precede it—at the close
of *Pym*. Better perhaps to proceed, as did Sir Thomas Browne,
who was fascinated by Pliny's account of the waters of Siberis,
which blackened the skin and frizzed the hair of white men—

who held, "What songs the Syrens sang, or what name Achilles assumed when he hid himself among women, though puzzling questions, are not beyond *all* conjecture." The solver of the end of *Barnaby Rudge* liked nothing more than a cryptogram, either one to be fashioned or decoded, and it was Poe himself, even as he began work on *Pym*, who held that "unity of effect" was not "indispensable" in "the common novel," which is "admired for its detached passages, without reference to the work as a whole—or . . . any general design. . . ."

What then is the meaning of the "secret writing" that Edgar Allan Poe fashioned and Arthur Gordon Pym of Edgartown found in the black fauna and flora of his mysterious Antarctic, in the black teeth of his black devils, in the polar water like warm milk, in the portentous words carved on the skeleton of the earth?

During the fall of 1833 the *Baltimore Sunday Visiter* awarded a hundred dollars to Poe for his prize story, "MS Found in a Bottle." At the close of this brief tale, a familiar Poeian hero, haunted by "nervous restlessness," finds himself aboard a ghost ship, which, drawn by an "impetuous undertow," is hurtling south through "colossal waters" in the "blackness of eternal night." Although he is filled with horror, "yet a curiosity to penetrate the mysteries of these awful regions" triumphs over his despair. In his MS he notes: "It is evident that we are hurrying onward to some exciting knowledge—some never-to-be-imparted secret, whose attainment is destruction. Perhaps this current leads us to the southern pole itself." Unlike Pym, this hero does not live to impart his secret: the white ice "opens suddenly" and the ship descends madly into the maelstrom of the "supernatural sea." A note that Poe appended to the tale a few years later relates that he has since become "acquainted with the maps of Mercator, in which the ocean is represented as rushing, by four mouths into the (northern) Polar Gulf, to be absorbed into the bowels of the earth; the Pole itself being represented by a black rock, towering to a prodigious height." What was this "exciting knowledge," this "never-to-be-imparted secret"? Was Poe simply indulging his penchant for mystification?

The note on Mercator is suggestive of another spur to the

imagination that created *Pym*. When Poe was a boy of nine, an ex-captain of infantry, one John Cleves Symmes, living in St. Louis, addressed to "all the World" a printed circular which he sent to learned societies and distinguished persons in America and Europe. "I declare the earth is hollow and habitable within . . . that it is open at the poles"—so began the manifesto that called for "one hundred brave companions," to hop off from Siberia for the North Pole, where, Symmes guaranteed, they would find "a warm and rich land stocked with thrifty vegetables and animals, if not men. . . ." The theory of "Symmes' Hole"— so Thoreau refers to it in *Walden*—was bandied about in the United States for a quarter of a century; the captain's son, Americus Symmes, tells us that it was "overwhelmed with ridicule as the production of a distempered imagination, or the result of partial insanity"—a "fruitful source of jest with the newspapers."

But the captain did have his champions. One of these, a pseudonymous shipmaster, Adam Seaborn, two years after Symmes had called on Sir Humphry Davy and Baron Alexander von Humboldt as "protectors," responded in a rough-hewn Gulliverian novel whose title was *Symzonia: A Voyage of Discovery*. In two basic ways Seaborn edited Symmes: first, his voyage was to the Antarctic; second, at the South Pole, or rather within it, he found men. Indeed, Symzonia, as he called the place, was "the abode of a race perfect in their kind." What amazes Seaborn more than anything else about the appearance of his polar Utopians is that they are perfectly white: "the sootiest African does not differ more from us in darkness of skin and grossness of features than they did from me in fairness of complexion and delicacy of form." On the conscious level Seaborn was suggesting no racist theory of color; in one of his final comments on the excellence of the Symzonians he makes the point that they are as fond of nature's freely given fruits as Americans are of those which are "wrung from the bloody sweat of slavery." Yet is it surprising that for an American, citizen of a land in which slaves are black, heir of a Christian moral-chromatic tradition in which God is white and the devil black, that the Perfect should be White?

Did Poe know the the theory of Symmes? Without a doubt.

Was he familiar with Seaborn's book? Probably. The work of another who believed in "holes at the Poles" he knew well. In April 1836, Jeremiah N. Reynolds, who a year after *Pym* would tell a story about Mocha Dick (like the Ethiopian Albino, as white as wool), urged Congress, in the House of Representatives, to explore the South Seas. In the issue of the *Messenger* that carried the first installment of *Pym*, Poe praised Reynolds' speech; indeed, he had already borrowed material from it for the tale. Reynolds was a public defender of Symmes. Years later, as Poe gasped his last breath in Baltimore, in his delirium he called loudly for "Reynolds."

The black rock that marked the North Pole ("Rupes nigra et altissima," Mercator labels it on his map of 1569); the hollow earth of Captain Symmes; the Antarctic Utopia of the Perfect Whites; from these in part Poe constructed—what shall we call it?—his Pymzonia, his world of Black and White, whose "exciting knowledge," undisclosed in "MS Found in a Bottle," will lurk in *Pym*'s chiaroscuro arabesque. "While . . . I cannot but lament the most unfortunate and bloody events which immediately arose from my advice," the Nantucket lad reflects after persuading the captain of the *Jane Guy* to solve "the great problem" of the Antarctic, "I must still be allowed to feel some degree of gratification at having been instrumental, however remotely, in opening to the eye of science one of the most intensely exciting secrets which has ever engrossed its attention."

Critics during the past half century, answering Poe's challenge, have now and then tried to discover the exciting secret of Tsalal and the Great White Avenger. For Henry James, thinking of *Pym* as a ghost story like "The Turn of the Screw," there was, in a sense, no secret at all. The "would-be portentous climax . . . where the indispensable history is absent, where the phenomena evoked, the moving accidents, coming straight . . . are immediate and flat, and the attempt is all at the horrific in itself" is a failure because it stops short. Concluded James: "There *are* no connections; not only . . . in the sense of further statement, but of our own further relation to the elements, which hang in the void: whereby we see the effect lost, the imaginative effort wasted"—a judgment to which F. O. Matthiessen objected,

pointing out that in "the mirror that James has held up to
Poe's narrative he has not caught the horror of its unrelieved
light, which had been the main intention of Poe's climax." For
S. Foster Damon, "the nature of the horrible whiteness which
sucked Gordon Pym down to his death [!] at the South Pole"
was "the same whiteness which, incarnate as Moby Dick, rose
from the depths and all but killed Ishmael." Poe recorded "a
mental voyage which had brought him to the edge of the unknown and to a point where he must find a new set of terms
for what he tremblingly descried beyond that edge," thought
Edward Shanks. In *Pym*'s last pages "realism turns to frank
fantasy"; when Poe finished, "he was conscious that, after many
and cruel misfortunes, he was hurrying into an awful obscurity,
able only to guess at its nature, helpless to save himself from
it." Less vague was Marie Bonaparte, in whose ears the names
of Tsalal sounded "like infant babble," the direction of whose
analysis may perhaps be seen in a montage of passages:

> . . . the black island represents a *cloacal* phantasy . . . *white* has
> reactivated memory-traces of infantile masturbation in Nu-Nu's un-
> conscious . . . pleasurable but vague feelings akin to those produced
> by tickling (*"Tekeli-li"*) . . . a terror of white, of milk-colour, among
> the natives of Tsalal, whose incest-wishes and sexuality appear to
> have been . . . precociously suppressed . . . the strangers' appar-
> ently milk-stained teeth implying incestuous relations with the mother.

To whose vengeance did Poe finally refer? asked Bonaparte. The
vengeance of the father was her answer: "For he in fact it was,
who, in prehistoric times established his taboos on the isle of
Tsalal. His prohibitions . . . hold the black wicked sons from
approaching the *whiteness* of the mother. . . . Thus the epilogue
to this story ends with a concrete though sibylline reference to
the father, from whom every primitive taboo, and our own
morals derive."

Whereas James could make out "no connections" in Pym's
end, critics of the past decade find the meaning and virtue of
the allegory precisely in its "No Exit" quality. Patrick Quinn
sees *Pym*'s chief merit in its taking us "from the most pedestrian
of beginnings to the most weirdly impressive of endings"; we
are "simply confronted at the end with the enigma of Pym's
final vision. . . . Throughout the last vertiginous chapters of

his story Poe multiplies the details which culminate in this cryptic apparition. . . . But at no point does Poe stop to read these signs. They retain the clouded complexity of dream images, composite of dread and longing." Dread of whom? Longing for what? Another critic, Edward Davidson, tries to be more specific. The end of the book, he maintains, is "either absurd, monstrous, or mysterious; for all that happens is a voyage in an oversize canoe into a blinding white light near the South Pole—as if Poe had no more to say and thus stopped his narrative short; he even increased the insult by adding an appendix in small type in which he essayed to clarify certain confusions—and clarified nothing." At the end of his journey, concludes Davidson, Pym is sailing toward

> that whiteness whose center lies beyond first things and whose nexus may be the creative impulse of the universe itself. Faced with this bewildering and ultimate reduction, Poe can use only one word, an idea of whiteness, the negation of fact and shape. Melville's Ishmael came back from this side of the ultimate illumination; but Pym went all the way through and never returned. He, like the primal order of matter itself, was reduced to a blinding One—or chaos. There was no word or term which could further report the vision of nothing on the other side. Nothing was all; there was no other word for it but "white."

Would Poe, the supremely conscious artist of our literature, have agreed with any or all of these interpretations? Perhaps a reading of the allegory, less Freudian, less existentialist, less oneiric, will turn up a surer meaning at the level of Poe's intention.

Poe—whom Valéry called "that great literary engineer"—once described his literary method as follows: ". . . having conceived with deliberate care, a certain unique or single effect to be wrought out, [the writer] then invents such incidents—he then combines such events as may best aid him in establishing this preconceived effect." At another time, arguing against Coleridge, he would write: "The fancy as nearly creates as the imagination, and neither at all. Novel conceptions are merely unusual combinations. The mind of man can imagine nothing which does not really exist; if it could, it would create not only ideally but substantially as do the thoughts of God."

The world of Tsalal is black to its core—so quintessentially black that it is divided by "chasmal differences" from whiteness in any form. The sea around it is "extraordinarily dark"; its fauna and flora are black; its granite and soil, the very dust in the bowels of its earth are black. Although Pym discovers white arrow flints in the chasms, he stresses the fact that there are "no light-colored substances of any kind upon the island." All this is passing strange. Not so strange, however, are the natives of the black world: "They were about the ordinary stature of Europeans, but of a more muscular and brawny frame. Their complexion a jet black, with thick and long wooly hair." The black women have "personal beauty" and a grace "not to be found in civilized society." The lips of the blacks are "thick and clumsy"; they have black teeth. Years after *Pym*, Poe wrote to a friend:

> Monk Lewis once was asked how he came . . . to introduce *black* banditti, when, in the country where the scene was laid, black people were quite unknown. His answer was: "I introduced them because I truly anticipated that blacks would have more *effect* on my audience than whites—and if I had taken it into my head that, by making them sky-blue the effect would have been greater, why sky-blue they should have been."

But it is not to create an effect of the totally fantastic that the banditti of Tsalal are black. In all, they are not different, except for their teeth—from the pure Negroes of Georgia or Virginia. Pym notes that when they are amused they clap their hands, slap their thighs and breasts, and laugh uproariously—and their favorite food is tame fowl. The image is the American stereotype of the minstrel Negro. Indeed, as Levin points out, the first view of the island is of a ledge that reminds Pym of another South, for it bears a "strong resemblance to corded bales of cotton." *

The name of the black island is Tsalal, the Hebrew verb for "to be dark"; its principal town is Klock-Klock, the Hebrew for "to be black"; its chief is Too-Wit, the Hebrew for "to be dirty"; the king of the archipelago is Tsalemon, the Hebrew for "shady." Poe knew little Hebrew; while writing *Pym*, when he needed a few Hebrew words for a review of a volume of Arabian travels he applied for help to a learned professor of New York. Why then invent names in the Biblical tongue? Was it simply play —another experiment in cryptography, of which he was so

---

* I have ignored the "problem" of the half-breed Peters—as Poe does in a way. At one point Pym remarks: "We were the only living white men on the island."

fond? "As we can scarcely imagine a time when there did not exist a necessity, or at least a desire, of transmitting information from one individual to another in such a manner as to elude general comprehension," he would later note, "so we may well suppose the practice of writing in cipher to be of great antiquity." Perhaps there is a hint of such mystification in these names; even to those who knew no Hebrew, Tsalemon sounded vaguely like Solomon. And there was a special effect in the whole idea: here were blacks, very like the slaves one saw in Virginia, speaking the language of Genesis. Was there also a deeper theory of language at work in Poe's choice, one that abused Emerson to make a point? "Albert, in his Hebrew Dictionary," he remarks in one of the "Pinakidia" printed in the *Messenger* as he is grinding out *Pym*, "pretends to discover in each word, in its root, in its letters, and in the manner of pronouncing them, the reason of its signification. Leescher in his treatise *De causis Linguae Hebreae*, carries the matter even farther." So, in Tsalal, the word is the thing—both were created together; and the word is in the language of the creation itself. "*Nullus enim locus sine genio est,*" he would cite from Servius as epigraph for "The Island of the Fay," continuing: "I love, indeed, to regard the dark valleys, and the grey rocks, and the waters that silently smile . . . I love to regard these as themselves but the colossal members of one vast animate and sentient whole—a whole whose . . . thought is that of God. . . ." How avid he was to pursue this line of thought may be seen in another of the "Pinakidia," where, pondering the black water of Tsalal, he writes: "The stream flowing through the middle of the Valley of Jehoshaphat is called, in the Gospel of St. John, 'the brook of cedars.' In the Septuagint the word is κέδρον, darkness, from the Hebrew Kiddar, black. . . ."

And not only are the names of the Tsalalians Hebrew; they speak a kind of Hebrew too. When the white handkerchief on Captain Guy's oar stops the black paddlers, they exclaim "Anamoo-moo! Lama-Lama!"—"What ship is this? What evil sent by God upon the water?" At sight of anything white the blacks, in fear, scream "Tekeli-li!"—as do the white birds who scare Nu-Nu ("to deny") to death. "Mene, Mene, Tekel,

Upharsin"—so read the handwriting on the wall, the words
that Daniel deciphered. "Tekel"—"Thou art weighed in the
balances, and art found wanting"—so Daniel revealed God's
word to Belshazzar, who was slain that night. When Captain
Guy asks malevolent Too-Wit why his men do not carry arms,
he replies, "Mattee non we pa pa si"—"There is no need of arms
when all are brothers"—the last five words of which are an
obvious macaronic of Latin, English, and Italian, while the
first is the Hebrew for "spear." To be sure, the "great men"
among the Tsalalians are Wampoos or Yampoos—a blend of
Swift's Yahoos and the race of Ham, one of whose sons was
Cush, in the Septuagint called Ethiops—that same Ham whose
posterity (as Genesis has it) occupied the southernmost regions
of the world.

The black Tsalalians are very wicked folk. It is not merely
that Too-Wit is the cunning savage who howls and kills in the
potboilers of Pacific adventure common in Poe's day. Like
Seymour, the brutal black cook of the "realistic" part of the tale,
he is "in all respects" no less than a "perfect demon." The
Tsalalians, says Pym, are "the most barbarous, subtle, and
bloodthirsty wretches that ever contaminated" the earth; and
again, more forcefully, "the most wicked, hypocritical, vindictive,
bloodthirsty, and altogether fiendish race of men upon the face
of the globe." The Tsalalians, in fact, are the people of the
Prince of Darkness. They do not fear the "formidable" serpents
that cross their path; they pronounce the names of their land
and king with a "prolonged hissing sound." Tsalal is Hell; its
water is Styx, a kind of dirty, imperfect blood flowing thickly
"in distinct veins, each of a distinct hue," which do not commingle. The color of the water is "every possible shade of
purple"—"*persa*," as Dante, whom Poe knew in the Italian,
describes it in the *Inferno*.* "The phenomena of this water,"
notes Pym, "formed the first definite link in that vast chain
of apparent miracles with which I was destined to be at length
encircled."

* Why purple? In 1845, as the first of his "Fifty Suggestions" printed
in *Graham's Magazine*, Poe wrote: "Your 'blue' . . . is black in *issimo*—
'*nigrum nigrius nigro*'—like the matter from which Raymond Lully first
manufactured his alcohol."

Tsalal is in the Antarctic, yet its landscape (despite a touch of the cotton South) is a blend of the terrains of Ethiopia, Sinai, and ruined Babylon. Its patterned gorges, reminiscent of the church of Abba Libanos hewn from the Ethiopian rock, traces out an Ethiopian word. On the black granite walls are carved Arabic and Egyptian letters, reminiscent of the writing on the Sinaitic rocks that so tantalized travelers passing through Arabia Petraea—whose accounts Poe read and reviewed as he wrote *Pym*. In the literature of Ethiopian travel—articles in encyclopedias like the *Britannica* and Rees's popular work, books by David Bruce and Job Ludolphus, Pliny's *Natural History* (which he used as a source for "Siope—A Fable," a sketch of 1837)—he had read of the mountains that "assume wild and fantastic forms, with sides frequently abrupt and precipitous . . . only accessible by very difficult passes," and of the Blue River, with its rocky formations "from the first to the last degree of the geological table"; of the Niger, so called by the Hebrews and Greeks "because it runs with black and muddy water," preserving its blackness even as it flows through Lake Tzanicum, coursing "through wildernesses full of black dust . . . cliffs and craggy rocks . . . scorched and burnt," where Ethiopians lived —some of whom "looked upon the sun . . . as their implacable enemy." And it was in Ethiopia that the rulers were descended from Solomon (Tsalemon) and Sheba—the same Sheba who gave to Solomon a gift of that black wood from which Poe wrought the clubs of the Tsalalians. When, driven by hunger, Pym stumbles on a place of singular wildness, "strewn with huge tumuli apparently the wreck of some gigantic structures of art," there comes into his mind "the descriptions given by travellers of those dreary regions marking the site of degraded Babylon" —founded by the line of Ham.

The Enemy of the Tsalalians is Whiteness—whether it be the "Four Beasts in One" furred in the white ermine of judge-ship (a visitor, like the red-eyed polar bear from the World of Whiteness), an egg, an open book, a pan of flour—or white men, from whose complexion the blacks "recoil." * "Tekeli-li!"

---

* In a note hidden away in a scholarly journal, Mrs. Mozelle S. Allen points out that Poe, a reader of Voltaire, describes the white snow of

the blacks cry out in "mingled horror, rage, and intense curiosity" when the chromatic icon of their damnation appears before them. It is the eternal hostility of black and white, figured forth when, in the beginning, "God divided the light from the darkness" and "formed man of the dust of the ground"—in the case of the Tsalalians, whose name is their meaning, from the black dust, three or four inches deep, on the floor of the chasms. "Enter into the rock, and hide thee in the dust," warned Isaiah, "for fear of the Lord and for the glory of His majesty." Poe will write it all, on the day of creation, into the very foundations of the universe.

As Pym explores the "perfect regularity" of the winding chasms at the bottom of the black pit he can scarcely bring himself to believe that the formations are "the work of nature." How then were the chasms made? Apparently by a careful, miraculous cleavage of the bedrock, for there are "minor cavities in the sides . . . each cavity having a corresponding protuberance opposite." It is the "Tekel" written by God's hand in and on the walls of the chasms, in the letters of the ancients, that decrees the timeless antipathy. Contrary to some critical opinion, the word that Poe says is the Ethiopian verbal root "to be shady" is not a hoax but a real Ethiopian word, the equivalent, in fact, as Poe ascertained in the *Lexicon* of Gesenius (published in Boston as he wrote *Pym*) of the Hebrew "Tsalal." And the same is true of the Arabic "to be white" (Gesenius gives it as "to be dazzling white") and of the Egyptian (Coptic) "The Region of the South"—all chipped, wonderfully, in single pieces by a supernatural hand from the black stone.

But what of the "human form," whose arm outstretched toward the south, ordains the sacred division: "to be shady"—"to be white"? Among the "Pinakidia" in the *Messenger* of August 1836, Poe notes that in "the Dutch Vondel's tragedy, 'The Deliverance of the Children of Israel,' one of the principal

---

divinity that falls on Pym as a "fine white powder, resembling ashes," and that in Voltaire's *History of the Voyages of Scarmantado* the black pirate lectures to his white captive: "You have a long nose and we have a flat nose; your hair is wholly straight and our wool is curly; you have skin the color of ashes [*cendre*] and ours is the color of ebony; consequently, we ought, by the sacred laws of nature, to be enemies."

characters is the Divinity himself." In the closing line of *Pym* this Divinity speaks: "*I have graven it within the hills, and my vengeance upon the dust within the rock.*" These words *are* a hoax, but only in a certain sense are they meant to deceive.*

The passage, quoted, sounds as if it comes from Scripture; in fact, it was written by Poe, who, in another tale, would engrave on an African stone the words "DESOLATION" and "SILENCE." The "I" in the passage is the "human figure" of the chasm. Both are Jehovah, who also not rarely wrote his word on stone. "Ethiopia shall soon stretch out her hands unto God"—so the Abolitionists untiringly quoted from the sixty-eighth Psalm; but the outstretched hand of the god of the chasm reaches out to the region of whiteness. "And now we rushed into the embraces of the cataract, where a chasm threw itself open to receive us. But there arose in our pathway a shrouded human figure, very far larger in its proportions than any dweller among men. And the hue of the skin of the figure was of the perfect whiteness of the snow." Pym feels no terror; unlike the hero of "MS Found in a Bottle," who descends in horror into the whirlpool, Gordon Pym, lulled in warm milk (it was Jonathan Edwards who said that milk, by its "whiteness and purity," was the image of "the word of God from the breasts of the church"), rushes away from the Black into the embracing arms of the comforting White, while the gigantic white birds shriek God's "Tekel" and Nu-Nu dies of fright. Why should Pym feel terror at the sight of Daniel's "Ancient of Days, whose garment was as white as snow, and the hair of his head like pure wool"? Or of the white Divinity whose voice, in the Vision of St. John, is as "the sound of many waters" and whose raiment, as St. Matthew saw it, was "white as the light"? For Melville, in his discourse on "The Whiteness of the Whale," behind the whiteness of the Divine, there lurked "an elusive something in the innermost idea of this hue, which strikes more of panic to the soul than that redness which affrights

---

* Many years ago, George Edward Woodberry pointed out another manipulation by Poe of a similar kind: "A more curious instance of Poe's dealing with authorities is his note on *Israfel,* which originally read, 'And the angel Israfel, who has the sweetest voice of all God's creatures: *Koran.*' The passage referred to is not in the Koran, but in Sale's *Preliminary Discourses* (iv, 71). Poe derived it from the notes to Moore's Lalla Rookh. . . ." Bayard Taylor in his *Diversions of the Echo Club* describes an "intellectual diversion" of Poe's time: "spurious quotations from various languages."

in blood." In *Pym,* it is blackness that affrights; for Poe the Revelation (II:17) was of a different order: "To him that overcometh will I give to eat of the hidden manna, and will give him a white stone, and in the stone a new name written, which no man knoweth saving he that receiveth it." Is it worthy of note that it is on the opening day of spring that Pym is taken by the white god?

Revelation is precisely what Poe is after. To those who have viewed him as an archetypal Rimbaud or Sartre it may come as a surprise that Poe was a Biblical fundamentalist of the most orthodox sort. Reviewing John L. Stephens' *Arabia Petraea* while *Pym* was in the works, what he singled out of principal value was its "direct tendency to throw light upon the Book of Books": by "dissipating the obscurities and determining the exact sense of the Scriptures" it could serve as an "instrument in the downfall of unbelief." In a piece of hack-work on "Palaestine," written a few months before, he had already viewed the blasted deserts of the Holy Land as "the visible effects of divine displeasure." Now, speaking with approval of Alexander Keith's *Evidence of Prophecy,* which defended the "long continued slavery of the Africans" as the curse on Ham, Poe saw in Stephens' book an argument for "the *literalness* of the understanding of the Bible predictions as an *essential* feature of prophecy." But there was in the Bible no prophecy of black damnation clear enough for his needs, and he therefore wrote his own: "*I have graven it within the hills. . . .*"

Does all this seem improbable? Is it possible that the critic who flayed allegory as used by Hawthorne because the technique was too artificial and transparent could himself be guilty of the heresy of an allegorical and didactic damning of the Negro from the beginning to the end of time? I will not labor the point that Poe, as critic and fictionist, was no friend of the Negro. This is common knowledge, and as Levin puts it, "The 'constant tendency to the south' in . . . *Pym* takes on a special inflection, when we are mindful of the Southern self-consciousness of the author. His letters and articles reveal him as an unyielding upholder of slavery, and as no great admirer of the Negro. . . . In the troubled depths of Poe's unconscious, there must have been not only the fantasy of a lost heritage, but a

resentment and a racial phobia." Jupiter in "The Gold Bug,"
Toby in "The Journal of Julius Rodman," and others are indeed
"comic stereotypes"; and Poe is tickled by Jim Jumble, who, in
Bird's *Sheppard Lee*, declines to be set free, by the "old negro
wench Juana (all lips)" in Tucker's *George Balcombe*, by the
"shovel-footed negro who waddles across the stage" in Ingraham's
Lafitte. In the simians of such tales as "Rue Morgue," "Marie
Roget," "Hop-Frog," and "The System of Dr. Tarr and Professor
Fether," there is perhaps a hint, as Levin shows, of "an old Southern bugbear: the fear of exposing a mother or a sister to the suspected brutality of a darker race." When Lowell in his *Fable
for Critics* wrote,

> Here comes Poe with his raven, like Barnaby Rudge—
> Three-fifths of him genius, and two-fifths sheer fudge,

it was not so much these lines that inflamed Poe as those which
read,

> Forty fathers of freedom, of whom twenty bred
> Their sons for the rice swamps at so much a head,
> And their daughters for—faugh! . . .

Whether berating Lowell as "the Anacharsis Cloots of American
letters," the "most rabid of the Abolition fanatics," no book of
whose a Southerner would touch, or warning his readers against
"giving a second thought to the political philosophies of Madame
Trollope" or "the sturdy prejudices" of Fanny Kemble, or prais-
ing Thomas Hood's "squib against Abolitionism," Poe, as Killis
Campbell long ago pointed out, held blacks, at best, in "good-
natured contempt." And sometimes he is less than good-natured.
"In his character of Nigger Tom," he writes in his review of
Sheppard Lee, "[Bird] gives us some very excellent chapters
upon abolition and the exciting effects of incendiary pamphlets
and pictures, among our slaves in the South. This part of the
narrative closes with a spirited picture of a negro insurrection,
and with the hanging of Nigger Tom." Although T. O. Mabbott
tells us that Poe had a Negro friend, one Armistead Gordon (is
Arthur Gordon an echo?), who was "the most interesting man
he had ever talked to," it is young Edgar who writes to his
foster father: "You suffer me to be subjected to the whims of
caprice, not only of your white family, but the complete authority
of the blacks."

All this is clear enough. But what Poe was after went deeper than contempt for the Negro. "Great geniuses are parts of the times, they themselves are the times and possess a correspondent coloring," Melville once said. Poe, who has seemed to many an anguished man set apart from his times, was, in fact, a part of the "American Nightmare." In the decade of the founding of Garrison's *Liberator,* of Nat Turner's conspiracy, of the formation of the American Anti-Slavery Society, of Theodore Weld's *The Bible Against Slavery,* he felt called upon to say a more basic piece—to show that slavemasters "violated no law divine or human," to defend the pigmentocracy in his own way. Thus, in reviewing Paulding's *Slavery in the United States* the year before *Pym* came off the press, he enthusiastically seconds its scriptural-genetic defense of slavery, "the basis of all our institutions." The argument, as he sees it, rests on the "peculiar nature" of the Negro.

> Let us reason upon it as we may, there is certainly a power, in causes inscrutable to us, which works essential changes in the different races of animals. . . . The color of the negro no man can deny, and therefore it was but the other day, that they who will believe nothing they cannot account for, made this manifest fact an authority for denying the truth of holy writ. Then comes the opposite extreme— they are, like ourselves, the sons of Adam, and must therefore, have like passions and wants and feelings and tempers in all respects. *This, we deny. . . .*

"Our theory is a short one," he concludes. *"It was the will of God it should be so."*

Poe was an expert arranger of nature to suit his themes. In "The Domain of Arnheim," the hero sees his fulfillment as poet in the creation of a magnificent landscape: "A poet, having very unusual pecuniary resources, might, while retaining the necessary idea of art . . . so imbue his designs at once with extent and novelty of beauty, as to convey the sentiment of spiritual interference . . . nature in the sense of the handiwork of the angels that hover between man and God." Tsalal was no garden of beauty but the intent was the same. It was the "will of God" that Poe tried to present in his allegory of black and white at the end of *Pym.*

University of Massachusetts   SIDNEY KAPLAN
April 18, 1960

PREFACE

Upon my return to the United States a few months ago, after the extraordinary series of adventure in the South Seas and elsewhere, of which an account is given in the following pages, accident threw me into the society of several gentlemen in Richmond, Virginia, who felt deep interest in all matters relating to the regions I had visited, and who were constantly urging it upon me, as a duty, to give my narrative to the public. I had several reasons, however, for declining to do so, some of which were of a nature altogether private, and concern no person but myself; others not so much so. One consideration which deterred me was, that, having kept no journal during a greater portion of the time in which I was absent, I feared I should not be able to write, from mere memory, a statement so minute and connected as to have the *appearance* of that truth it would really possess, barring only the natural and unavoidable exaggeration to which all of us are prone when detailing events which have had powerful influence in exciting the imaginative faculties. Another reason was that the incidents to be narrated were of a nature so positively marvelous that, unsupported as my assertions must necessarily be (except by the evidence of a single individual, and he a half-breed Indian), I could only hope for belief among my family, and those of my friends who have had reason, through life, to put faith in my veracity—the probability being that the public at large would regard what I should put forth as merely an impudent and ingenious fiction. A distrust in my own abilities as a writer was, nevertheless, one of the principal causes which prevented me from complying with the suggestions of my advisers.

Among those gentlemen in Virginia who expressed the greatest interest in my statement, more particularly in regard to that

1

portion of it which related to the Antarctic Ocean, was Mr. Poe, lately editor of the Southern Literary Messenger, a monthly magazine, published by Mr. Thomas W. White, in the city of Richmond. He strongly advised me, among others, to prepare at once a full account of what I had seen and undergone, and trust to the shrewdness and common sense of the public—insisting, with great plausibility, that however roughly, as regards mere authorship, my book should be got up, its very uncouthness, if there were any, would give it all the better chance of being received as truth.

Notwithstanding this representation, I did not make up my mind to do as he suggested. He afterward proposed (finding that I would not stir in the matter) that I should allow him to draw up, in his own words, a narrative of the earlier portion of my adventures, from facts afforded by myself, publishing it in the Southern Messenger *under the garb of fiction*. To this, perceiving no objection, I consented, stipulating only that my real name should be retained. Two numbers of the pretended fiction appeared, consequently, in the Messenger for January and February (1837), and, in order that it might certainly be regarded as fiction, the name of Mr. Poe was affixed to the articles in the table of contents of the magazine.

The manner in which this *ruse* was received has induced me at length to undertake a regular compilation and publication of the adventures in question; for I found that, in spite of the air of fable which had been so ingeniously thrown around that portion of my statement which appeared in the Messenger (without altering or distorting a single fact), the public were still not at all disposed to receive it as fable, and several letters were sent to Mr. P.'s address, distinctly expressing a conviction to the contrary. I thence concluded that the facts of my narrative would prove of such a nature as to carry with them sufficient evidence of their own authenticity, and that I had consequently little to fear on the score of popular incredulity.

This *exposé* being made, it will be seen at once how much of what follows I claim to be my own writing; and it will also be understood that no fact is misrepresented in the first few pages which were written by Mr. Poe. Even to those readers who have not seen the Messenger, it will be unnecessary to point out where his portion ends and my own commences; the difference in point of style will be readily perceived.

A. G. PYM

New York, July, 1838.

CHAPTER 1

MY NAME is Arthur Gordon Pym. My father was a respectable trader in sea stores at Nantucket, where I was born. My maternal grandfather was an attorney in good practice. He was fortunate in everything, and had speculated very successfully in stocks of the Edgarton New-Bank, as it was formerly called. By these and other means he had managed to lay by a tolerable sum of money. He was more attached to myself, I believe, than to any other person in the world, and I expected to inherit the most of his property at his death. He sent me, at six years of age, to the school of old Mr. Ricketts, a gentleman with only one arm, and of eccentric manners—he is well known to almost every person who has visited New Bedford. I stayed at his school until I was sixteen, when I left him for Mr. E. Ronald's academy on the hill. Here I became intimate with the son of Mr. Barnard, a sea captain, who generally sailed in the employ of Lloyd and Vredenburgh—Mr. Barnard is also very well known in New Bedford, and has many relations, I am certain, in Edgarton. His son was named Augustus, and he was nearly two years older than myself. He had been on a whaling voyage with his father in the *John Donaldson*, and was always talking to me of his adventures in the South Pacific Ocean. I used frequently to go home with him, and remain all day, and sometimes all night. We occupied the same bed, and he would be sure to keep me awake until almost light, telling me stories of the natives of the Island of Tinian, and other places he had visited in his travels. At last I could not help being interested in what he said, and by degrees I felt the greatest desire to go to sea. I owned a sailboat called the *Ariel*, and worth about seventy-five dollars. She had a half deck or cuddy, and was rigged sloop-fashion—I forget her tonnage, but she would hold ten persons without much crowding. In this boat we were in the habit of going on some of the maddest freaks in the world; and, when I now think of them, it appears to me a thousand wonders that I am alive today.

I will relate one of these adventures by way of introduction to a longer and more momentous narrative. One night there was a party at Mr. Barnard's, and both Augustus and myself were not a little intoxicated towards the close of it. As usual, in such cases, I took part of his bed in preference to going home. He went to sleep, as I thought, very quietly (it being near one when the party broke up), and without saying a word on his favorite topic. It might have been half an hour from the time of our getting in bed, and I was just about falling into a doze, when he suddenly started up, and swore with a terrible oath that he would not go to sleep for any Arthur Pym in Christendom, when there was so glorious a breeze from the southwest. I never was so astonished in my life, not knowing what he intended, and thinking that the wines and liquors he had drunk had set him entirely beside himself. He proceeded to talk very coolly, however, saying he knew that I supposed him intoxicated, but that he was never more sober in his life. He was only tired, he added, of lying in bed on such a fine night like a dog, and was determined to get up and dress, and go out on a frolic with the boat. I can hardly tell what possessed me, but the words were no sooner out of his mouth than I felt a thrill of the greatest excitement and pleasure, and thought his mad idea one of the most delightful and most reasonable things in the world. It was blowing almost a gale, and the weather was very cold—it being late in October. I sprang out of bed, nevertheless, in a kind of ecstasy, and told him I was quite as brave as himself, and quite as tired as he was of lying in bed like a dog, and quite as ready for any fun or frolic as any Augustus Barnard in Nantucket.

We lost no time in getting on our clothes and hurrying down to the boat. She was lying at the old decayed wharf by the lumberyard of Pankey & Co., and almost thumping her sides out against the rough logs. Augustus got into her and bailed her, for she was nearly half full of water. This being done, we hoisted jib and mainsail, kept full, and started boldly out to sea.

The wind, as I before said, blew freshly from the southwest. The night was very clear and cold. Augustus had taken the helm, and I stationed myself by the mast, on the deck of the cuddy. We flew along at a great rate—neither of us having said a word since casting loose from the wharf. I now asked my companion what course he intended to steer, and what time he thought it probable we should get back. He whistled for a few minutes, and then said crustily, "I am going to sea—*you* may go home if you think proper." Turning my eyes upon him, I perceived at once that, in spite of his assumed *nonchalance,* he was greatly agitated. I could see him distinctly by the light of the moon—his face was paler than any marble, and his hand shook so excessively that he could scarcely retain hold of the tiller. I found that something had gone wrong, and became seriously alarmed. At this period I knew little about the management of a boat, and was now depending entirely upon the nautical skill of my friend. The wind, too, had suddenly increased, and we were fast getting out of the lee of the land—still I was ashamed to betray any trepidation, and for almost half an hour maintained a resolute silence. I could stand it no longer, however, and spoke to Augustus about the propriety of turning back. As before, it was nearly a minute before he made answer, or took any notice of my suggestion. "By-and-by," said he at length—"time enough—home by-and-by." I had expected such a reply, but there was something in the tone of these words which filled me with an indescribable feeling of dread. I again looked at the speaker attentively. His lips were perfectly livid, and his knees shook so violently together that he seemed scarcely able to stand. "For God's sake, Augustus," I screamed, now heartily frightened, "what ails you?—what is the matter?—what *are* you going to do?" "Matter!" he stammered, in the greatest apparent surprise, letting go the tiller at the same moment, and falling forward into the bottom of the boat—"matter —why, nothing is the—matter—going home—d—d—don't you see?" The whole truth now flashed upon me. I flew to him and raised him up. He was drunk—beastly drunk—he could no longer either stand, speak, or see. His eyes were perfectly glazed; and as I let him go in the extremity of my despair, he rolled like a mere log into the bilge water from which I had lifted him. It was evident that, during the evening, he had drunk far more than I suspected, and that his conduct in bed had been the result of a highly concentrated state of intoxication—a state which, like madness, frequently enables the victim to imitate the out·ward demeanor of one in perfect possession of his senses. The coolness of the night air, however, had had its usual effect—the mental energy began to yield before its influence—and the confused perception which he no doubt then had of his perilous situation had assisted in hastening the catastrophe. He was now thoroughly insensible, and there was no probability that he would be otherwise for many hours.

It is hardly possible to conceive the extremity of my terror. The fumes of the wine lately taken had evaporated, leaving me doubly timid and irresolute. I knew that I was altogether incapable of managing the boat, and that a fierce wind and strong ebb tide were hurrying us to destruction. A storm was evidently gathering behind us; we had neither compass nor provisions; and it was clear that, if we held our present course, we should be out of sight of land before daybreak. These thoughts, with a crowd of others equally fearful, flashed through my mind with a bewildering rapidity, and for some moments paralyzed me beyond the possibility of making any exertion. The boat was going through the water at a terrible rate—full before the wind—no reef in either jib or mainsail—running her bows completely under the foam. It was a thousand wonders she did not broach to— Augustus having let go the tiller, as I said before, and I being too much agitated to think of taking it myself. By good luck, however, she kept steady, and gradually I recovered some degree of presence of mind. Still the wind was increasing fearfully; and whenever we rose from a plunge forward, the sea behind fell combing over our counter, and deluged us with water. I was so utterly benumbed, too, in every limb, as to be nearly unconscious of sensation. At length I summoned up the resolution of despair, and rushing to the mainsail, let it go by the run. As might have been expected, it flew over the bows, and, getting drenched with water, carried away the mast short off by the board. This latter accident alone saved me from instant destruction. Under the jib only, I now boomed along before the wind, shipping heavy seas occasionally over the counter, but relieved from the terror of immediate death. I took the helm, and breathed with greater freedom, as I found that there yet remained to us a chance of ultimate escape. Augustus still lay senseless in the bottom of the boat; and as there was imminent danger of his drowning (the water being nearly a foot deep just where he fell), I contrived to raise him partially up, and keep him in a sitting position, by passing a rope round his waist, and lashing it to a ringbolt in the deck of the cuddy. Having thus arranged everything as well as I could in my chilled and agitated condition, I recommended myself to God, and made up my mind to bear whatever might happen with all the fortitude in my power.

Hardly had I come to this resolution when, suddenly, a loud and long scream or yell, as if from the throats of a thousand demons, seemed to pervade the whole atmosphere around and above the boat. Never while I live shall I forget the intense agony of terror I experienced at that moment. My hair stood erect on my head—I felt the blood congealing in my veins—my heart ceased utterly to beat, and without having once raised my eyes to learn the source of my alarm, I tumbled headlong and insensible upon the body of my fallen companion.

I found myself, upon reviving, in the cabin of a large whaling-ship (the *Penguin*) bound to Nantucket. Several persons were standing over me, and Augustus, paler than death, was busily occupied in chafing my hands. Upon seeing me open my eyes, his exclamations of gratitude and joy excited alternate laughter and tears from the rough-looking personages who were present. The mystery of our being in existence was now soon explained. We had been run down by the whaling-ship, which was close hauled, beating up to Nantucket with every sail she could venture to set, and consequently running almost at right angles to our own course. Several men were on the lookout forward, but did not perceive our boat until it was an impossibility to avoid coming in contact—their shouts of warning upon seeing us were what so terribly alarmed me. The huge ship, I was told, rode immediately over us with as much ease as our own little vessel would have passed over a feather, and without the least perceptible impediment to her progress. Not a scream arose from the deck of the victim—there was a slight grating sound to be heard mingling with the roar of wind and water, as the frail bark which was swallowed up rubbed for a moment along the keel of her destroyer —but this was all. Thinking our boat (which it will be remembered was dismasted) some mere shell cut adrift as useless, the captain (Captain E. T. V. Block of New London) was for proceeding on his course without troubling himself further about the matter. Luckily, there were two of the lookout who swore positively to having seen some person at our helm, and represented the possibility of yet saving him. A discussion ensued, when Block grew angry, and, after awhile, said that "it was no business of his to be eternally watching for eggshells; that the ship should *not* put about for any such nonsense; and if there was a man run down, it was nobody's fault but his own—he might drown and be d—d," or some language to that effect. Henderson, the first mate, now took the matter up, being justly indignant, as well as the whole ship's crew, at a speech evincing so base a degree of heartless atrocity. He spoke plainly, seeing himself upheld by the men, told the captain he considered him a fit subject for the gallows, and that he would disobey his orders if he were hanged for it the moment he set his foot on shore. He strode aft, jostling Block (who turned very pale and made no answer) on one side, and seizing the helm, gave the word, in a firm voice, *Hard-a-lee!* The men flew to their posts, and the ship went cleverly about. All this had occupied nearly five minutes, and it was supposed to be hardly within the bounds of possibility that any individual could be saved—allowing any to have been on board the boat. Yet, as the reader has seen, both Augustus and myself were rescued; and our deliverance seemed to have been brought about by two of those almost inconceivable pieces of good fortune which are attributed by the wise and pious to the special interference of Providence.

While the ship was yet in stays, the mate lowered the jolly boat and jumped into her with the very two men, I believe, who spoke up as having seen me at the helm. They had just left the lee of the vessel (the moon still shining brightly) when she made a long and heavy roll to windward, and Henderson, at the same moment, starting up in his seat, bawled out to his crew to *back water*. He would say nothing else—repeating his cry impatiently, *back water! back water!* The men put back as speedily as possible; but by this time the ship had gone round, and gotten fully under headway, although all hands on board were making great exertions to take in sail. In despite of the danger of the attempt, the mate clung to the main-chains as soon as they came within his reach. Another huge lurch now brought the starboard side of the vessel out of water nearly as far as her keel, when the cause of his anxiety was rendered obvious enough. The body of a man was seen to be affixed in the most singular manner to the smooth and shining bottom (the *Penguin* was coppered and copper-fastened), and beating violently against it with every movement of the hull. After several ineffectual efforts, made during the lurches of the ship, and at the imminent risk of swamping the boat, I was finally disengaged from my perilous situation and taken on board—for the body proved to be my own. It appeared that one of the timber bolts having started and broken a passage through the copper, it had arrested my progress as I passed under the ship, and fastened me in so extraordinary a manner to her bottom. The head of the bolt had made its way through the collar of the green baize jacket I had on, and through the back part of my neck, forcing itself out between two sinews and just below the right ear. I was immediately put to bed—although life seemed to be totally extinct. There was no surgeon on board. The captain, however, treated me with every attention—to make

amends, I presume, in the eyes of his crew, for his atrocious behavior in the previous portion of the adventure.

In the meantime, Henderson had again put off from the ship,
although the wind was now blowing almost a hurricane. He had
not been gone many minutes when he fell in with some fragments
of our boat, and shortly afterward one of the men with him
asserted that he could distinguish a cry for help at intervals amid
the roaring of the tempest. This induced the hardy seamen to
persevere in their search for more than half an hour, although
repeated signals to return were made them by Captain Block,
and although every moment on the water in so frail a boat was
fraught to them with the most imminent and deadly peril. Indeed,
it is nearly impossible to conceive how the small jolly they were
in could have escaped destruction for a single instant. She was
built, however, for the whaling service, and was fitted, as I have
since had reason to believe, with air boxes, in the manner of some
lifeboats used on the coast of Wales.

After searching in vain for about the period of time just
mentioned, it was determined to get back to the ship. They had
scarcely made this resolve when a feeble cry arose from a dark
object that floated rapidly by. They pursued and soon overtook
it. It proved to be the entire deck of the *Ariel*'s cuddy. Augustus
was struggling near it, apparently in the last agonies. Upon
getting hold of him it was found that he was attached by a rope
to the floating timber. This rope, it will be remembered, I had
myself tied round his waist, and made fast to a ringbolt, for the
purpose of keeping him in an upright position, and my so doing,
it appeared, had been ultimately the means of preserving his
life. The *Ariel* was slightly put together, and in going down her
frame naturally went to pieces; the deck of the cuddy, as might
be expected, was lifted, by the force of the water rushing in,
entirely from the main timbers, and floated (with other fragments, no doubt) to the surface—Augustus was buoyed up with
it, and thus escaped a terrible death.

It was more than an hour after being taken on board the
Penguin before he could give any account of himself, or be made

to comprehend the nature of the accident which had befallen our
boat. At length he became thoroughly aroused, and spoke much
of his sensations while in the water. Upon his first attaining any
degree of consciousness, he found himself beneath the surface,
whirling round and round with inconceivable rapidity, and with
a rope wrapped in three or four folds tightly about his neck. In an
instant afterward he felt himself going rapidly upward, when, his
head striking violently against a hard substance, he again relapsed
into insensibility. Upon once more reviving he was in fuller
possession of his reason—this was still, however, in the greatest
degree clouded and confused. He now knew that some accident
had occurred, and that he was in the water, although his mouth
was above the surface, and he could breathe with some freedom.
Possibly, at this period, the deck was drifting rapidly before the
wind, and drawing him after it, as he floated upon his back. Of
course, as long as he could have retained this position, it would
have been nearly impossible that he should be drowned. Presently a surge threw him directly athwart the deck; and this post
he endeavored to maintain, screaming at intervals for help. Just
before he was discovered by Mr. Henderson, he had been obliged
to relax his hold through exhaustion, and, falling into the sea,
had given himself up for lost. During the whole period of his
struggles he had not the faintest recollection of the *Ariel*, nor
of any matters in connection with the source of his disaster. A
vague feeling of terror and despair had taken entire possession of
his faculties. When he was finally picked up, every power of his
mind had failed him; and, as before said, it was nearly an hour
after getting on board the *Penguin* before he became fully aware
of his condition. In regard to myself—I was resuscitated from a
state bordering very nearly upon death (and after every other
means had been tried in vain for three hours and a half) by
vigorous friction with flannels bathed in hot oil—a proceeding
suggested by Augustus. The wound in my neck, although of an
ugly appearance, proved of little real consequence, and I soon
recovered from its effects.

The *Penguin* got into port about nine o'clock in the morning, after encountering one of the severest gales ever experienced off Nantucket. Both Augustus and myself managed to appear at Mr. Barnard's in time for breakfast—which, luckily, was somewhat late, owing to the party over night. I suppose all at the table were too much fatigued themselves to notice our jaded appearance—of course, it would not have borne a very rigid scrutiny. School-boys, however, can accomplish wonders in the way of deception, and I verily believe not one of our friends in Nantucket had the slightest suspicion that the terrible story told by some sailors in town of their having run down a vessel at sea and drowned some thirty or forty poor devils, had reference either to the *Ariel*, my companion, or myself. We two have since very frequently talked the matter over—but never without a shudder. In one of our conversations Augustus frankly confessed to me, that in his whole life he had at no time experienced so excruciating a sense of dismay, as when on board our little boat he first discovered the extent of his intoxication, and felt himself sinking beneath its influence.

CHAPTER 2

IN NO AFFAIRS of mere prejudice, pro or con, do we deduce inferences with entire certainty even from the most simple data. It might be supposed that a catastrophe such as I have just related would have effectually cooled my incipient passion for the sea. On the contrary, I never experienced a more ardent longing for the wild adventures incident to the life of a navigator than within a week after our miraculous deliverance. This short period proved amply long enough to erase from my memory the shadows, and bring out in vivid light all the pleasurably exciting points of color, all the picturesqueness of the late perilous accident. My conversations with Augustus grew daily more frequent and more intensely full of interest. He had a manner of relating his stories of the ocean (more than one half of which I now suspect to have been sheer fabrications) well adapted to have weight with one of my enthusiastic temperament, and somewhat gloomy although glowing imagination. It is strange, too, that he most strongly enlisted my feelings in behalf of the life of a seaman, when he depicted his more terrible moments of suffering and despair. For the bright side of the painting I had a limited sympathy. My visions were of shipwreck and famine; of death or captivity among barbarian hordes; of a lifetime dragged out in sorrow and tears, upon some gray and desolate rock, in an ocean unapproachable and unknown. Such visions or desires—for they amounted to desires—are common, I have since been assured, to the whole numerous race of the melancholy among men—at the time of which I speak I regarded them only as prophetic glimpses of a destiny which I felt myself in a measure bound to fulfill. Augustus thoroughly entered into my state of mind. It is probable, indeed, that our intimate communion had resulted in a partial interchange of character.

About eighteen months after the period of the *Ariel's* disaster, the firm of Lloyd and Vredenburgh (a house connected in some manner with the Messieurs Enderby, I believe, of Liverpool) were engaged in repairing and fitting out the brig *Grampus* for a whaling voyage. She was an old hulk, and scarcely seaworthy when all was done to her that could be done. I hardly know why she was chosen in preference to other good vessels belonging to the same owners—but so it was. Mr. Barnard was appointed to command her, and Augustus was going with him. While the brig was getting ready, he frequently urged upon me the excellency of the opportunity now offered for indulging my desire of travel. He found me by no means an unwilling listener— yet the matter could not be so easily arranged. My father made no direct opposition; but my mother went into hysterics at the bare mention of the design; and, more than all, my grandfather, from whom I expected much, vowed to cut me off with a shilling if I should ever broach the subject to him again. These difficulties, however, so far from abating my desire, only added fuel to the flame. I determined to go at all hazards; and, having made known my intention to Augustus, we set about arranging a plan by which it might be accomplished. In the meantime I forbore speaking to any of my relations in regard to the voyage, and, as I busied myself ostensibly with my usual studies, it was supposed that I had abandoned the design. I have since frequently examined my conduct on this occasion with sentiments of displeasure as well as of surprise. The intense hypocrisy I made use of for the furtherance of my project—an hypocrisy pervading every word and action of my life for so long a period of time— could only have been rendered tolerable to myself by the wild and burning expectation with which I looked forward to the fulfillment of my long-cherished visions of travel.

In pursuance of my scheme of deception, I was necessarily obliged to leave much to the management of Augustus, who was employed for the greater part of every day on board the *Grampus*, attending to some arrangements for his father in the cabin and cabin hold. At night, however, we were sure to have a conference and talk over our hopes. After nearly a month passed in this manner, without our hitting upon any plan we thought likely to succeed, he told me at last that he had determined upon everything necessary. I had a relation living in New Bedford, a Mr. Ross, at whose house I was in the habit of spending occasionally two or three weeks at a time. The brig was to sail about the middle of June (June, 1827), and it was agreed that, a day or two before her putting to sea, my father was to receive a note, as usual, from Mr. Ross, asking me to come over and spend a fortnight with Robert and Emmet (his sons). Augustus charged himself with the inditing of this note and getting it delivered. Having set out, as supposed, for New Bedford, I was then to report myself to my companion, who would contrive a hiding place for me in the *Grampus*. This hiding place, he assured me, would be rendered sufficiently comfortable for a residence of many days, during which I was not to make my appearance. When the brig had proceeded so far on her course as to make any turning back a matter out of question, I should then, he said, be formally installed in all the comforts of the cabin; and as to his father, he would only laugh heartily at the joke. Vessels enough would be met with by which a letter might be sent home explaining the adventure to my parents.

The middle of June at length arrived, and everything had been matured. The note was written and delivered, and on a Monday morning I left the house for the New Bedford packet, as supposed. I went, however, straight to Augustus, who was waiting for me at the corner of a street. It had been our original plan that I should keep out of the way until dark, and then slip on board the brig; but, as there was now a thick fog in our favor, it was agreed to lose no time in secreting me. Augustus led the way to the wharf, and I followed at a little distance, enveloped in a thick seaman's cloak, which he had brought with him, so that my person might not be easily recognized. Just as we turned the second corner, after passing Mr. Edmunds' well, who should appear, standing right in front of me, and looking me full in the face, but old Mr. Peterson, my grandfather. "Why, bless my soul, Gordon," said he, after a long pause, "why, why—*whose* dirty cloak is that you have on?" "Sir!" I replied, assuming, as well as I could, in the exigency of the moment, an air of offended surprise, and talking in the gruffest of all imaginable tones—"sir! you are a sum'mat mistaken; my name, in the first place, bee'nt nothing at all like Goddin, and I'd want you for to know better, you black-guard, than to call my new obercoat a darty one." For my life I could hardly refrain from screaming with laughter at the odd manner in which the old gentleman received this handsome rebuke. He started back two or three steps, turned first pale and then excessively red, threw up his spectacles, then putting them down, ran full tilt at me, with his umbrella uplifted. He stopped short, however, in his career, as if struck with a sudden recollec-tion; and presently, turning round, hobbled off down the street, shaking all the while with rage, and muttering between his teeth, "Won't do—new glasses—thought it was Gordon—d—d good-for-nothing salt water Long Tom."

After this narrow escape we proceeded with greater caution, and arrived at our point of destination in safety. There were only one or two of the hands on board, and these were busy forward, doing something to the forecastle combings. Captain Barnard, we knew very well, was engaged at Lloyd and Vredenburgh's, and would remain there until late in the evening, so we had little to apprehend on his account. Augustus went first up the vessel's side, and in a short while I followed him, without being noticed by the men at work. We proceeded at once into the cabin, and found no person there. It was fitted up in the most comfortable style—a thing somewhat unusual in a whaling vessel. There were four very excellent staterooms, with wide and convenient berths. There was also a large stove, I took notice, and a remarkably thick and valuable carpet covering the floor of both the cabin and staterooms. The ceiling was full seven feet high, and, in short, everything appeared of a more roomy and agreeable nature than I had anticipated. Augustus, however, would allow me but little time for observation, insisting upon the necessity of my concealing myself as soon as possible. He led the way into his own state-room, which was on the starboard side of the brig, and next to the bulkheads. Upon entering, he closed the door and bolted it. I thought I had never seen a nicer little room than the one in which I now found myself. It was about ten feet long, and had only one berth, which, as I said before, was wide and convenient. In that portion of the closet nearest the bulkheads there was a space of four feet square, containing a table, a chair, and a set of hang-ing shelves full of books, chiefly books of voyages and travels. There were many other little comforts in the room, among which I ought not to forget a kind of safe or refrigerator, in which Augus-tus pointed out to me a host of delicacies, both in the eating and drinking department.

He now pressed with his knuckles upon a certain spot of the carpet in one corner of the space just mentioned, letting me know that a portion of the flooring, about sixteen inches square, had been neatly cut out and again adjusted. As he pressed, this portion rose up at one end sufficiently to allow the passage of his finger beneath. In this manner he raised the mouth of the trap (to which the carpet was still fastened by tacks), and I found that it led into the afterhold. He next lit a small taper by means of a phos-phorus match, and, placing the light in a dark lantern, descended with it through the opening, bidding me follow. I did so, and he then pulled the cover upon the hole, by means of a nail driven into the underside—the carpet, of course, resuming its original position on the floor of the stateroom, and all traces of the aperture being concealed.

The taper gave out so feeble a ray that it was with the greatest difficulty I could grope my way through the confused mass of lumber among which I now found myself. By degrees, however, my eyes became accustomed to the gloom, and I proceeded with less trouble, holding on to the skirts of my friend's coat. He brought me, at length, after creeping and winding through innumerable narrow passages, to an ironbound box, such as is used sometimes for packing fine earthenware. It was nearly four

feet high, and full six long, but very narrow. Two large empty
oil casks lay on the top of it, and above these, again, a vast quantity of straw matting, piled up as high as the floor of the cabin. In
every other direction around was wedged as closely as possible,
even up to the ceiling, a complete chaos of almost every species
of ship-furniture, together with a heterogeneous medley of crates,
hampers, barrels, and bales, so that it seemed a matter no less
than miraculous that we had discovered any passage at all to the
box. I afterward found that Augustus had purposely arranged
the stowage in this hold with a view to affording me a thorough
concealment, having had only one assistant in the labor, a man not
going out in the brig.

My companion now showed me that one of the ends of the
box could be removed at pleasure. He slipped it aside and
displayed the interior, at which I was excessively amused. A
mattress from one of the cabin berths covered the whole of its
bottom, and it contained almost every article of mere comfort
which could be crowded into so small a space, allowing me, at
the same time, sufficient room for my accommodation, either in
a sitting position or lying at full length. Among other things,
there were some books, pen, ink, and paper, three blankets, a
large jug full of water, a keg of sea biscuit, three or four immense
Bologna sausages, an enormous ham, a cold leg of roast mutton,
and half a dozen bottles of cordials and liqueurs. I proceeded
immediately to take possession of my little apartment, and this
with feelings of higher satisfaction, I am sure, than any monarch
ever experienced upon entering a new palace. Augustus now
pointed out to me the method of fastening the open end of the
box, and then, holding the taper close to the deck, showed me a
piece of dark whipcord lying along it. This, he said, extended
from my hiding place throughout all the necessary windings
among the lumber, to a nail which was driven into the deck of the
hold, immediately beneath the trap door leading into his stateroom. By means of this cord I should be enabled readily to trace
my way out without his guidance, provided any unlooked-for
accident should render such a step necessary. He now took his

departure, leaving with me the lantern, together with a copious supply of tapers and phosphorus, and promising to pay me a visit as often as he could contrive to do so without observation. This was on the seventeenth of June.

I remained three days and nights (as nearly as I could guess) in my hiding place without getting out of it at all, except twice for the purpose of stretching my limbs by standing erect between two crates just opposite the opening. During the whole period I saw nothing of Augustus; but this occasioned me little uneasiness, as I knew the brig was expected to put to sea every hour, and in the bustle he would not easily find opportunities of coming down to me. At length I heard the trap open and shut, and presently he called in a low voice, asking if all was well, and if there was anything I wanted. "Nothing," I replied; "I am as comfortable as can be; when will the brig sail?" "She will be under weigh in less than half an hour," he answered. "I came to let you know, and for fear you should be uneasy at my absence. I shall not have a chance of coming down again for some time— perhaps for three or four days more. All is going on right aboveboard. After I go up and close the trap, do you creep along by the whipcord to where the nail is driven in. You will find my watch there—it may be useful to you, as you have no daylight to keep time by. I suppose you can't tell how long you have been buried—only three days—this is the twentieth. I would bring the watch to your box, but am afraid of being missed." With this he went up.

In about an hour after he had gone I distinctly felt the brig in motion, and congratulated myself upon having at length fairly commenced a voyage. Satisfied with this idea, I determined to make my mind as easy as possible, and await the course of events until I should be permitted to exchange the box for the more roomy, although hardly more comfortable, accommodations of the cabin. My first care was to get the watch. Leaving the taper burning, I groped along in the dark, following the cord through windings innumerable, in some of which I discovered that, after toiling a long distance, I was brought back within a foot or two of a former position. At length I reached the nail, and securing the object of my journey, returned with it in safety. I now looked over the books which had been so thoughtfully provided, and selected the expedition of Lewis and Clark to the mouth of the Columbia. With this I amused myself for some time, when, growing sleepy, I extinguished the light with great care, and soon fell into a sound slumber.

Upon awaking I felt strangely confused in mind, and some time elapsed before I could bring to recollection all the various circumstances of my situation. By degrees, however, I remembered all. Striking a light, I looked at the watch; but it was run down, and there were, consequently, no means of determining how long I slept. My limbs were greatly cramped, and I was forced to relieve them by standing between the crates. Presently, feeling an almost ravenous appetite, I bethought myself of the cold mutton, some of which I had eaten just before going to sleep, and found excellent. What was my astonishment at discovering it to be in a state of absolute putrefaction! This circumstance occasioned me great disquietude; for, connecting it with the disorder of mind I experienced upon awaking, I began to suppose that I must have slept for an inordinately long period of time. The close atmosphere of the hold might have something to do with this, and might, in the end, be productive of the most serious results. My head ached excessively; I fancied that I drew every breath with difficulty; and, in short, I was oppressed with a multitude of gloomy feelings. Still I could not venture to make any disturbance by opening the trap or otherwise, and having wound up the watch, contented myself as well as possible.

Throughout the whole of the next tedious twenty-four hours no person came to my relief, and I could not help accusing Augustus of the grossest inattention. What alarmed me chiefly was, that the water in my jug was reduced to about half a pint, and I was suffering much from thirst, having eaten freely of the Bologna sausages after the loss of my mutton. I became very uneasy, and could no longer take any interest in my books. I was overpowered, too, with a desire to sleep, yet trembled at the thought of indulging it, lest there might exist some pernicious influence, like that of burning charcoal, in the confined air of the hold. In the meantime the roll of the brig told me that we were far in the main ocean, and a dull humming sound, which reached my ears as if from an immense distance, convinced me no ordinary gale was blowing. I could not imagine a reason for the absence of Augustus. We were surely far enough advanced on our voyage to allow of my going up. Some accident might have happened to him—but I could think of none which would account for his suffering me to remain so long a prisoner, except, indeed, his having suddenly died or fallen overboard, and upon this idea I could not dwell with any degree of patience. It was possible that we had been baffled by head winds, and were still in the near vicinity of Nantucket. This notion, however, I was forced to abandon; for such being the case, the brig must have frequently gone about; and I was entirely satisfied, from her continual inclination to the larboard, that she had been sailing all along with a steady breeze on her starboard quarter. Besides, granting that we were still in the neighborhood of the island, why should not Augustus have visited me and informed me of the circumstance? Pondering in this manner upon the difficulties of my solitary and cheerless condition, I resolved to wait yet another twenty-four hours, when, if no relief were obtained, I would make my way to the trap, and endeavor either to hold a parley with my friend, or get at least a little fresh air through the opening, and a further supply of water from his stateroom. While occupied with this thought, however, I fell, in spite of every exertion to the contrary, into a state of profound sleep, or rather stupor. My dreams were of the most terrific description. Every species of calamity and horror befell me. Among other miseries, I was smothered to death between huge pillows, by demons of the most ghastly and ferocious aspect. Immense serpents held me in their embrace, and looked earnestly in my face with their fearfully shining eyes. Then deserts, limitless, and of the most forlorn and awe-inspiring character, spread themselves out before me. Immensely tall trunks of trees, gray and leafless, rose up in endless succession as far as the eye could reach. Their roots were concealed in wide-spreading morasses, whose dreary water lay intensely black, still, and altogether terrible, beneath. And the strange trees seemed endowed with a human vitality, and, waving to and fro their skeleton arms, were crying to the silent waters for mercy, in the shrill and piercing accents of the most acute agony and despair. The scene changed; and I stood, naked and alone, amid the burning sand plains of Zahara. At my feet lay crouched a fierce lion of the tropics. Suddenly his wild eyes opened and fell upon me. With a convulsive bound he sprang to his feet, and laid bare his horrible teeth. In another instant there burst from his red throat a roar like the thunder of the firmament, and I fell impetuously to the earth. Stifling in a paroxysm of terror, I at last found myself partially awake. My dream, then, was not all a dream. Now, at least, I was in possession of my senses. The paws of some huge and real monster were pressing heavily upon my bosom—his hot breath was in my ear—and his white and ghastly fangs were gleaming upon me through the gloom.

Had a thousand lives hung upon the movement of a limb or the utterance of a syllable, I could have neither stirred nor spoken. The beast, whatever it was, retained his position without attempting any immediate violence, while I lay in an utterly helpless, and, I fancied, a dying condition beneath him. I felt that my powers of body and mind were fast leaving me—in a word, that I was perishing, and perishing of sheer fright. My brain swam—I grew deadly sick—my vision failed—even the glaring eyeballs above me grew dim. Making a last strong effort, I at length breathed a faint ejaculation to God, and resigned myself to die. The sound of my voice seemed to arouse all the latent fury of the animal. He precipitated himself at full length upon my body; but what was my astonishment, when, with a long and low whine, he commenced licking my face and hands with the greatest eagerness, and with the most extravagant demonstration of affection and joy! I was bewildered, utterly lost in amazement—but I could not forget the peculiar whine of my Newfoundland dog Tiger, and the odd manner of his caresses I well knew. It was he.

I experienced a sudden rush of blood to my temples—a giddy and overpowering sense of deliverance and reanimation. I rose hurriedly from the mattress upon which I had been lying, and throwing myself upon the neck of my faithful follower and friend, relieved the long oppression of my bosom in a flood of the most passionate tears.

As upon a former occasion, my conceptions were in a state of the greatest indistinctness and confusion after leaving the mattress. For a long time I found it nearly impossible to connect any ideas—but, by very slow degrees, my thinking faculties returned, and I again called to memory the several incidents of my condition. For the presence of Tiger I tried in vain to account; and after busying myself with a thousand different conjectures respecting him, was forced to content myself with rejoicing that he was with me to share my dreary solitude, and render me comfort by his caresses. Most people love their dogs—but for Tiger I had an affection far more ardent than common; and never, certainly, did any creature more truly deserve it. For seven years he had been my inseparable companion, and in a multitude of instances had given evidence of all the noble qualities for which we value the animal. I had rescued him, when a puppy, from the clutches of a malignant little villain in Nantucket, who was leading him, with a rope around his neck, to the water; and the grown dog repaid the obligation, about three years afterward, by saving me from the bludgeon of a street robber.

Getting now hold of the watch, I found, upon applying it to my ear, that it had again run down; but at this I was not at all surprised, being convinced, from the peculiar state of my feelings, that I had slept, as before, for a very long period of time; how long, it was of course impossible to say. I was burning up with fever, and my thirst was almost intolerable. I felt about the box for my little remaining supply of water; for I had no light, the taper having burnt to the socket of the lantern, and the phosphorus box not coming readily to hand. Upon finding the jug, however, I discovered it to be empty—Tiger, no doubt, having been tempted to drink it, as well as to devour the remnant of mutton, the bone of which lay, well picked, by the opening of the box. The spoiled meat I could well spare, but my heart sank as I thought of the water. I was feeble in the extreme—so much so that I shook all over, as with an ague, at the slightest movement or exertion. To add to my troubles, the brig was pitching and rolling with great violence, and the oil casks which lay upon my box were in momentary danger of falling down, so as to block up the only way of ingress or egress. I felt, also, terrible sufferings from seasickness. These considerations determined me to make my way, at all hazards, to the trap, and obtain immediate relief, before I should be incapacitated from doing so altogether. Having come to this resolve, I again felt about for the phosphorus box and tapers. The former I found after some little trouble; but, not discovering the tapers as soon as I had expected (for I remembered very nearly the spot in which I had placed them), I gave up the search for the present, and bidding Tiger lie quiet, began at once my journey towards the trap.

In this attempt my great feebleness became more than ever apparent. It was with the utmost difficulty I could crawl along at all, and very frequently my limbs sank suddenly from beneath me; when, falling prostrate on my face, I would remain for some minutes in a state bordering on insensibility. Still I struggled forward by slow degrees, dreading every moment that I should swoon amid the narrow and intricate windings of the lumber, in which event I had nothing but death to expect as the result. At length, upon making a push forward with all the energy I could command, I struck my forehead violently against the sharp corner of an ironbound crate. The accident only stunned me for a few moments; but I found, to my inexpressible grief, that the quick and violent roll of the vessel had thrown the crate entirely across my path, so as effectually to block up the passage. With my utmost exertions I could not move it a single inch from its position, it being closely wedged in among the surrounding boxes and ship-furniture. It became necessary, therefore, enfeebled as I was, either to leave the guidance of the whipcord and seek out a new passage, or to climb over the obstacle, and resume the path on the other side. The former alternative presented too many difficulties and dangers to be thought of without a shudder. In my present weak state of both mind and body, I should infallibly lose my way if I attempted it, and perish miserably amid the dismal and disgusting labyrinths of the hold. I proceeded, therefore, without hesitation, to summon up all my remaining strength and fortitude, and endeavor, as I best might, to clamber over the crate.

Upon standing erect, with this end in view, I found the undertaking even a more serious task than my fears had led me to imagine. On each side of the narrow passage arose a complete wall of various heavy lumber, which the least blunder on my part might be the means of bringing down upon my head; or, if this accident did not occur, the path might be effectually blocked up against my return by the descending mass, as it was in front by the obstacle there. The crate itself was a long and unwieldy box, upon which no foothold could be obtained. In vain I attempted, by every means in my power, to reach the top, with the hope of being thus enabled to draw myself up. Had I succeeded in reaching it, it is certain that my strength would have proved utterly inadequate to the task of getting over, and it was better in every respect that I failed. At length, in a desperate effort to force the crate from its ground, I felt a strong vibration in the side next me. I thrust my hand eagerly to the edge of the planks, and found that a very large one was loose. With my pocketknife, which luckily, I had with me, I succeeded after great labor, in prying it entirely off; and getting through the aperture, discovered, to my exceeding joy, that there were no boards on the opposite side —in other words, that the top was wanting, it being the bottom through which I had forced my way. I now met with no important difficulty in proceeding along the line until I finally reached the nail. With a beating heart I stood erect, and with a gentle touch pressed against the cover of the trap. It did not rise as soon as I had expected, and I pressed it with somewhat more determination, still dreading lest some other person than Augustus might be in his stateroom. The door, however, to my astonish-

ment, remained steady, and I became somewhat uneasy, for I
knew that it had formerly required little or no effort to remove
it. I pushed it strongly—it was nevertheless firm: with all my
strength—it still did not give way: with rage, with fury, with
despair—it set at defiance my utmost efforts; and it was evident,
from the unyielding nature of the resistance, that the hole had
either been discovered and effectually nailed up, or that some
immense weight had been placed upon it, which it was useless
to think of removing.

My sensations were those of extreme horror and dismay. In
vain I attempted to reason on the probable cause of my being
thus entombed. I could summon up no connected chain of reflection, and, sinking on the floor, gave way, unresistingly, to the
most gloomy imaginings, in which the dreadful deaths of thirst,
famine, suffocation, and premature interment, crowded upon
me as the prominent disasters to be encountered. At length there
returned to me some portion of presence of mind. I arose, and
felt with my fingers for the seams or cracks of the aperture.
Having found them, I examined them closely to ascertain if they
emitted any light from the stateroom; but none was visible. I
then forced the pen blade of my knife through them, until I met
with some hard obstacle. Scraping against it, I discovered it to be
a solid mass of iron which, from its peculiar wavy feel as I passed
the blade along it, I concluded to be a chain cable. The only
course now left me was to retrace my way to the box, and there
either yield to my sad fate, or try so to tranquilize my mind as
to admit of my arranging some plan of escape. I immediately
set about the attempt, and succeeded, after innumerable difficulties, in getting back. As I sank, utterly exhausted, upon the mattress, Tiger threw himself at full length by my side, and seemed
as if desirous, by his caresses, of consoling me in my troubles, and
urging me to bear them with fortitude.

The singularity of his behavior at length forcibly arrested
my attention. After licking my face and hands for some minutes,
he would suddenly cease doing so, and utter a low whine. Upon
reaching out my hand towards him, I then invariably found him

lying on his back, with his paws uplifted. This conduct, so frequently repeated, appeared strange, and I could in no manner account for it. As the dog seemed distressed, I concluded that he had received some injury; and, taking his paws in my hands, I examined them one by one, but found no sign of any hurt. I then supposed him hungry, and gave him a large piece of ham, which he devoured with avidity—afterward, however, resuming his extraordinary maneuvers. I now imagined that he was suffering, like myself, the torments of thirst, and was about adopting this conclusion as the true one, when the idea occurred to me that I had as yet only examined his paws, and that there might possibly be a wound upon some portion of his body or head. The latter I felt carefully over, but found nothing. On passing my hand, however, along his back, I perceived a slight erection of the hair extending completely across it. Probing this with my finger, I discovered a string, and tracing it up, found that it encircled the whole body. Upon a closer scrutiny, I came across a small slip of what had the feeling of letter paper, through which the string had been fastened in such a manner as to bring it immediately beneath the left shoulder of the animal.

CHAPTER 3

THE THOUGHT instantly occurred to me that the paper was a note from Augustus, and that some unaccountable accident having happened to prevent his relieving me from my dungeon, he had devised this method of acquainting me with the true state of affairs. Trembling with eagerness, I now commenced another search for my phosphorus matches and tapers. I had a confused recollection of having put them carefully away just before falling asleep; and, indeed, previously to my last journey to the trap, I had been able to remember the exact spot where I had deposited them. But now I endeavored in vain to call it to mind, and busied myself for a full hour in a fruitless and vexatious search for the missing articles; never, surely, was there a more tantalizing state of anxiety and suspense. At length, while groping about, with my head close to the ballast, near the opening of the box, and outside of it, I perceived a faint glimmering of light in the direction of the steerage. Greatly surprised, I endeavored to make my way towards it, as it appeared to be but a few feet from my position. Scarcely had I moved with this intention, when I lost sight of the glimmer entirely, and, before I could bring it into view again, was obliged to feel along by the box until I had exactly resumed my original situation. Now, moving my head with caution to and fro, I found that, by proceeding slowly, with great care, in an opposite direction to that in which I had at first started, I was enabled to draw near the light, still keeping it in view. Presently I came directly upon it (having squeezed my way through innumerable narrow windings), and found that it proceeded from some fragments of my matches lying in an empty barrel turned upon its side. I was wondering how they came in such a place, when my hand fell upon two or three pieces of taperwax, which had been evidently

30

mumbled by the dog. I concluded at once that he had devoured the whole of my supply of candles, and I felt hopeless of being ever able to read the note of Augustus. The small remnants of the wax were so smashed up among other rubbish in the barrel, that I despaired of deriving any service from them, and left them as they were. The phosphorus, of which there was only a speck or two, I gathered up as well as I could, and returned with it, after much difficulty, to my box, where Tiger had all the while remained.

What to do next I could not tell. The hold was so intensely dark that I could not see my hand, however close I would hold it to my face. The white slip of paper could barely be discerned, and not even that when I looked at it directly; by turning the exterior portions of the retina towards it, that is to say, by surveying it slightly askance, I found that it became in some measure perceptible. Thus the gloom of my prison may be imagined, and the note of my friend, if indeed it were a note from him, seemed only likely to throw me into further trouble, by disquieting to no purpose my already enfeebled and agitated mind. In vain I revolved in my brain a multitude of absurd expedients for procuring light—such expedients precisely as a man in the perturbed sleep occasioned by opium would be apt to fall upon for a similar purpose—each and all of which appear by turns to the dreamer the most reasonable and the most preposterous of conceptions, just as the reasoning or imaginative faculties flicker, alternately, one above the other. At last an idea occurred to me which seemed rational, and which gave me cause to wonder, very justly, that I had not entertained it before. I placed the slip of paper on the back of a book, and, collecting the fragments of the phosphorus matches which I had brought from the barrel, laid them together upon the paper. I then, with the palm of my hand, rubbed the whole over quickly, yet steadily. A clear light diffused itself immediately throughout the whole surface; and had there been any writing upon it, I should not have experienced the least difficulty, I am sure, in reading it. Not a syllable was there, however—nothing but a dreary and unsatisfactory blank; the illumination died away in a few seconds, and my heart died away within me as it went.

I have before stated more than once that my intellect, for some period prior to this, had been in a condition nearly bordering on idiocy. There were, to be sure, momentary intervals of perfect sanity, and, now and then, even of energy, but these were few. It must be remembered that I had been, for many days certainly, inhaling the almost pestilential atmosphere of a close hold in a whaling vessel, and a long portion of that time but scantily supplied with water. For the last fourteen or fifteen hours I had none—nor had I slept during that time. Salt provisions of the most exciting kind had been my chief, and, indeed, since the loss of the mutton, my only supply of food, with the exception of the sea biscuit; and these latter were utterly useless to me, as they were too dry and hard to be swallowed in the swollen and parched condition of my throat. I was now in a high state of fever, and in every respect exceedingly ill. This will account for the fact that many miserable hours of despondency elapsed after my last adventure with the phosphorus, before the thought suggested itself that I had examined only one side of the paper. I shall not attempt to describe my feelings of rage (for I believe I was more angry than anything else) when the egregious oversight I had committed flashed suddenly upon my perception. The blunder itself would have been unimportant, had not my own folly and impetuosity rendered it otherwise— in my disappointment at not finding some words upon the slip, I had childishly torn it in pieces and thrown it away, it was impossible to say where.

From the worst part of this dilemma I was relieved by the sagacity of Tiger. Having got, after a long search, a small piece of the note, I put it to the dog's nose, and endeavored to make him understand that he must bring me the rest of it. To my astonishment (for I had taught him none of the usual tricks for which his breed are famous), he seemed to enter at once into my meaning, and, rummaging about for a few moments, soon found another considerable portion. Bringing me this, he paused

awhile, and, rubbing his nose against my hand, appeared to be
waiting for my approval of what he had done. I patted him on
the head, when he immediately made off again. It was now some
minutes before he came back—but when he did come, he brought
with him a large slip, which proved to be all the paper missing
—it having been torn, it seems, only into three pieces. Luckily, I
had no trouble in finding what few fragments of the phosphorus
were left—being guided by the indistinct glow one or two of
the particles still emitted. My difficulties had taught me the
necessity of caution, and I now took time to reflect upon what
I was about to do. It was very probable, I considered, that
some words were written upon that side of the paper which had
not been examined—but which side was that? Fitting the pieces
together gave me no clue in this respect, although it assured
me that the words (if there were any) would be found all on one
side, and connected in a proper manner, as written. There was
the greater necessity of ascertaining the point in question beyond
a doubt, as the phosphorus remaining would be altogether in-
sufficient for a third attempt, should I fail in the one I was now
about to make. I placed the paper on a book as before, and sat
for some minutes thoughtfully revolving the matter over in my
mind. At last I thought it barely possible that the written side
might have some unevenness on its surface, which a delicate
sense of feeling might enable me to detect. I determined to make
the experiment, and passed my finger very carefully over the
side which first presented itself—nothing, however, was perceptible, and I turned the paper, adjusting it on the book. I now again
carried my forefinger cautiously along, when I was aware of
an exceedingly slight, but still discernible glow, which followed
as it proceeded. This, I knew, must arise from some very
minute remaining particles of the phosphorus with which I had
covered the paper in my previous attempt. The other, or underside, then, was that on which lay the writing, if writing there
should finally prove to be. Again I turned the note, and went
to work as I had previously done. Having rubbed in the phosphorus, a brilliancy ensued as before—but this time several

lines of MS. in a large hand, and apparently in red ink, became distinctly visible. The glimmer, although sufficiently bright, was but momentary. Still, had I not been too greatly excited, there would have been ample time enough for me to peruse the whole three sentences before me—for I saw there were three. In my anxiety, however, to read all at once, I succeeded only in reading the seven concluding words, which thus appeared —"*blood—your life depends upon lying close.*"

Had I been able to ascertain the entire contents of the note —the full meaning of the admonition which my friend had thus attempted to convey, that admonition, even although it should have revealed a story of disaster the most unspeakable, could not, I am firmly convinced, have imbued my mind with one tithe of the harrowing and yet indefinable horror with which I was inspired by the fragmentary warning thus received. And "*blood,*" too, that word of all words—so rife at all times with mystery, and suffering, and terror—how trebly full of import did it now appear —how chillily and heavily (disjointed, as it thus was, from any foregoing words to qualify or render it distinct) did its vague syllables fall, amid the deep gloom of my prison, into the innermost recesses of my soul!

Augustus had, undoubtedly, good reasons for wishing me to remain concealed, and I formed a thousand surmises as to what they could be—but I could think of nothing affording a satisfactory solution of the mystery. Just after returning from my last journey to the trap, and before my attention had been otherwise directed by the singular conduct of Tiger, I had come to the resolution of making myself heard at all events by those on board, or, if I could not succeed in this directly, of trying to cut my way through the orlop deck. The half certainty which I felt of being able to accomplish one of these two purposes in the last emergency, had given me courage (which I should not otherwise have had) to endure the evils of my situation. The few words I had been able to read, however, had cut me off from these final resources, and I now, for the first time, felt all the misery of my fate. In a paroxysm of despair I threw myself again upon the mattress, where, for about the period of a day and night, I lay in a kind of stupor, relieved only by momentary intervals of reason and recollection.

At length I once more arose, and busied myself in reflection upon the horrors which encompassed me. For another twenty-four hours it was barely possible that I might exist without water —for a longer time I could not do so. During the first portion of my imprisonment I had made free use of the cordials with which Augustus had supplied me, but they only served to excite fever, without in the least degree assuaging my thirst. I had now only about a gill left, and this was of a species of strong peach liqueur at which my stomach revolted. The sausages were entirely consumed; of the ham nothing remained but a small piece of the skin; and all the biscuit, except a few fragments of one, had been eaten by Tiger. To add to my troubles, I found that my headache was increasing momentarily, and with it the species of delirium which had distressed me more or less since my first falling asleep. For some hours past it had been with the greatest difficulty I could breathe at all, and now each attempt at so doing was attended with the most distressing spasmodic action of the chest. But there was still another and very different source of disquietude, and one, indeed, whose harassing terrors had been the chief means of arousing me to exertion from my stupor on the mattress. It arose from the demeanor of the dog.

I first observed an alteration in his conduct while rubbing in the phosphorus on the paper in my last attempt. As I rubbed, he ran his nose against my hand with a slight snarl; but I was too greatly excited at the time to pay much attention to the circumstance. Soon afterward, it will be remembered, I threw myself on the mattress, and fell into a species of lethargy. Presently I became aware of a singular hissing sound close at my ears, and discovered it to proceed from Tiger, who was panting and wheezing in a state of the greatest apparent excitement, his eyeballs flashing fiercely through the gloom. I spoke to him, when he replied with a low growl, and then remained quiet. Presently I relapsed into my stupor, from which I was again awakened in a similar manner. This was repeated three or four times, until finally his behavior inspired me with so great a degree of fear, that I became fully aroused. He was now lying close by the door of the box, snarling fearfully, although in a kind of undertone, and grinding his teeth as if strongly convulsed. I had no doubt whatever that the want of water or the confined atmosphere of the hold had driven him mad, and I was at a loss what course to pursue. I could not endure the thought of killing him, yet it seemed absolutely necessary for my own safety. I could distinctly perceive his eyes fastened upon me with an expression of the most deadly animosity, and I expected every instant that he would attack me. At last I could endure my terrible situation no longer, and determined to make my way from the box at all hazards, and dispatch him, if his opposition should render it necessary for me to do so. To get out, I had to pass directly over his body, and he already seemed to anticipate my design—raising himself upon his forelegs (as I perceived by the altered position of his eyes), and displaying the whole of his white fangs, which were easily discernible. I took the remains of the hamskin, and the bottle containing the liqueur, and secured them about my person, together with a large carving knife which Augustus had left me—then, folding my cloak around me as closely as possible, I made a movement towards the mouth of the box. No sooner did I do this, than the dog sprang with a loud growl towards my throat. The whole weight of his body struck me on the right shoulder, and I fell violently to the left, while the enraged animal passed entirely over me. I had fallen upon my knees, with my head buried among the blankets, and these protected me from a second furious assault, during which I felt the sharp teeth pressing vigorously upon the woolen which enveloped my neck—yet, luckily, without being able to penetrate all the folds. I was now beneath the dog, and a few moments would place me completely in his power. Despair gave me strength, and I rose bodily up, shaking him from me by main force, and dragging with me the blankets from the mattress. These I now threw over him, and before he could extricate himself, I had got through the door and closed it effectually against his pursuit. In this struggle, however, I had been forced to drop the morsel of hamskin, and I now found my whole stock of provisions reduced to a single gill of liqueur. As this reflection crossed my mind, I felt myself actuated by one of those fits of perverseness which might be supposed to influence a spoiled child in similar circumstances, and, raising the bottle to my lips, I drained it to the last drop, and dashed it furiously upon the floor.

Scarcely had the echo of the crash died away, when I heard my name pronounced in an eager but subdued voice, issuing from the direction of the steerage. So unexpected was anything of the kind, and so intense was the emotion excited within me by the sound, that I endeavored in vain to reply. My powers of speech totally failed, and, in an agony of terror lest my friend should conclude me dead, and return without attempting to reach me, I stood up between the crates near the door of the box, trembling convulsively, and gasping and struggling for utterance. Had a thousand worlds depended upon a syllable, I could not have spoken it. There was a slight movement now audible among the lumber somewhere forward of my station. The sound presently grew less distinct, then again less so, and still less. Shall I ever forget my feelings at this moment? He was going—my friend— my companion, from whom I had a right to expect so much—he was going—he would abandon me—he was gone! He would leave me to perish miserably, to expire in the most horrible and loathsome of dungeons—and one word—one little syllable would save me—yet that single syllable I could not utter! I felt, I am sure, more than ten thousand times the agonies of death itself. My brain reeled, and I fell, deadly sick, against the end of the box.

As I fell, the carving knife was shaken out from the waistband of my pantaloons, and dropped with a rattling sound to the floor. Never did any strain of the richest melody come so sweetly to my ears! With the intensest anxiety I listened to ascertain the effect of the noise upon Augustus—for I knew that the person who called my name could be no one but himself. All was silent

for some moments. At length I again heard the word *Arthur!*
repeated in a low tone, and one full of hesitation. Reviving
hope loosened at once my powers of speech, and I now screamed,
at the top of my voice, "*Augustus! oh, Augustus!*" "Hush—
for God's sake be silent!" he replied, in a voice trembling with
agitation; "I will be with you immediately—as soon as I can
make my way through the hold." For a long time I heard him
moving among the lumber, and every moment seemed to me
an age. At length I felt his hand upon my shoulder, and he
placed at the same moment a bottle of water to my lips. Those
only who have been suddenly redeemed from the jaws of the
tomb, or who have known the insufferable torments of thirst
under circumstances as aggravated as those which encompassed
me in my dreary prison, can form any idea of the unutterable
transports which that one long draught of the richest of all
physical luxuries afforded.

When I had in some degree satisfied my thirst, Augustus produced from his pocket three or four cold boiled potatoes, which
I devoured with the greatest avidity. He had brought with him
a light in a dark lantern, and the grateful rays afforded me
scarcely less comfort than the food and drink. But I was im-
patient to learn the cause of his protracted absence, and he proceeded to recount what had happened on board during my
incarceration.

CHAPTER 4

THE BRIG put to sea, as I had supposed, in about an hour after he had left the watch. This was on the twentieth of June. It will be remembered that I had then been in the hold for three days; and, during this period, there was so constant a bustle on board, and so much running to and fro, especially in the cabin and staterooms, that he had had no chance of visiting me without the risk of having the secret of the trap discovered. When at length he did come, I had assured him that I was doing as well as possible; and, therefore, for the two next days he felt but little uneasiness on my account—still, however, watching an opportunity of going down. It was not *until the fourth day* that he found one. Several times during this interval he had made up his mind to let his father know of the adventure, and have me come up at once; but we were still within reaching distance of Nantucket, and it was doubtful, from some expressions which had escaped Captain Barnard, whether he would not immediately put back if he discovered me to be on board. Besides, upon thinking the matter over, Augustus, so he told me, could not imagine that I was in immediate want, or that I would hesitate, in such case, to make myself heard at the trap. When, therefore, he considered everything, he concluded to let me stay until he could meet with an opportunity of visiting me unobserved. This, as I said before, did not occur until the fourth day after his bringing me the watch, and the seventh since I had first entered the hold. He then went down without taking with him any water or provisions, intending in the first place merely to call my attention, and get me to come from the box to the trap —when he would go up to the stateroom and thence hand me down a supply. When he descended for this purpose he found that I was asleep, for it seems that I was snoring very loudly.

From all the calculations I can make on the subject, this must have been the slumber into which I fell just after my return from the trap with the watch, and which, consequently, must have lasted *for more than three entire days and nights* at the very least. Latterly, I have had reason, both from my own experience and the assurance of others, to be acquainted with the strong soporific effects of the stench arising from old fish oil when closely confined; and when I think of the condition of the hold in which I was imprisoned, and the long period during which the brig had been used as a whaling vessel, I am more inclined to wonder that I awoke at all, after once falling asleep, than that I should have slept uninterruptedly for the period specified above.

Augustus called to me at first in a low voice and without closing the trap—but I made him no reply. He then shut the trap and spoke to me in a louder, and finally in a very loud tone—still I continued to snore. He was now at a loss what to do. It would take him some time to make his way through the lumber to my box, and in the meanwhile his absence would be noticed by Captain Barnard, who had occasion for his services every minute, in arranging and copying papers connected with the business of the voyage. He determined, therefore, upon reflection, to ascend, and await another opportunity of visiting me. He was the more easily induced to this resolve, as my slumber appeared to be of the most tranquil nature, and he could not suppose that I had undergone any inconvenience from my incarceration. He had just made up his mind on these points when his attention was arrested by an unusual bustle, the sound of which proceeded apparently from the cabin. He sprang through the trap as quickly as possible, closed it, and threw open the door of his stateroom. No sooner had he put his foot over the threshold than a pistol flashed in his face, and he was knocked down, at the same moment, by a blow from a handspike.

A strong hand held him on the cabin floor, with a tight grasp upon his throat—still he was able to see what was going on around him. His father was tied hand and foot, and lying along the steps of the companionway with his head down, and a deep wound in the forehead, from which the blood was flowing in a continued stream. He spoke not a word, and was apparently dying. Over him stood the first mate, eying him with an expression of fiendish derision, and deliberately searching his pockets, from which he presently drew forth a large wallet and a chronometer. Seven of the crew (among whom was the cook, a Negro) were rummaging the staterooms on the larboard for arms, where they soon equipped themselves with muskets and ammunition. Besides Augustus and Captain Barnard, there were nine men altogether in the cabin, and these among the most ruffianly of the brig's company. The villains now went upon deck, taking my friend with them, after having secured his arms behind his back. They proceeded straight to the forecastle, which was fastened down—two of the mutineers standing by it with axes—two also at the main hatch. The mate called out in a loud voice, "Do you hear there below? tumble up with you—one by one—now, mark that—and no grumbling!" It was some minutes before anyone appeared: —at last an Englishman, who had shipped as a raw hand, came up, weeping piteously, and entreating the mate, in the most humble manner, to spare his life. The only reply was a blow on the forehead from an ax. The poor fellow fell to the deck, without a groan, and the black cook lifted him up in his arms as he would a child, and tossed him deliberately into the sea. Hearing the blow and the plunge of the body, the men below could now be induced to venture on deck neither by threats nor promises, until a proposition was made to smoke them out. A general rush then ensued, and for a moment it seemed possible that the brig might be retaken. The mutineers, however, succeeded at last in closing the forecastle effectually before more than six of their opponents could get up. These six, finding themselves so greatly outnumbered and without arms, submitted after a brief struggle. The mate gave them fair words—no doubt with a view of inducing those below to yield, for they had no difficulty in hearing all that was said on deck. The result proved his sagacity, no less than his diabolical villainy. All in the forecastle presently signified their intention of submitting, and, ascending one by one, were pinioned and then thrown on their backs, together with the first six—there being, in all of the crew who were not concerned in the mutiny, twenty-seven.

A scene of the most horrible butchery ensued. The bound seamen were dragged to the gangway. Here the cook stood with an ax, striking each victim on the head as he was forced over the side of the vessel by the other mutineers. In this manner twenty-two perished, and Augustus had given himself up for lost, expecting every moment his own turn to come next. But it seemed that the villains were now either weary, or in some measure disgusted with their bloody labor; for the four remaining prisoners, together with my friend, who had been thrown on the deck with the rest, were respited while the mate sent below for rum, and the whole murderous party held a drunken carouse, which lasted until sunset. They now fell to disputing in regard to the fate of the survivors, who lay not more than four paces off, and could distinguish every word said. Upon some of the mutineers the liquor appeared to have a softening effect, for several voices were heard in favor of releasing the captives altogether, on condition of joining the mutiny and sharing the profits. The black cook, however (who in all respects was a perfect demon, and who seemed to exert as much influence, if not more, than the mate himself), would listen to no proposition of the kind, and rose repeatedly for the purpose of resuming his work at the gangway. Fortunately, he was so far overcome by intoxication as to be easily restrained by the less bloodthirsty of the party, among whom was a line manager, who went by the name of Dirk Peters. This man was the son of an Indian squaw of the tribe of Upsarokas, who live among the fastnesses of the Black Hills near the source of the Missouri. His father was a fur trader, I believe, or at least connected in some manner with the Indian trading posts on Lewis River. Peters himself was one of the most purely ferocious-looking men I ever beheld. He was short in stature—not more than four feet eight inches high—but his limbs were of the most Herculean mold. His hands, especially, were so enormously thick and broad as hardly to retain a human shape. His arms, as well as legs, were *bowed* in the most singular manner, and appeared to possess no flexibility whatever. His head was equally deformed, being of immense size, with an indentation on the crown (like that on the head of most Negroes), and entirely bald. To conceal this latter deficiency, which did not proceed from old age, he usually wore a wig formed of any hairlike material which presented itself—occasionally the skin of a Spanish dog or American grizzly bear. At the time spoken of he had on a portion of one of these bearskins; and it added no little to the natural ferocity of his countenance, which betook of the Upsaroka character. The mouth extended nearly from ear to ear; the lips were thin, and seemed, like some other portions of his frame, to be devoid of natural pliancy, so that the ruling expression never varied under the influence of any emotion whatever. This ruling expression may be conceived when it is considered that the teeth were exceedingly long and protruding, and never even partially covered, in any instance, by the lips. To pass this man with a casual glance, one might imagine him to be convulsed with laughter—but a second look would induce a shuddering acknowledgment, that if such an expression were indicative of merriment, the merriment must be that of a demon. Of this singular being many anecdotes were prevalent among the seafaring men of Nantucket. These anecdotes went to prove his prodigious strength when under excitement, and some of them had given rise to a doubt of his sanity. But on board the *Grampus*, it seems, he was regarded at the time of the mutiny with feelings more of derision than of anything else. I have been thus particular in speaking of Dirk Peters, because, ferocious as he appeared, he proved the main instrument in preserving the life of Augustus, and because I shall have frequent occasion to mention him hereafter in the course of my narrative—a narrative, let me here say, which, in its latter portions, will be found to include incidents of a nature so entirely out of the range of human experience, and for this reason so far beyond the limits of human credulity, that I proceed in utter hopelessness of obtaining credence for all that I shall tell, yet confidently trusting in time and progressing science to verify

some of the most important and most improbable of my statements.

After much indecision and two or three violent quarrels, it
was determined at last that all the prisoners (with the exception
of Augustus, whom Peters insisted in a jocular manner upon keeping as his clerk) should be set adrift in one of the smallest whale-
boats. The mate went down into the cabin to see if Captain Barnard was still living—for, it will be remembered, he was left
below when the mutineers came up. Presently the two made their
appearance, the captain pale as death, but somewhat recovered
from the effects of his wound. He spoke to the men in a voice
hardly articulate, entreated them not to set him adrift, but to
return to their duty, and promising to land them wherever they
chose, and to take no steps for bringing them to justice. He might
as well have spoken to the winds. Two of the ruffians seized him
by the arms and hurled him over the brig's side into the boat,
which had been lowered while the mate went below. The four
men who were lying on the deck were then untied and ordered
to follow, which they did without attempting any resistance—
Augustus being still left in his painful position, although he struggled and prayed only for the poor satisfaction of being permitted
to bid his father farewell. A handful of sea biscuit and a jug of
water were now handed down; but neither mast, sail, oar, nor
compass. The boat was towed astern for a few minutes, during
which the mutineers held another consultation—it was then
finally cut adrift. By this time night had come on—there were
neither moon nor stars visible—and a short and ugly sea was
running, although there was no great deal of wind. The boat was
instantly out of sight, and little hope could be entertained for the
unfortunate sufferers who were in it. This event happened, however, in latitude 35° 30′ north, longitude 61° 20′ west, and consequently at no very great distance from the Bermuda Islands.
Augustus therefore endeavored to console himself with the idea
that the boat might either succeed in reaching the land, or come
sufficiently near to be fallen in with by vessels off the coast.

All sail was now put upon the brig, and she continued her

original course to the southwest—the mutineers being bent upon
some piratical expedition, in which, from all that could be understood, a ship was to be intercepted on her way from the Cape
Verd Islands to Porto Rico. No attention was paid to Augustus,
who was untied and suffered to go about anywhere forward of
the cabin companionway. Dirk Peters treated him with some
degree of kindness, and on one occasion saved him from the
brutality of the cook. His situation was still one of the most
precarious, as the men were continually intoxicated, and there
was no relying upon their continued good humor or carelessness
in regard to himself. His anxiety on my account he represented,
however, as the most distressing result of his condition; and,
indeed, I had never reason to doubt the sincerity of his friendship. More than once he had resolved to acquaint the mutineers
with the secret of my being on board, but was restrained from so
doing, partly through recollection of the atrocities he had already
beheld, and partly through a hope of being able soon to bring
me relief. For the latter purpose he was constantly on the watch;
but, in spite of the most constant vigilance, three days elapsed
after the boat was cut adrift before any chance occurred. At
length, on the night of the third day, there came on a heavy blow
from the eastward, and all hands were called up to take in sail.
During the confusion which ensued, he made his way below unobserved, and into the stateroom. What was his grief and horror
in discovering that the latter had been rendered a place of deposit
for a variety of sea stores and ship furniture, and that several
fathoms of old chain cable, which had been stowed away beneath
the companion ladder, had been dragged thence to make room
for a chest, and were now lying immediately upon the trap! To
remove it without discovery was impossible, and he returned on
deck as quickly as he could. As he came up the mate seized him
by the throat, and demanding what he had been doing in the
cabin, was about flinging him over the larboard bulwark, when
his life was again preserved through the interference of Dirk
Peters. Augustus was now put in handcuffs (of which there were
several pairs on board), and his feet lashed tightly together. He

was then taken into the steerage, and thrown into a lower berth next to the forecastle bulkheads, with the assurance that he should never put his foot on deck again "until the brig was no longer a brig." This was the expression of the cook, who threw him into the berth—it is hardly possible to say what precise meaning was intended by the phrase. The whole affair, however, proved the ultimate means of my relief, as will presently appear.

CHAPTER 5

FOR SOME MINUTES after the cook had left the fore-castle, Augustus abandoned himself to despair, never hoping to leave the berth alive. He now came to the resolution of acquainting the first of the men who should come down with my situation, thinking it better to let me take my chance with the mutineers than perish of thirst in the hold—for it had been ten days since I was first imprisoned, and my jug of water was not a plentiful supply even for four. As he was thinking on this subject, the idea came all at once into his head that it might be possible to communicate with me by way of the main hold. In any other circumstances, the difficulty and hazard of the undertaking would have prevented him from attempting it; but now he had, at all events, little prospect of life, and consequently little to lose—he bent his whole mind, therefore, upon the task.

His handcuffs were the first consideration. At first he saw no method of removing them, and feared that he should thus be baffled in the very outset; but, upon a closer scrutiny, he discovered that the irons could be slipped off and on at pleasure, with very little effort or inconvenience, merely by squeezing his hands through them—this species of manacle being altogether ineffectual in confining young persons, in whom the smaller bones readily yield to pressure. He now untied his feet, and, leaving the cord in such a manner that it could easily be readjusted in the event of any person's coming down, proceeded to examine the bulkhead where it joined the berth. The partition here was of soft pine board, an inch thick, and he saw that he should have little trouble in cutting his way through. A voice was now heard at the forecastle companionway, and he had just time to put his right hand into its handcuff (the left had not been removed), and to draw the rope in a slipknot around his ankle, when Dirk

Peters came below, followed by Tiger, who immediately leaped into the berth and lay down. The dog had been brought on board by Augustus, who knew my attachment to the animal, and thought it would give me pleasure to have him with me during the voyage. He went up to our house for him immediately after first taking me into the hold, but did not think of mentioning the circumstance upon his bringing the watch. Since the mutiny, Augustus had not seen him before his appearance with Dirk Peters, and had given him up for lost, supposing him to have been thrown overboard by some of the malignant villains belonging to the mate's gang. It appeared afterward that he had crawled into a hole beneath a whaleboat, from which, not having room to turn round, he could not extricate himself. Peters at last let him out, and with a species of good feeling which my friend knew well how to appreciate, had now brought him to him in the forecastle as a companion, leaving at the same time some salt junk and potatoes, with a can of water: he then went on deck, promising to come down with something more to eat on the next day.

When he had gone, Augustus freed both hands from the manacles and unfastened his feet. He then turned down the head of the mattress on which he had been lying, and with his penknife (for the ruffians had not thought it worth while to search him) commenced cutting vigorously across one of the partition planks, as closely as possible to the floor of the berth. He chose to cut here, because, if suddenly interrupted, he would be able to conceal what had been done by letting the head of the mattress fall into its proper position. For the remainder of the day, however, no disturbance occurred, and by night he had completely divided the plank. It should here be observed that none of the crew occupied the forecastle as a sleeping place, living altogether in the cabin since the mutiny, drinking the wines, and feasting on the sea stores of Captain Barnard, and giving no more heed than was absolutely necessary to the navigation of the brig. These circumstances proved fortunate both for myself and Augustus; for, had matters been otherwise, he would have found it impossible to reach me. As it was, he proceeded with confidence in his design. It was near daybreak, however, before he completed the second division of the board (which was about a foot above the first cut), thus making an aperture quite large enough to admit his passage through with facility to the main orlop deck. Having got here, he made his way with but little trouble to the lower main hatch, although in so doing he had to scramble over tiers of oil casks piled nearly as high as the upper deck, there being barely room enough left for his body. Upon reaching the hatch, he found that Tiger had followed him below, squeezing between two rows of the casks. It was now too late, however, to attempt getting to me before dawn, as the chief difficulty lay in passing through the close stowage in the lower hold. He therefore resolved to return, and wait till the next night. With this design, he proceeded to loosen the hatch, so that he might have as little detention as possible when he should come again. No sooner had he loosened it than Tiger sprang eagerly to the small opening produced, snuffed for a moment, and then uttered a long whine, scratching at the same time, as if anxious to remove the covering with his paws. There could be no doubt, from his behavior, that he was aware of my being in the hold, and Augustus thought it possible that he would be able to get to me if he put him down. He now hit upon the expedient of sending the note, as it was especially desirable that I should make no attempt at forcing my way out, at least under existing circumstances, and there could be no certainty of his getting to me himself on the morrow as he intended. After events proved how fortunate it was that the idea occurred to him as it did: for, had it not been for the receipt of the note, I should undoubtedly have fallen upon some plan, however desperate, of alarming the crew, and both our lives would most probably have been sacrificed in consequence.

Having concluded to write, the difficulty was now to procure the materials for so doing. An old toothpick was soon made into a pen; and this by means of feeling altogether, for the between-decks were as dark as pitch. Paper enough was obtained from the back of a letter—a duplicate of the forged letter from Mr.

Ross. This had been the original draught; but the handwriting not being sufficiently well imitated, Augustus had written another, thrusting the first, by good fortune, into his coat pocket, where it was most opportunely discovered. Ink alone was thus wanting, and a substitute was immediately found for this by means of a slight incision with the penknife on the back of a finger just above the nail—a copious flow of blood ensuing, as usual, from wounds in that vicinity. The note was now written, as well as it could be in the dark and under the circumstances. It briefly explained that a mutiny had taken place; that Captain Barnard was set adrift; and that I might expect immediate relief as far as provisions were concerned, but must not venture upon making any disturbance. It concluded with these words: *"I have scrawled this with blood —your life depends upon lying close."*

The slip of paper being tied upon the dog, he was now put down the hatchway, and Augustus made the best of his way back to the forecastle, where he found no reason to believe that any of the crew had been in his absence. To conceal the hole in the partition, he drove his knife in just above it, and hung up a pea jacket which he found in the berth. His handcuffs were then replaced, and also the rope around his ankles.

These arrangements were scarcely completed when Dirk Peters came below, very drunk, but in excellent humor, and bringing with him my friend's allowance of provision for the day. This consisted of a dozen large Irish potatoes roasted, and a pitcher of water. He sat for some time on a chest by the berth, and talked freely about the mate, and the general concerns of the brig. His demeanor was exceedingly capricious, and even grotesque. At one time Augustus was much alarmed by his odd conduct. At last, however, he went on deck, muttering a promise to bring his prisoner a good dinner on the morrow. During the day two of the crew (harpooners) came down, accompanied by the cook, all three in nearly the last stage of intoxication. Like Peters, they made no scruple of talking unreservedly about their plans. It appeared that they were much divided among themselves as to their ultimate course, agreeing in no point except the attack on the ship from the Cape Verd Islands, with which they were in hourly expectation of meeting. As far as could be ascertained, the mutiny had not been brought about altogether for the sake of booty; a private pique of the chief mate's against Captain Barnard having been the main instigation. There now seemed to be two principal factions among the crew—one headed by the mate, the other by the cook. The former party were for seizing the first suitable vessel which should present itself, and equipping it at some of the West India Islands for a piratical cruise. The latter division, however, which was the stronger, and included Dirk Peters among its partisans, was bent upon pursuing the course originally laid out for the brig into the South Pacific; there either to take whale, or act otherwise, as circumstances should suggest. The representations of Peters, who had frequently visited these regions, had great weight, apparently, with the mutineers, wavering, as they were, between half-engendered notions of profit and pleasure. He dwelt on the world of novelty and amusement to be found among the innumerable islands of the Pacific, on the perfect security and freedom from all restraint to be enjoyed, but, more particularly, on the deliciousness of the climate, on the abundant means of good living, and on the voluptuous beauty of the women. As yet, nothing had been absolutely determined upon; but the pictures of the hybrid line manager were taking strong hold upon the ardent imaginations of the seamen, and there was every probability that his intentions would be finally carried into effect.

The three men went away in about an hour, and no one else entered the forecastle all day. Augustus lay quiet until nearly night. He then freed himself from the rope and irons, and prepared for his attempt. A bottle was found in one of the berths, and this he filled with water from the pitcher left by Peters, storing his pockets at the same time with cold potatoes. To his great joy he also came across a lantern, with a small piece of tallow candle in it. This he could light at any moment, as he had in his possession a box of phosphorus matches. When it was quite dark, he got through the hole in the bulkhead, having taken the

precaution to arrange the bedclothes in the berth so as to convey
the idea of a person covered up. When through, he hung up the
pea jacket on his knife, as before, to conceal the aperture—this
maneuver being easily effected, as he did not readjust the piece
of plank taken out until afterward. He was now on the main
orlop deck, and proceeded to make his way, as before, between
the upper deck and the oil casks to the main hatchway. Having
reached this, he lit the piece of candle, and descended, groping
with extreme difficulty among the compact stowage of the hold.
In a few moments he became alarmed at the insufferable stench
and the closeness of the atmosphere. He could not think it possible that I had survived my confinement for so long a period
breathing so oppressive an air. He called my name repeatedly,
but I made him no reply, and his apprehensions seemed thus to
be confirmed. The brig was rolling violently, and there was so
much noise in consequence, that it was useless to listen for any
weak sound, such as those of my breathing or snoring. He threw
open the lantern, and held it as high as possible, whenever an
opportunity occurred, in order that, by observing the light, I
might, if alive, be aware that succor was approaching. Still nothing
was heard from me, and the supposition of my death began to
assume the character of certainty. He determined, nevertheless,
to force a passage, if possible, to the box, and at least ascertain
beyond a doubt the truth of his surmises. He pushed on for some
time in a most pitiable state of anxiety, until, at length, he found
the pathway utterly blocked up, and that there was no possibility
of making any farther way by the course in which he had set out.
Overcome now by his feelings, he threw himself among the
lumber in despair, and wept like a child. It was at this period
that he heard the crash occasioned by the bottle which I had
thrown down. Fortunate, indeed, was it that the incident occurred
—for, upon this incident, trivial as it appears, the thread of my
destiny depended. Many years elapsed, however, before I was
aware of this fact. A natural shame and regret for his weakness
and indecision prevented Augustus from confiding to me at once
what a more intimate and unreserved communion afterward

induced him to reveal. Upon finding his further progress in the
hold impeded by obstacles which he could not overcome, he had
resolved to abandon his attempt at reaching me, and return at
once to the forecastle. Before condemning him entirely on this
head, the harassing circumstances which embarrassed him should
be taken into consideration. The night was fast wearing away,
and his absence from the forecastle might be discovered; and,
indeed, would necessarily be so, if he should fail to get back to
the berth by daybreak. His candle was expiring in the socket,
and there would be the greatest difficulty in retracing his way to
the hatchway in the dark. It must be allowed, too, that he had
every good reason to believe me dead; in which event no benefit
could result to me from his reaching the box, and a world of
danger would be encountered to no purpose by himself. He had
repeatedly called, and I had made him no answer. I had been
now eleven days and nights with no more water than that contained in the jug which he had left with me—a supply which it was
not at all probable I had hoarded in the beginning of my confinement, as I had had every cause to expect a speedy release. The
atmosphere of the hold, too, must have appeared to him, coming
from the comparatively open air of the steerage, of a nature
absolutely poisonous, and by far more intolerable than it had
seemed to me upon my first taking up my quarters in the box—
the hatchways at that time having been constantly open for
many months previous. Add to these considerations that of the
scene of bloodshed and terror so lately witnessed by my friend;
his confinement, privations, and narrow escapes from death;
together with the frail and equivocal tenure by which he still
existed—circumstances all so well calculated to prostrate every
energy of mind—and the reader will be easily brought, as I have
been, to regard his apparent falling off in friendship and in faith
with sentiments rather of sorrow than of anger.

The crash of the bottle was distinctly heard, yet Augustus was
not sure that it proceeded from the hold. The doubt, however, was
sufficient inducement to persevere. He clambered up nearly to the
orlop deck by means of the stowage, and then, watching for a lull

in the pitchings of the vessel, he called out to me in as loud a tone as he could command—regardless, for the moment, of the danger of being overheard by the crew. It will be remembered that on this occasion the voice reached me, but I was so entirely overcome by violent agitation as to be incapable of reply. Confident, now, that his worst apprehensions were well founded, he descended, with a view of getting back to the forecastle without loss of time. In his haste some small boxes were thrown down, the noise occasioned by which I heard, as will be recollected. He had made considerable progress on his return when the fall of the knife again caused him to hesitate. He retraced his steps immediately, and, clambering up the stowage a second time, called out my name, loudly as before, having watched for a lull. This time I found voice to answer. Overjoyed at discovering me to be still alive, he now resolved to brave every difficulty and danger in reaching me. Having extricated himself as quickly as possible from the labyrinth of lumber by which he was hemmed in, he at length struck into an opening which promised better, and finally, after a series of struggles, arrived at the box in a state of utter exhaustion.

CHAPTER 6

THE LEADING PARTICULARS of this narration were all that Augustus communicated to me while we remained near the box. It was not until afterward that he entered fully into all the details. He was apprehensive of being missed, and I was wild with impatience to leave my detested place of confinement. We resolved to make our way at once to the hole in the bulkhead, near which I was to remain for the present, while he went through to reconnoiter. To leave Tiger in the box was what neither of us could endure to think of; yet, how to act otherwise was the question. He now seemed to be perfectly quiet, and we could not even distinguish the sound of his breathing upon applying our ears closely to the box. I was convinced that he was dead, and determined to open the door. We found him lying at full length, apparently in a deep stupor, yet still alive. No time was to be lost, yet I could not bring myself to abandon an animal who had now been twice instrumental in saving my life, without some attempt at preserving him. We therefore dragged him along with us as well as we could, although with the greatest difficulty and fatigue; Augustus, during part of the time, being forced to clamber over the impediments in our way with the huge dog in his arms—a feat to which the feebleness of my frame rendered me totally inadequate. At length we succeeded in reaching the hole, when Augustus got through, and Tiger was pushed in afterward. All was found to be safe, and we did not fail to return sincere thanks to God for our deliverance from the imminent danger we had escaped. For the present, it was agreed that I should remain near the opening, through which my companion could readily supply me with a part of his daily provision, and where I could have the advantages of breathing an atmosphere comparatively pure.

In explanation of some portions of this narrative, wherein I have spoken of the stowage of the brig, and which may appear ambiguous to some of my readers who may have seen a proper or regular stowage, I must here state that the manner in which this most important duty had been performed on board the *Grampus* was a most shameful piece of neglect on the part of Captain Barnard, who was by no means as careful or as experienced a seaman as the hazardous nature of the service on which he was employed would seem necessarily to demand. A proper stowage cannot be accomplished in a careless manner, and many most disastrous accidents, even within the limits of my own experience, have arisen from neglect or ignorance in this particular. Coasting vessels, in the frequent hurry and bustle attendant upon taking in or discharging cargo, are the most liable to mishap from the want of a proper attention to stowage. The great point is to allow no possibility of the cargo or ballast's shifting position even in the most violent rollings of the vessel. With this end, great attention must be paid, not only to the bulk taken in, but to the nature of the bulk, and whether there be a full or only a partial cargo. In most kinds of freight the stowage is accomplished by means of a screw. Thus, in a load of tobacco or flour, the whole is screwed so tightly into the hold of the vessel that the barrels or hogsheads, upon discharging, are found to be completely flattened, and take some time to regain their original shape. This screwing, however, is resorted to principally with a view of obtaining more room in the hold; for in a *full* load of any such commodities as flour or tobacco, there can be no danger of any shifting whatever, at least none from which inconvenience can result. There have been instances, indeed, where this method of screwing has resulted in the most lamentable consequences, arising from a cause altogether distinct from the danger attendant upon a shifting of cargo. A load of cotton, for example, tightly screwed while in certain conditions, has been known, through the expansion of its bulk, to rend a vessel asunder at sea. There can be no doubt, either, that the same result would ensue in the case of tobacco, while undergoing its usual course of fermentation, were it not for the interstices consequent upon the rotundity of the hogsheads.

It is when a partial cargo is received that danger is chiefly to be apprehended from shifting, and that precaution should be always taken to guard against such misfortune. Only those who have encountered a violent gale of wind, or, rather, who have experienced the rolling of a vessel in a sudden calm after the gale, can form an idea of the tremendous force of the plunges, and of the consequent terrible impetus given to all loose articles in the vessel. It is then that the necessity of a cautious stowage, when there is a partial cargo, becomes obvious. When lying to (especially with a small head sail), a vessel which is not properly modeled in the bows is frequently thrown upon her beam-ends; this occurring even every fifteen or twenty minutes upon an average, yet without any serious consequences resulting, *provided there be a proper stowage*. If this, however, has not been strictly attended to, in the first of these heavy lurches the whole of the cargo tumbles over to the side of the vessel which lies upon the water, and, being thus prevented from regaining her equilibrium, as she would otherwise necessarily do, she is certain to fill in a few seconds and go down. It is not too much to say that at least one half of the instances in which vessels have foundered in heavy gales at sea may be attributed to a shifting of cargo or of ballast.

When a partial cargo of any kind is taken on board, the whole, after being first stowed as compactly as may be, should be covered with a layer of stout shifting boards, extending completely across the vessel. Upon these boards strong temporary stanchions should be erected, reaching to the timbers above, and thus securing everything in its place. In cargoes consisting of grain, or any similar matter, additional precautions are requisite. A hold filled entirely with grain upon leaving port will be found not more than three-fourths full upon reaching its destination—this, too, although the freight, when measured bushel by bushel by the consignee, will overrun by a vast deal (on account of the swelling of the grain) the quantity consigned. This result is occasioned by *settling* during the voyage, and is the more perceptible in proportion to the roughness of the weather experienced. If grain loosely thrown in a vessel, then, is ever so well secured by shifting boards and stanchions, it will be liable to shift in a long passage so greatly as to bring the most distressing calamities. To prevent these, every method should be employed before leaving port to *settle* the cargo as much as possible; and for this there are many contrivances, among which may be mentioned the driving of wedges into the grain. Even after all this is done, and unusual pains taken to secure the shifting boards, no seaman who knows what he is about will feel altogether secure in a gale of any violence with a cargo of grain on board, and, least of all, with a partial cargo. Yet there are hundreds of our coasting vessels, and, it is likely, many more from the ports of Europe, which sail daily with partial cargoes, even of the most dangerous species, and without any precautions whatever. The wonder is that no more accidents occur than do actually happen. A lamentable instance of this heedlessness occurred to my knowledge in the case of Captain Joel Rice of the schooner *Firefly*, which sailed from Richmond, Virginia, to Madeira, with a cargo of corn, in the year 1825. The captain had gone many voyages without serious accident, although he was in the habit of paying no attention whatever to his stowage, more than to secure it in the ordinary manner. He had never before sailed with a cargo of grain, and on this occasion had the corn thrown on board loosely, when it did not much more than half fill the vessel. For the first portion of the voyage he met with nothing more than light breezes; but when within a day's sail of Madeira there came on a strong gale from the N. N. E. which forced him to lie to. He brought the schooner to the wind under a double-reefed foresail alone, when she rode as well as any vessel could be expected to do, and shipped not a drop of water. Towards night the gale somewhat abated, and she rolled with more unsteadiness than before, but still did very well, until a heavy lurch threw her upon her beam-ends to starboard. The corn was then heard to shift bodily,

the force of the movement bursting open the main hatchway.
The vessel went down like a shot. This happened within hail of
a small sloop from Madeira, which picked up one of the crew
(the only person saved), and which rode out the gale in perfect
security, as indeed a jolly boat might have done under proper
management.

The stowage on board the *Grampus* was most clumsily done, if
stowage that could be called which was little better than a
promiscuous huddling together of oil casks* and ship-furniture.
I have already spoken of the condition of articles in the hold. On
the orlop deck there was space enough for my body (as I have
stated) between the oil casks and the upper deck; a space was
left open around the main hatchway; and several other large
spaces were left in the stowage. Near the hole cut through the
bulkhead by Augustus there was room enough for an entire cask,
and in this space I found myself comfortably situated for the
present.

By the time my friend had got safely into the berth, and
readjusted his handcuffs and the rope, it was broad daylight. We
had made a narrow escape indeed; for scarcely had he arranged
all matters, when the mate came below with Dirk Peters and the
cook. They talked for some time about the vessel from the Cape
Verds, and seemed to be excessively anxious for her appearance.
At length the cook came to the berth in which Augustus was
lying, and seated himself in it near the head. I could see and hear
everything from my hiding place, for the piece cut out had not
been put back, and I was in momentary expectation that the
Negro would fall against the pea jacket, which was hung up to
conceal the aperture, in which case all would have been discovered, and our lives would, no doubt, have been instantly
sacrificed. Our good fortune prevailed, however; and although he
frequently touched it as the vessel rolled, he never pressed against
it sufficiently to bring about a discovery. The bottom of the jacket
had been carefully fastened to the bulkhead, so that the hole

---

* Whaling vessels are usually fitted with iron oil tanks—why the *Grampus*
was not I have never been able to ascertain. (Poe's note.)

might not be seen by its swinging to one side. All this time Tiger was lying in the foot of the berth, and appeared to have recovered in some measure his faculties, for I could see him occasionally open his eyes and draw a long breath.

After a few minutes the mate and cook went above, leaving Dirk Peters behind, who, as soon as they were gone, came and sat himself down in the place just occupied by the mate. He began to talk very sociably with Augustus, and we could now see that the greater part of his apparent intoxication, while the two others were with him, was a feint. He answered all my companion's questions with perfect freedom; told him that he had no doubt of his father's having been picked up, as there were no less than five sail in sight just before sundown on the day he was cut adrift; and used other language of a consolatory nature, which occasioned me no less surprise than pleasure. Indeed, I began to entertain hopes, that through the instrumentality of Peters we might be finally enabled to regain possession of the brig, and this idea I mentioned to Augustus as soon as I found an opportunity. He thought the matter possible, but urged the necessity of the greatest caution in making the attempt, as the conduct of the hybrid appeared to be instigated by the most arbitrary caprice alone; and, indeed, it was difficult to say if he was at any moment of sound mind. Peters went upon deck in about an hour, and did not return again until noon, when he brought Augustus a plentiful supply of junk beef and pudding. Of this, when we were left alone, I partook heartily, without returning through the hole. No one else came down into the forecastle during the day, and at night I got into Augustus' berth, where I slept soundly and sweetly until nearly daybreak, when he awakened me upon hearing a stir upon deck and I regained my hiding place as quickly as possible. When the day was fully broke, we found that Tiger had recovered his strength almost entirely, and gave no indications of hydrophobia, drinking a little water that was offered him with great apparent eagerness. During the day he regained all his former vigor and appetite. His strange conduct had been brought on, no doubt, by the deleterious quality of the air of the hold, and had no connection with canine madness. I could not sufficiently rejoice that I had persisted in bringing him with me from the box. This day was the thirtieth of June, and the thirteenth since the *Grampus* made sail from Nantucket.

On the second of July the mate came below, drunk as usual, and in an excessively good humor. He came to Augustus' berth, and, giving him a slap on the back, asked him if he thought he could behave himself if he let him loose, and whether he would promise not to be going into the cabin again. To this, of course, my friend answered in the affirmative, when the ruffian set him at liberty, after making him drink from a flask of rum which he drew from his coat pocket. Both now went on deck, and I did not see Augustus for about three hours. He then came below with the good news that he had obtained permission to go about the brig as he pleased anywhere forward of the mainmast, and that he had been ordered to sleep, as usual, in the forecastle. He brought me, too, a good dinner, and a plentiful supply of water. The brig was still cruising for the vessel from the Cape Verds, and a sail was now in sight, which was thought to be the one in question. As the events of the ensuing eight days were of little importance, and had no direct bearing upon the main incidents of my narrative, I will here throw them into the form of a journal, as I do not wish to omit them altogether.

July 3. Augustus furnished me with three blankets, with which I contrived a comfortable bed in my hiding place. No one came below, except my companion, during the day. Tiger took his station in the berth just by the aperture, and slept heavily, as if not yet entirely recovered from the effects of his sickness. Towards night a flaw of wind struck the brig before sail could be taken in, and very nearly capsized her. The puff died away immediately, however, and no damage was done beyond the splitting of the foretopsail. Dirk Peters treated Augustus all this day with great kindness, and entered into a long conversation with him respecting the Pacific Ocean, and the islands he had visited in that region. He asked him whether he would not like to go with the mutineers on a kind of exploring and pleasure voyage in those quarters, and said that the men were gradually coming over to the mate's views. To this Augustus thought it best to reply that he would be glad to go on such an adventure, since nothing better could be done, and that anything was preferable to a piratical life.

July 4. The vessel in sight proved to be a small brig from Liverpool, and was allowed to pass unmolested. Augustus spent most of his time on deck, with a view of obtaining all the information in his power respecting the intentions of the mutineers. They had frequent and violent quarrels among themselves, in one of which a harpooner, Jim Bonner, was thrown overboard. The party of the mate was gaining ground. Jim Bonner belonged to the cook's gang, of which Peters was a partisan.

July 5. About daybreak there came on a stiff breeze from the west, which at noon freshened into a gale, so that the brig could carry nothing more than her trysail and foresail. In taking in the foretopsail, Simms, one of the common hands, and belonging also to the cook's gang, fell overboard, being very much in liquor, and was drowned—no attempt being made to save him. The whole number of persons on board was now thirteen, to wit: Dirk Peters; Seymour, the black cook; —— Jones; —— Greely; Hartman Rogers, and William Allen, of the cook's party; the mate, whose name I never learned; Absalom Hicks; —— Wilson; John Hunt; and Richard Parker, of the mate's party—besides Augustus and myself.

July 6. The gale lasted all this day, blowing in heavy squalls, accompanied with rain. The brig took in a good deal of water through her seams, and one of the pumps was kept continually going, Augustus being forced to take his turn. Just at twilight a large ship passed close by us, without having been discovered until within hail. The ship was supposed to be the one for which the mutineers were on the lookout. The mate hailed her, but the reply was drowned in the roaring of the gale. At eleven, a sea was shipped amidships, which tore away a great portion of the larboard bulwarks, and did some other slight damage. Towards morning the weather moderated, and at sunrise there was very little wind.

July 7. There was a heavy swell running all this day, during which the brig, being light, rolled excessively, and many articles broke loose in the hold, as I could hear distinctly from my hiding place. I suffered a great deal from seasickness. Peters had a long conversation this day with Augustus, and told him that two of his gang, Greely and Allen, had gone over to the mate, and were resolved to turn pirates. He put several questions to Augustus which he did not then exactly understand. During a part of this evening the leak gained upon the vessel; and little could be done to remedy it, as it was occasioned by the brig's straining, and taking in the water through her seams. A sail was thrummed, and got under the bows, which aided us in some measure, so that we began to gain upon the leak.

July 8. A light breeze sprang up at sunrise from the eastward when the mate headed the brig to the southwest, with the intention of making some of the West India Islands, in pursuance of his piratical designs. No opposition was made by Peters or the cook; at least none in the hearing of Augustus. All idea of taking the vessel from the Cape Verds was abandoned. The leak was now easily kept under by one pump going every three quarters of an hour. The sail was drawn from beneath the bows. Spoke two small schooners during the day.

July 9. Fine weather. All hands employed in repairing bulwarks. Peters had again a long conversation with Augustus, and spoke more plainly than he had done heretofore. He said nothing should induce him to come into the mate's views, and even hinted his intention of taking the brig out of his hands. He asked my friend if he could depend upon his aid in such case, to which Augustus said, "Yes," without hesitation. Peters then said he would sound the others of his party upon the subject, and went away. During the remainder of the day Augustus had no opportunity of speaking with him privately.

CHAPTER 7

JULY 10. Spoke a brig from Rio, bound to Norfolk. Weather hazy, with a light baffling wind from the eastward. Today Hartman Rogers died, having been attacked on the eighth with spasms after drinking a glass of grog. This man was of the cook's party, and one upon whom Peters placed his main reliance. He told Augustus that he believed the mate had poisoned him, and that he expected, if he did not be on the lookout, his own turn would come shortly. There were now only himself, Jones, and the cook belonging to his own gang—on the other side there were five. He had spoken to Jones about taking the command from the mate; but the project having been coolly received, he had been deterred from pressing the matter any further, or from saying anything to the cook. It was well, as it happened, that he was so prudent, for in the afternoon the cook expressed his determination of siding with the mate, and went over formally to that party; while Jones took an opportunity of quarreling with Peters, and hinted that he would let the mate know of the plan in agitation. There was now, evidently, no time to be lost, and Peters expressed his determination of attempting to take the vessel at all hazards, provided Augustus would lend him his aid. My friend at once assured him of his willingness to enter into any plan for that purpose, and, thinking the opportunity a favorable one, made known the fact of my being on board. At this the hybrid was not more astonished than delighted, as he had no reliance whatever upon Jones, whom he already considered as belonging to the party of the mate. They went below immediately, when Augustus called to me by name, and Peters and myself were soon made acquainted. It was agreed that we should attempt to retake the vessel upon the first good opportunity, leaving Jones altogether out of our councils. In the event of success, we were to run the brig into the first port that offered, and deliver her up. The desertion of his party had frustrated Peters' design of going into the Pacific—an adventure which could not be accomplished without a crew, and he depended upon either getting acquitted upon trial, on the score of insanity (which he solemnly averred had actuated him in lending his aid to the mutiny), or upon obtaining a pardon, if found guilty, through the representations of Augustus and myself. Our deliberations were interrupted for the present by the cry of "All hands take in sail," and Peters and Augustus ran up on deck.

As usual, the crew were nearly all drunk; and, before sail could be properly taken in, a violent squall laid the brig on her beam-ends. By keeping her away, however, she righted, having shipped a good deal of water. Scarcely was everything secure, when another squall took the vessel, and immediately afterward another—no damage being done. There was every appearance of a gale of wind, which, indeed, shortly came on, with great fury, from the northward and westward. All was made as snug as possible, and we laid to, as usual, under a close-reefed foresail. As night drew on, the wind increased in violence, with a remarkably heavy sea. Peters now came into the forecastle with Augustus, and we resumed our deliberations.

We agreed that no opportunity could be more favorable than the present for carrying our design into effect, as an attempt at such a moment would never be anticipated. As the brig was snugly laid to, there would be no necessity of maneuvering her until good weather, when, if we succeeded in our attempt, we might liberate one, or perhaps two of the men, to aid us in taking her into port. The main difficulty was the great disproportion in our forces. There were only three of us, and in the cabin there were nine. All the arms on board, too, were in their possession, with the exception of a pair of small pistols which Peters had concealed about his person, and the large seaman's knife which he always wore in the waistband of his pantaloons. From certain indications too, such, for example, as there being no such thing as an ax or a handspike lying in their customary places, we began to fear that the mate had his suspicions, at least in regard to

Peters, and that he would let slip no opportunity of getting rid of him. It was clear, indeed, that what we should determine to do could not be done too soon. Still the odds were too much against us to allow of our proceeding without the greatest caution.

Peters proposed that he should go up on deck, and enter into conversation with the watch (Allen), when he would be able to throw him into the sea without trouble, and without making any disturbance, by seizing a good opportunity; that Augustus and myself should then come up, and endeavor to provide ourselves with some kind of weapons from the deck; and that we should then make a rush together, and secure the companionway before any opposition could be offered. I objected to this, because I could not believe that the mate (who was a cunning fellow in all matters which did not affect his superstitious prejudices) would suffer himself to be so easily entrapped. The very fact of there being a watch on deck at all was sufficient proof that he was upon the alert—it not being usual, except in vessels where discipline is most rigidly enforced, to station a watch on deck when a vessel is lying to in a gale of wind. As I address myself principally, if not altogether, to persons who have never been to sea, it may be as well to state the exact condition of a vessel under such circumstances. Lying to, or, in sea parlance, "laying to," is a measure resorted to for various purposes, and effected in various manners. In moderate weather it is frequently done with a view of merely bringing the vessel to a standstill, to wait for another vessel, or any similar object. If the vessel which lies to is under full sail, the maneuver is usually accomplished by throwing round some portion of her sails so as to let the wind take them aback, when she becomes stationary. But we are now speaking of lying to in a gale of wind. This is done when the wind is ahead, and too violent to admit of carrying sail without danger of capsizing; and sometimes even when the wind is fair, but the sea too heavy for the vessel to be put before it. If a vessel be suffered to scud before the wind in a very heavy sea, much damage is usually done her by the shipping of water over her stern, and sometimes by the violent plunges she makes forward.

This maneuver, then, is seldom resorted to in such case, unless through necessity. When the vessel is in a leaky condition, she is often put before the wind even in the heaviest seas; for, when lying to, her seams are sure to be greatly opened by her violent straining, and it is not so much the case when scudding. Often, too, it becomes necessary to scud a vessel, either when the blast is so exceedingly furious as to tear in pieces the sail which is employed with a view of bringing her head to the wind, or when, through the false modeling of the frame or other causes, this main object cannot be effected.

Vessels in a gale of wind are laid to in different manners, according to their peculiar construction. Some lie to best under a foresail, and this, I believe, is the sail most usually employed. Large square-rigged vessels have sails for the express purpose, called storm-staysails. But the jib is occasionally employed by itself—sometimes the jib and foresail, or a double-reefed foresail, and not unfrequently the aftersails, are made use of. Foretopsails are very often found to answer the purpose better than any other species of sail. The *Grampus* was generally laid to under a close-reefed foresail.

When a vessel is to be laid to, her head is brought up to the wind just so nearly as to fill the sail under which she lies, when hauled flat aft, that is, when brought diagonally across the vessel. This being done, the bows point within a few degrees of the direction from which the wind issues, and the windward bow of course receives the shock of the waves. In this situation a good vessel will ride out a very heavy gale of wind without shipping a drop of water, and without any further attention being requisite on the part of the crew. The helm is usually lashed down, but this is altogether unnecessary (except on account of the noise it makes when loose), for the rudder has no effect upon the vessel when lying to. Indeed, the helm had far better be left loose than lashed very fast, for the rudder is apt to be torn off by heavy seas if there be no room for the helm to play. As long as the sail holds, a well-modeled vessel will maintain her situation, and ride every sea, as if instinct with life and reason. If the violence of the wind, however, should tear the sail into pieces (a feat which it requires a perfect hurricane to accomplish under ordinary circumstances), there is then imminent danger. The vessel falls off from the wind, and, coming broadside to the sea, is completely at its mercy; the only resource in this case is to put her quickly before the wind, letting her scud until some other sail can be set. Some vessels will lie to under no sail whatever, but such are not to be trusted at sea.

But to return from this digression. It had never been customary with the mate to have any watch on deck when lying to in a gale of wind, and the fact that he had now one, coupled with the circumstances of the missing axes and handspikes, fully convinced us that the crew were too well on the watch to be taken by surprise in the manner Peters had suggested. Something, however, was to be done, and that with as little delay as practicable, for there could be no doubt that a suspicion having been once entertained against Peters, he would be sacrificed upon the earliest occasion, and one would certainly be either found or made upon the breaking of the gale.

Augustus now suggested that if Peters could contrive to remove, under any pretext, the piece of chain cable which lay over the trap in the stateroom, we might possibly be able to come upon them unawares by means of the hold; but a little reflection convinced us that the vessel rolled and pitched too violently for any attempt of that nature.

By good fortune I at length hit upon the idea of working upon the superstitious terrors and guilty conscience of the mate. It will be remembered that one of the crew, Hartman Rogers, had died during the morning, having been attacked two days before with spasms after drinking some spirits and water. Peters had expressed to us his opinion that this man had been poisoned by the mate, and for this belief he had reasons, so he said, which were incontrovertible, but which he could not be prevailed upon to explain to us—this wayward refusal being only in keeping with other points of his singular character. But whether or not he had any better grounds for suspecting the mate than we had ourselves, we were easily led to fall in with his suspicion, and determined to act accordingly.

Rogers had died about eleven in the forenoon, in violent convulsions; and the corpse presented in a few minutes after death one of the most horrid and loathsome spectacles I ever remember to have seen. The stomach was swollen immensely, like that of a man who has been drowned and lain under water for many weeks. The hands were in the same condition, while the face was shrunken, shriveled, and of a chalky whiteness, except where relieved by two or three glaring red splotches, like those occasioned by the erysipelas: one of these splotches extended diagonally across the face, completely covering up an eye as if with a band of red velvet. In this disgusting condition the body had been brought up from the cabin at noon to be thrown overboard, when the mate getting a glimpse of it (for he now saw it for the first time), and being either touched with remorse for his crime or struck with terror at so horrible a sight, ordered the men to sew the body up in its hammock, and allow it the usual rites of sea burial. Having given these directions he went below, as if to avoid any further sight of his victim. While preparations were making to obey his orders, the gale came on with great fury, and the design was abandoned for the present. The corpse, left to itself, was washed into the larboard scuppers, where it still lay at the time of which I speak, floundering about with the furious lurches of the brig.

Having arranged our plan, we set about putting it in execution as speedily as possible. Peters went upon deck, and, as he had anticipated, was immediately accosted by Allen, who appeared to be stationed more as a watch upon the forecastle than for any other purpose. The fate of this villain, however, was speedily and silently decided; for Peters, approaching him in a careless manner, as if about to address him, seized him by the throat, and, before he could utter a single cry, tossed him over the bulwarks. He then called to us, and we came up. Our first precaution was to look about for something with which to arm ourselves, and in doing this we had to proceed with great care, for it was impossible to stand on deck an instant without holding fast, and violent seas broke over the vessel at every plunge forward. It was indispensable, too, that we should be quick in our operations, for every minute we expected the mate to be up to set the pumps going, as it was evident the brig must be taking in water very fast. After searching about for some time, we could find nothing more fit for our purpose than the two pump handles, one of which Augustus took, and I the other. Having secured these, we stripped off the shirt of the corpse and dropped the body overboard. Peters and myself then went below, leaving Augustus to watch upon deck, where he took his station just where Allen had been placed, and with his back to the cabin companionway, so that, if any one of the mate's gang should come up, he might suppose it was the watch.

As soon as I got below I commenced disguising myself so as to represent the corpse of Rogers. The shirt which we had taken from the body aided us very much, for it was of a singular form and character, and easily recognizable—a kind of smock, which the deceased wore over his other clothing. It was a blue stockinet, with large white stripes running across. Having put this on, I proceeded to equip myself with a false stomach, in imitation of the horrible deformity of the swollen corpse. This was soon effected by means of stuffing with some bedclothes. I then gave the same appearance to my hands by drawing on a pair of white woolen mittens, and filling them in with any kind of rags that offered themselves. Peters then arranged my face, first rubbing it well over with white chalk, and afterward splotching it with blood, which he took from a cut in his finger. The streak across the eye was not forgotten, and presented a most shocking appearance.

CHAPTER 8

As I VIEWED myself in a fragment of looking glass which hung up in the cabin, and by the dim light of a kind of battle lantern, I was so impressed with a sense of vague awe at my appearance, and at the recollection of the terrific reality which I was thus representing, that I was seized with a violent tremor, and could scarcely summon resolution to go on with my part. It was necessary, however, to act with decision, and Peters and myself went up on deck.

We there found everything safe, and, keeping close to the bulwarks, the three of us crept to the cabin companionway. It was only partially closed, precautions having been taken to prevent its being suddenly pushed to from without, by means of placing billets of wood on the upper step so as to interfere with the shutting. We found no difficulty in getting a full view of the interior of the cabin through the cracks where the hinges were placed. It now proved to have been very fortunate for us that we had not attempted to take them by surprise, for they were evidently on the alert. Only one was asleep, and he lying just at the foot of the companion ladder, with a musket by his side. The rest were seated on several mattresses, which had been taken from the berths and thrown on the floor. They were engaged in earnest conversation; and although they had been carousing, as appeared from two empty jugs, with some tin tumblers which lay about, they were not as much intoxicated as usual. All had knives, one or two of them pistols, and a great many muskets were lying in a berth close at hand.

We listened to their conversation for some time before we could make up our minds how to act, having as yet resolved on nothing determinate, except that we would attempt to paralyze their exertions, when we should attack them, by means of the apparition of Rogers. They were discussing their piratical plans, in which all we could hear distinctly was, that they would unite with the crew of a schooner *Hornet*, and, if possible, get the schooner herself into their possession preparatory to some attempt on a large scale, the particulars of which could not be made out by either of us.

One of the men spoke of Peters, when the mate replied to him in a low voice which could not be distinguished, and afterward added more loudly, that "he could not understand his being so much forward with the captain's brat in the forecastle, and he thought the sooner both of them were overboard the better." To this no answer was made, but we could easily perceive that the hint was well received by the whole party, and more particularly by Jones. At this period I was excessively agitated, the more so as I could see that neither Augustus nor Peters could determine how to act. I made up my mind, however, to sell my life as dearly as possible, and not to suffer myself to be overcome by any feelings of trepidation.

The tremendous noise made by the roaring of the wind in the rigging, and the washing of the sea over the deck, prevented us from hearing what was said, except during momentary lulls. In one of these, we all distinctly heard the mate tell one of the men to "go forward, and order the d—d lubbers to come into the cabin, where he could have an eye upon them, for he wanted no such secret doings on board the brig." It was well for us that the pitching of the vessel at this moment was so violent as to prevent this order from being carried into instant execution. The cook got up from his mattress to go for us, when a tremendous lurch, which I thought would carry away the masts, threw him headlong against one of the larboard stateroom doors, bursting it open, and creating a good deal of other confusion. Luckily, neither of our party was thrown from his position, and we had time to make a precipitate retreat to the forecastle, and arrange a hurried plan of action before the messenger made his appearance, or rather before he put his head out of the companion hatch, for he did not come on deck. From this station he could not notice the absence of Allen, and he accordingly bawled out, as if to him, repeating the orders of the mate. Peters cried out, "Ay, ay," in a disguised voice, and the cook immediately went below, without entertaining a suspicion that all was not right.

My two companions now proceeded boldly aft and down into the cabin, Peters closing the door after him in the same manner he had found it. The mate received them with feigned cordiality, and told Augustus that, since he had behaved himself so well of late, he might take up his quarters in the cabin and be one of them for the future. He then poured him out a tumbler half full of rum, and made him drink it. All this I saw and heard, for I followed my friends to the cabin as soon as the door was shut, and took up my old point of observation. I had brought with me the two pump handles, one of which I secured near the companionway, to be ready for use when required.

I now steadied myself as well as possible so as to have a good view of all that was passing within, and endeavored to nerve myself to the task of descending among the mutineers when Peters should make a signal to me as agreed upon. Presently he contrived to turn the conversation upon the bloody deeds of the mutiny, and by degrees led the men to talk of the thousand superstitions which are so universally current among seamen. I could not make out all that was said, but I could plainly see the effects of the conversation in the countenances of those present. The mate was evidently much agitated, and presently, when some-one mentioned the terrific appearance of Rogers' corpse, I thought he was upon the point of swooning. Peters now asked him if he did not think it would be better to have the body thrown overboard at once, as it was too horrible a sight to see it floundering about in the scuppers. At this the villain absolutely gasped for breath, and turned his head slowly round upon his companions, as if imploring someone to go up and perform the task. No one, however, stirred, and it was quite evident that the whole party were wound up to the highest pitch of nervous excitement. Peters now made me the signal. I immedi-ately threw open the door of the companionway, and, descending, without uttering a syllable, stood erect in the midst of the party.

The intense effect produced by this sudden apparition is not at all to be wondered at when the various circumstances are taken into consideration. Usually, in cases of a similar nature, there is left in the mind of the spectator some glimmering of doubt as to the reality of the vision before his eyes; a degree of hope, however feeble, that he is the victim of chicanery, and that the apparition is not actually a visitant from the world of shadows. It is not too much to say that such remnants of doubt have been at the bottom of almost every such visitation, and that the appalling horror which has sometimes been brought about, is to be attributed, even in the cases most in point, and where most suffering has been experienced, more to a kind of anticipative horror, lest the apparition *might possibly be* real, than to an unwavering belief in its reality. But, in the present instance, it will be seen immediately, that in the minds of the mutineers there was not even the shadow of a basis upon which to rest a doubt that the apparition of Rogers was indeed a revivification of his disgusting corpse, or at least its spiritual image. The isolated situation of the brig, with its entire inaccessibility on account of the gale, confined the apparently possible means of deception within such narrow and definite limits, that they must have thought themselves enabled to survey them all at a glance. They had now been at sea twenty-four days without holding more than a speaking communication with any vessel whatever. The whole of the crew, too, at least all whom they had the most remote reason for suspecting to be on board, were assembled in the cabin, with the exception of Allen, the watch; and his gigantic stature (he was six feet six inches high) was too familiar in their eyes to permit the notion that he was the apparition before them to enter their minds even for an instant. Add to these considerations the awe-inspiring nature of the tempest, and that of the conversation brought about by Peters; the deep impression which the loathsomeness of the actual corpse had made in the morning upon the imaginations of the men; the excellence of the imitation in my person, and the uncertain and wavering light in which they beheld me, as the glare of the cabin lantern, swinging violently to and fro, fell dubiously and fitfully upon my figure, and there will be no reason to wonder that the deception had even more than the entire effect which we had anticipated. The mate sprang up from the mattress on which he was lying, and without uttering a syllable, fell back, stone dead, upon the cabin floor, and was hurled to the leeward like a log by a heavy roll of the brig. Of the remaining seven, there were but three who had at first any degree of presence of mind. The four others sat for some time rooted apparently to the floor, the most pitiable objects of horror and utter despair my eyes ever encountered. The only opposition we experienced at all was from the cook, John Hunt, and Richard Parker; but they made but a feeble and irresolute defense. The two former were shot instantly by Peters, and I felled Parker with a blow on the head from the pump handle which I had brought with me. In the meantime Augustus seized one of the muskets lying on the floor and shot another mutineer (—— Wilson) through the breast. There were now but three remaining; but by this time they had become aroused from their lethargy, and perhaps began to see that a deception had been practiced upon them, for they fought with great resolution and fury, and, but for the immense muscular strength of Peters, might have ultimately got the better of us. These three men were —— Jones, —— Greely, and Absalom Hicks. Jones had thrown Augustus on the floor, stabbed him in several places along the right arm, and would no doubt have soon dispatched him (as neither Peters nor myself could immediately get rid of our own antagonists), had it not been for the timely aid of a friend, upon whose assistance we surely had never depended. This friend was no other than Tiger. With a low growl, he bounded into the cabin, at a most critical moment for Augustus, and throwing himself upon Jones, pinned him to the floor in an instant. My friend, however, was now too much injured to render us any aid whatever, and I was so encumbered with my disguise that I could do but little. The dog would not leave his hold upon the throat of Jones—Peters, nevertheless, was far more than a match for the two men who remained, and would, no doubt, have dispatched them sooner, had it not been for the narrow space in which he had to act, and the tremendous lurches of the vessel. Presently he was enabled to get hold of a heavy stool, several of which lay about the floor. With this he beat out the brains of Greely as he was in the act of discharging a musket at me, and immediately afterward a roll of the brig throwing him in contact with Hicks, he seized him by the throat, and, by dint of sheer strength, strangled him instantaneously. Thus, in far less time than I have taken to tell it, we found ourselves masters of the brig.

The only person of our opponents who was left alive was Richard Parker. This man, it will be remembered, I had knocked down with a blow from the pump handle at the commencement of the attack. He now lay motionless by the door of the shattered stateroom; but, upon Peters touching him with his foot, he spoke, and entreated for mercy. His head was only slightly cut, and otherwise he had received no injury, having been merely stunned by the blow. He now got up, and, for the present, we secured his hands behind his back. The dog was still growling over Jones; but, upon examination, we found him completely dead, the blood issuing in a stream from a deep wound in the throat, inflicted, no doubt, by the sharp teeth of the animal.

It was now about one o'clock in the morning, and the wind was still blowing tremendously. The brig evidently labored much more than usual, and it became absolutely necessary that something should be done with a view of easing her in some measure. At almost every roll to leeward she shipped a sea, several of which came partially down into the cabin during our scuffle, the hatchway having been left open by myself when I descended. The entire range of bulwarks to larboard had been swept away, as well as the caboose, together with the jolly boat from the counter. The creaking and working of the mainmast, too, gave indication that it was nearly sprung. To make room for more stowage in the afterhold, the heel of this mast had been stepped between decks (a very reprehensible practice, occasionally resorted to by ignorant shipbuilders), so that it was in imminent danger of working from its step. But, to crown all our difficulties, we plumbed the well, and found no less than seven feet water.

Leaving the bodies of the crew lying in the cabin, we got to work immediately at the pumps—Parker, of course, being set at liberty to assist us in the labor. Augustus' arm was bound up as well as we could effect it, and he did what he could, but that was not much. However, we found that we could just manage to keep the leak from gaining upon us by having one pump constantly going. As there were only four of us, this was severe labor; but we endeavored to keep up our spirits, and looked anxiously for daybreak, when we hoped to lighten the brig by cutting away the mainmast.

In this manner we passed a night of terrible anxiety and fatigue, and, when the day at length broke, the gale had neither abated in the least, nor were there any signs of its abating. We now dragged the bodies on deck and threw them overboard. Our next care was to get rid of the mainmast. The necessary preparations having been made, Peters cut away at the mast (having found axes in the cabin), while the rest of us stood by the stays and lanyards. As the brig gave a tremendous lee lurch, the word was given to cut away the weather lanyards, which being done, the whole mass of wood and rigging plunged into the sea, clear of the brig, and without doing any material injury. We now found that the vessel did not labor quite as much as before, but our situation was still exceedingly precarious, and, in spite of the utmost exertions, we could not gain upon the leak without the aid of both pumps. The little assistance which Augustus could render us was not really of any importance. To add to our distress, a heavy sea, striking the brig to windward, threw her off several points from the wind, and, before she could regain her position, another broke completely over her, and hurled her full upon her beam-ends. The ballast now shifted in a mass to leeward (the stowage had been knocking about perfectly at random for some time), and for a few moments we thought nothing could save us from capsizing. Presently, however, we partially righted;

but the ballast still retaining its place to larboard, we lay so much along that it was useless to think of working the pumps, which indeed we could not have done much longer in any case, as our hands were entirely raw with the excessive labor we had undergone, and were bleeding in the most horrible manner.

Contrary to Parker's advice, we now proceeded to cut away the foremast, and at length accomplished it after much difficulty, owing to the position in which we lay. In going overboard the wreck took with it the bowsprit, and left us a complete hulk.

So far we had had reason to rejoice in the escape of our longboat, which had received no damage from any of the huge seas which had come on board. But we had not long to congratulate ourselves; for the foremast having gone, and, of course, the foresail with it, by which the brig had been steadied, every sea now made a complete breach over us, and in five minutes our deck was swept from stem to stern, the longboat and starboard bulwarks torn off, and even the windlass shattered into fragments. It was, indeed, hardly possible for us to be in a more pitiable condition.

At noon there seemed to be some slight appearance of the gale's abating, but in this we were sadly disappointed, for it only lulled for a few minutes to blow with redoubled fury. About four in the afternoon it was utterly impossible to stand up against the violence of the blast; and, as the night closed in upon us, I had not a shadow of hope that the vessel would hold together until morning.

By midnight we had settled very deep in the water, which was now up to the orlop deck. The rudder went soon afterward, the sea which tore it away lifting the afterportion of the brig entirely from the water, against which she thumped in her descent with such a concussion as would be occasioned by going ashore. We had all calculated that the rudder would hold its own to the last, as it was unusually strong, being rigged as I have never seen one rigged either before or since. Down its main timber there ran a succession of stout iron hooks, and others in the same manner down the sternpost. Through these hooks there extended a very thick wrought-iron rod, the rudder being thus held to the sternpost, and swinging freely on the rod. The tremendous force of the sea which tore it off may be estimated by the fact, that the hooks in the sternpost, which ran entirely through it, being clinched on the inside, were drawn every one of them completely out of the solid wood.

We had scarcely time to draw breath after the violence of this shock, when one of the most tremendous waves I had then ever known broke right on board of us, sweeping the companionway clear off, bursting in the hatchways, and filling every inch of the vessel with water.

CHAPTER 9

LUCKILY, just before night, all four of us had lashed ourselves firmly to the fragments of the windlass, lying in this manner as flat upon the deck as possible. This precaution alone saved us from destruction. As it was we were all more or less stunned by the immense weight of water which tumbled upon us, and which did not roll from above us until we were nearly exhausted. As soon as I could recover breath, I called aloud to my companions. Augustus alone replied, saying, "It is all over with us, and may God have mercy upon our souls." By-and-by both the others were enabled to speak, when they exhorted us to take courage, as there was still hope; it being impossible, from the nature of the cargo, that the brig could go down, and there being every chance that the gale would blow over by the morning. These words inspired me with new life; for, strange as it may seem, although it was obvious that a vessel with a cargo of empty oil casks would not sink, I had been hitherto so confused in mind as to have overlooked this consideration altogether; and the danger which I had for some time regarded as the most imminent was that of foundering. As hope revived within me, I made use of every opportunity to strengthen the lashings which held me to the remains of the windlass, and in this occupation I soon discovered that my companions were also busy. The night was as dark as it could possibly be, and the horrible shrieking din and confusion which surrounded us it is useless to attempt describing. Our deck lay level with the sea, or rather we were encircled with a towering ridge of foam, a portion of which swept over us every instant. It is not too much to say that our heads were not fairly out of water more than one second in three. Although we lay close together, no one of us could see the other, or, indeed, any portion of the brig itself, upon which we were so tempestuously hurled about.

At intervals we called one to the other, thus endeavoring to keep alive hope, and render consolation and encouragement to such of us as stood most in need of it. The feeble condition of Augustus made him an object of solicitude with us all; and as, from the lacerated condition of his right arm, it must have been impossible for him to secure his lashings with any degree of firmness, we were in momentary expectation of finding that he had gone overboard—yet to render him aid was a thing altogether out of the question. Fortunately, his station was more secure than that of any of the rest of us; for the upper part of his body lying just beneath a portion of the shattered windlass, the seas, as they tumbled in upon him, were greatly broken in their violence. In any other situation than this (into which he had been accidentally thrown after having lashed himself in a very exposed spot) he must inevitably have perished before morning. Owing to the brig's lying so much along, we were all less liable to be washed off than otherwise would have been the case. The heel, as I have before stated, was to larboard, about one half of the deck being constantly under water. The seas, therefore, which struck us to starboard were much broken by the vessel's side, only reaching us in fragments as we lay flat on our faces; while those which came from larboard, being what are called backwater seas, and obtaining little hold upon us on account of our posture, had not sufficient force to drag us from our fastenings.

In this frightful situation we lay until the day broke so as to show us more fully the horrors which surrounded us. The brig was a mere log, rolling about at the mercy of every wave; the gale was upon the increase, if anything, blowing indeed a complete hurricane, and there appeared to us no earthly prospect of deliverance. For several hours we held on in silence, expecting every moment that our lashings would either give way, that the remains of the windlass would go by the board, or that some of the huge seas, which roared in every direction around us and above us, would drive the hulk so far beneath the water that we should be drowned before it could regain the surface. By the mercy of God, however, we were preserved from these imminent dangers, and about midday were cheered by the light of the blessed sun. Shortly afterward we could perceive a sensible diminution in the force of the wind, when, now for the first time since the latter part of the evening before, Augustus spoke, asking Peters, who lay closest to him, if he thought there was any possibility of our being saved. As no reply was at first made to this question, we all concluded that the hybrid had been drowned where he lay; but presently, to our great joy, he spoke, although very feebly, saying that he was in great pain, being so cut by the tightness of his lashings across the stomach, that he must either find means of loosening them or perish, as it was impossible that he could endure his misery much longer. This occasioned us great distress, as it was altogether useless to think of aiding him in any manner while the sea continued washing over us as it did. We exhorted him to bear his sufferings with fortitude, and promised to seize the first opportunity which should offer itself to relieve him. He replied that it would soon be too late; that it would be all over with him before we could help him; and then, after moaning for some minutes, lay silent, when we concluded that he had perished.

As the evening drew on, the sea had fallen so much that scarcely more than one wave broke over the hulk from windward in the course of five minutes, and the wind had abated a great deal, although still blowing a severe gale. I had not heard any of my companions speak for hours, and now called to Augustus. He replied, although very feebly, so that I could not distinguish what he said. I then spoke to Peters and to Parker, neither of whom returned any answer.

Shortly after this period I fell into a state of partial insensibility, during which the most pleasing images floated in my imagination; such as green trees, waving meadows of ripe grain, processions of dancing girls, troops of cavalry, and other phantasies. I now remembered that, in all which passed before my mind's eye, *motion* was a predominant idea. Thus, I never fancied any stationary object, such as a house, a mountain, or anything of that kind; but windmills, ships, large birds, balloons, people on horseback, carriages driving furiously, and similar moving objects, presented themselves in endless succession. When I recovered from this state, the sun was, as near as I could guess, an hour high. I had the greatest difficulty in bringing to recollection the various circumstances connected with my situation, and for some time remained firmly convinced that I was still in the hold of the brig, near the box, and that the body of Parker was that of Tiger.

When I at length completely came to my senses, I found that the wind blew no more than a moderate breeze, and that the sea was comparatively calm; so much so that it only washed over the brig amidships. My left arm had broken loose from its lashings, and was much cut about the elbow; my right was entirely benumbed, and the hand and wrist swollen prodigiously by the pressure of the rope, which had worked from the shoulder downward. I was also in great pain from another rope which went about my waist, and had been drawn to an insufferable degree of tightness. Looking round upon my companions, I saw that Peters still lived, although a thick line was pulled so forcibly around his loins as to give him the appearance of being cut nearly in two; as I stirred, he made a feeble motion to me with his hand, pointing to the rope. Augustus gave no indication of life whatever, and was bent nearly double across a splinter of the windlass. Parker spoke to me when he saw me moving, and asked me if I had not sufficient strength to release him from his situation; saying, that if I would summon up what spirits I could, and contrive to untie him, we might yet save our lives; but that otherwise we must all perish. I told him to take courage, and I would endeavor to free him. Feeling in my pantaloons' pocket, I got hold of my penknife, and after several ineffectual attempts, at length succeeded in opening it. I then, with my left hand, managed to free my right from its fastenings, and afterward cut the other ropes which held me. Upon attempting, however, to move from my position, I found that my legs failed me altogether, and that I could not get up; neither could I move my right arm in any direction. Upon mentioning this to Parker, he advised me to lie quiet for a few minutes, holding on to the windlass with my left hand, so as to allow time for the blood to circulate. Doing this, the numbness

presently began to die away so that I could move first one of my
legs, and then the other; and, shortly afterward I regained the
partial use of my right arm. I now crawled with great caution
towards Parker, without getting on my legs, and soon cut loose
all the lashings about him, when, after a short delay, he also
recovered the partial use of his limbs. We now lost no time in
getting loose the rope from Peters. It had cut a deep gash
through the waistband of his woolen pantaloons, and through
two shirts, and made its way into his groin, from which the blood
flowed out copiously as we removed the cordage. No sooner had
we removed it, however, than he spoke, and seemed to experience
instant relief—being able to move with much greater ease than
either Parker or myself—this was no doubt owing to the discharge
of blood.

We had little hope that Augustus would recover, as he evinced
no signs of life; but, upon getting to him, we discovered that
he had merely swooned from loss of blood, the bandages we had
placed around his wounded arm having been torn off by the
water; none of the ropes which held him to the windlass were
drawn sufficiently tight to occasion his death. Having relieved
him from the fastenings, and got him clear of the broken wood
about the windlass, we secured him in a dry place to windward,
with his head somewhat lower than his body, and all three of us
busied ourselves in chafing his limbs. In about half an hour he
came to himself, although it was not until the next morning that
he gave signs of recognizing any of us, or had sufficient strength
to speak. By the time we had thus got clear of our lashings it was
quite dark, and it began to cloud up, so that we were again in the
greatest agony lest it should come on to blow hard, in which
event nothing could have saved us from perishing, exhausted as
we were. By good fortune it continued very moderate during
the night, the sea subsiding every minute, which gave us great
hopes of ultimate preservation. A gentle breeze still blew from
the N.W., but the weather was not at all cold. Augustus was
lashed carefully to windward in such a manner as to prevent him
from slipping overboard with the rolls of the vessel, as he was still

too weak to hold on at all. For ourselves there was no such necessity. We sat close together, supporting each other with the aid of the broken ropes about the windlass, and devising methods of escape from our frightful situation. We derived much comfort from taking off our clothes and wringing the water from them. When we put them on after this, they felt remarkably warm and pleasant, and served to invigorate us in no little degree. We helped Augustus off with his, and wrung them for him, when he experienced the same comfort.

Our chief sufferings were now those of hunger and thirst, and, when we looked forward to the means of relief in this respect, our hearts sunk within us, and we were induced to regret that we had escaped the less dreadful perils of the sea. We endeavored, however, to console ourselves with the hope of being speedily picked up by some vessel, and encouraged each other to bear with fortitude the evils that might happen.

The morning of the fourteenth at length dawned, and the weather still continued clear and pleasant, with a steady but very light breeze from the N.W. The sea was now quite smooth and as, from some cause which we could not determine, the brig did not lie so much along as she had done before, the deck was comparatively dry, and we could move about with freedom. We had now been better than three entire days and nights without either food or drink, and it became absolutely necessary that we should make an attempt to get up something from below. As the brig was completely full of water, we went to this work despondingly, and with but little expectation of being able to obtain anything. We made a kind of drag by driving some nails which we broke out from the remains of the companion hatch into two pieces of wood. Tying these across each other, and fastening them to the end of a rope, we threw them into the cabin, and dragged them to and fro, in the faint hope of being thus able to entangle some article which might be of use to us for food, or which might at least render us assistance in getting it. We spent the greater part of the morning in this labor without effect, fishing up nothing more than a few bedclothes, which were readily caught by the nails. Indeed, our contrivance was so very clumsy that any greater success was hardly to be anticipated.

We now tried the forecastle, but equally in vain, and were upon the brink of despair, when Peters proposed that we should fasten a rope to his body, and let him make an attempt to get up something by diving into the cabin. This proposition we hailed with all the delight which reviving hope could inspire. He proceeded immediately to strip off his clothes with the exception of his pantaloons; and a strong rope was then carefully fastened around his middle, being brought up over his shoulders in such a manner that there was no possibility of its slipping. The undertaking was one of great difficulty and danger; for, as we could hardly expect to find much, if any, provision in the cabin itself, it was necessary that the diver, after letting himself down, should make a turn to the right, and proceed under water a distance of ten or twelve feet, in a narrow passage, to the storeroom, and return, without drawing breath.

Everything being ready, Peters now descended into the cabin, going down the companion ladder until the water reached his chin. He then plunged in, head first, turning to the right as he plunged, and endeavoring to make his way to the storeroom. In this first attempt, however, he was altogether unsuccessful. In less than half a minute after his going down we felt the rope jerked violently (the signal we had agreed upon when he desired to be drawn up). We accordingly drew him up instantly, but so incautiously as to bruise him badly against the ladder. He had brought nothing with him, and had been unable to penetrate more than a very little way into the passage, owing to the constant exertions he found it necessary to make in order to keep himself from floating up against the deck. Upon getting out he was very much exhausted, and had to rest full fifteen minutes before he could again venture to descend.

The second attempt met with even worse success; for he remained so long under water without giving the signal, that, becoming alarmed for his safety, we drew him out without it, and found that he was almost at the last gasp, having, as he said, repeatedly jerked at the rope without our feeling it. This was probably owing to a portion of it having become entangled in the balustrade at the foot of the ladder. This balustrade was, indeed, so much in the way, that we determined to remove it, if possible, before proceeding with our design. As we had no means of getting it away except by main force, we all descended into the water as far as we could on the ladder, and giving a pull against it with our united strength, succeeded in breaking it down.

The third attempt was equally unsuccessful with the two first, and it now became evident that nothing could be done in this manner without the aid of some weight with which the diver might steady himself, and keep to the floor of the cabin while making his search. For a long time we looked about in vain for something which might answer this purpose; but at length, to our great joy, we discovered one of the weather forechains so loose that we had not the least difficulty in wrenching it off. Having fastened this securely to one of his ankles, Peters now made his fourth descent into the cabin, and this time succeeded in making his way to the door of the steward's room. To his inexpressible grief, however, he found it locked, and was obliged to return without effecting an entrance, as, with the greatest exertion, he could remain under water not more, at the utmost extent, than a single minute. Our affairs now looked gloomy indeed, and neither Augustus nor myself could refrain from bursting into tears, as we thought of the host of difficulties which encompassed us, and the slight probability which existed of our finally making an escape. But this weakness was not of long duration. Throwing ourselves on our knees to God, we implored His aid in the many dangers which beset us; and arose with renewed hope and vigor to think what could yet be done by mortal means towards accomplishing our deliverance.

CHAPTER 10

SHORTLY AFTERWARD an incident occurred which I am induced to look upon as more intensely productive of emotion, as far more replete with the extremes first of delight and then of horror, than even any of the thousand chances which afterward befell me in nine long years, crowded with events of the most startling and, in many cases, of the most unconceived and unconceivable character. We were lying on the deck near the companionway, and debating the possibility of yet making our way into the storeroom, when, looking towards Augustus, who lay fronting myself, I perceived that he had become all at once deadly pale, and that his lips were quivering in the most singular and unaccountable manner. Greatly alarmed, I spoke to him, but he made me no reply, and I was beginning to think that he was suddenly taken ill, when I took notice of his eyes, which were glaring apparently at some object behind me. I turned my head, and shall never forget the ecstatic joy which thrilled through every particle of my frame, when I perceived a large brig bearing down upon us, and not more than a couple of miles off. I sprung to my feet as if a musket bullet had suddenly struck me to the heart; and, stretching out my arms in the direction of the vessel, stood in this manner, motionless, and unable to articulate a syllable. Peters and Parker were equally affected, although in different ways. The former danced about the deck like a madman, uttering the most extravagant rodomontades, intermingled with howls and imprecations, while the latter burst into tears, and continued for many minutes weeping like a child.

The vessel in sight was a large hermaphrodite brig, of a Dutch build, and painted black, with a tawdry gilt figurehead. She had evidently seen a good deal of rough weather, and, we supposed, had suffered much in the gale which had proved so disastrous to ourselves; for her foretopmast was gone, and some of her starboard bulwarks. When we first saw her, she was, as I have already said, about two miles off and to windward, bearing down upon us. The breeze was very gentle, and what astonished us chiefly was, that she had no other sails set than her foresail and mainsail, with a flying jib—of course she came down but slowly, and our impatience amounted nearly to frenzy. The awkward manner in which she steered, too, was remarked by all of us, even excited as we were. She yawed about so considerably, that once or twice we thought it impossible she could see us, or imagined that, having seen us, and discovered no person on board, she was about to tack and make off in another direction. Upon each of these occasions we screamed and shouted at the top of our voices, when the stranger would appear to change for a moment her intention, and again hold on towards us—this singular conduct being repeated two or three times, so that at last we could think of no other manner of accounting for it than by supposing the helmsman to be in liquor.

No person was seen upon her decks until she arrived within about a quarter of a mile of us. We then saw three seamen, whom by their dress we took to be Hollanders. Two of these were lying on some old sails near the forecastle, and the third, who appeared to be looking at us with great curiosity, was leaning over the starboard bow near the bowsprit. This last was a stout and tall man, with a very dark skin. He seemed by his manner to be encouraging us to have patience, nodding to us in a cheerful although rather odd way, and smiling constantly, so as to display a set of the most brilliantly white teeth. As his vessel drew nearer, we saw a red flannel cap which he had on fall from his head into the water; but of this he took little or no notice, continuing his odd smiles and gesticulations. I relate these things and circumstances minutely, and I relate them, it must be understood, precisely as they *appeared* to us.

The brig came on slowly, and now more steadily than before, and—I cannot speak calmly of this event—our hearts leaped up wildly within us, and we poured out our whole souls in shouts and thanksgiving to God for the complete, unexpected, and glorious deliverance that was so palpably at hand. Of a sudden, and all at once, there came wafted over the ocean from the strange vessel (which was now close upon us) a smell, a stench, such as the whole world has no name for—no conception of—hellish—utterly suffocating—insufferable, inconceivable. I gasped for breath, and turning to my companions, perceived that they were paler than marble. But we had now no time left for question or surmise—the brig was within fifty feet of us, and it seemed to be her intention to run under our counter, that we might board her without her putting out a boat. We rushed aft, when, suddenly, a wide yaw threw her off full five or six points from the course she had been running, and, as she passed under our stern at the distance of about twenty feet, we had a full view of her decks. Shall I ever forget the triple horror of that spectacle? Twenty-five or thirty human bodies, among whom were several females, lay scattered about between the counter and the galley in the last and most loathsome state of putrefaction. We plainly saw that not a soul lived in that fated vessel! Yet we could not help shouting to the dead for help! Yes, long and loudly did we beg, in the agony of the moment, that those silent and disgusting images would stay for us, would not abandon us to become like them, would receive us among their goodly company! We were raving with horror and despair—thoroughly mad through the anguish of our grievous disappointment.

As our first loud yell of terror broke forth, it was replied to by something, from near the bowsprit of the stranger, so closely resembling the scream of a human voice that the nicest ear might have been startled and deceived. At this instant another sudden yaw brought the region of the forecastle for a moment into view, and we beheld at once the origin of the sound. We saw the tall stout figure still leaning on the bulwark, and still nodding his head to and fro, but his face was now turned from us so that we could not behold it. His arms were extended over the rail, and the palms of his hands fell outward. His knees were lodged upon a stout rope, tightly stretched, and reaching from the heel of the bowsprit to a cathead. On his back, from which a portion of the shirt had been torn, leaving it bare, there sat a huge seagull, busily gorging itself with the horrible flesh, its bill and talons deep buried, and its white plumage spattered all over with blood. As the brig moved further round so as to bring us close in view, the bird, with much apparent difficulty, drew out its crimsoned head, and, after eying us for a moment as if stupefied, arose lazily from the body upon which it had been feasting, and, flying directly above our deck, hovered there a while with a portion of clotted and liverlike substance in its beak. The horrid morsel dropped at length with a sullen splash immediately at the feet of Parker. May God forgive me, but now, for the first time, there flashed through my mind a thought, a thought which I will not mention, and I felt myself making a step towards the ensanguined spot. I looked upward, and the eyes of Augustus met my own with a degree of intense and eager meaning which immediately brought me to my senses. I sprang forward quickly, and, with a deep shudder, threw the frightful thing into the sea.

The body from which it had been taken, resting as it did upon the rope, had been easily swayed to and fro by the exertions of the carnivorous bird, and it was this motion which had at first impressed us with the belief of its being alive. As the gull relieved it of its weight, it swung round and fell partially over, so that the face was fully discovered. Never, surely, was any object so terribly full of awe! The eyes were gone, and the whole flesh around the mouth, leaving the teeth utterly naked. This, then, was the smile which had cheered us on to hope! this the—but I forbear. The brig, as I have already told, passed under our stern, and made its way slowly but steadily to leeward. With her and with her terrible crew went all our gay visions of deliverance and joy. Deliberately as she went by, we might possibly have found means of boarding her, had not our sudden disappointment, and the appalling nature of the discovery which accompanied it, laid entirely prostrate every active faculty of mind and body. We had seen and felt, but we could neither think nor act, until, alas, too late. How much our intellects had been weakened by this

incident may be estimated by the fact that, when the vessel had
proceeded so far that we could perceive no more than the half of
her hull, the proposition was seriously entertained of attempting
to overtake her by swimming!

I have, since this period, vainly endeavored to obtain some
clew to the hideous uncertainty which enveloped the fate of the
stranger. Her build and general appearance, as I have before
stated, led us to the belief that she was a Dutch trader, and the
dresses of the crew also sustained this opinion. We might have
easily seen the name upon her stern, and, indeed, taken other
observations which would have guided us in making out her character; but the intense excitement of the moment blinded us to
everything of that nature. From the saffronlike hue of such of
the corpses as were not entirely decayed, we concluded that the
whole of her company had perished by the yellow fever, or some
other virulent disease of the same fearful kind. If such were the
case (and I know not what else to imagine), death, to judge from
the positions of the bodies, must have come upon them in a
manner awfully sudden and overwhelming, in a way totally distinct from that which generally characterizes even the most
deadly pestilences with which mankind are acquainted. It is
possible, indeed, that poison, accidentally introduced into some
of their sea stores, may have brought about the disaster; or that
the eating some unknown venomous species of fish, or other
marine animal, or oceanic bird, might have induced it—but it is
utterly useless to form conjectures where all is involved, and will,
no doubt, remain forever involved, in the most appalling and
unfathomable mystery.

CHAPTER 11

WE SPENT the remainder of the day in a condition of stupid lethargy, gazing after the retreating vessel until the darkness, hiding her from our sight, recalled us in some measure to our senses. The pangs of hunger and thirst then returned, absorbing all other cares and considerations. Nothing, however, could be done until the morning, and, securing ourselves as well as possible, we endeavored to snatch a little repose. In this I succeeded beyond my expectations, sleeping until my companions, who had not been so fortunate, aroused me at daybreak to renew our attempts at getting up provision from the hull.

It was now a dead calm, with the sea as smooth as I have ever known it—the weather warm and pleasant. The brig was out of sight. We commenced our operations by wrenching off, with some trouble, another of the forechains; and having fastened both to Peters' feet, he again made an endeavor to reach the door of the storeroom, thinking it possible that he might be able to force it open, provided he could get at it in sufficient time; and this he hoped to do, as the hulk lay much more steadily than before.

He succeeded very quickly in reaching the door, when, loosening one of the chains from his ankle, he made every exertion to force a passage with it, but in vain, the framework of the room being far stronger than was anticipated. He was quite exhausted with his long stay under water, and it became absolutely necessary that some other one of us should take his place. For this service Parker immediately volunteered; but, after making three ineffectual efforts, found that he could never even succeed in getting near the door. The condition of Augustus' wounded arm rendered it useless for him to attempt going down, as he would be unable to force the room open should he reach it, and it accordingly now devolved upon me to exert myself for our common deliverance.

Peters had left one of the chains in the passage, and I found, upon plunging in, that I had not sufficient ballast to keep me firmly down. I determined, therefore, to attempt no more, in my first effort, than merely to recover the other chain. In groping along the floor of the passage for this I felt a hard substance, which I immediately grasped, not having time to ascertain what it was, but returning and ascending instantly to the surface. The prize proved to be a bottle, and our joy may be conceived when I say that it was found to be full of port wine. Giving thanks to God for this timely and cheering assistance, we immediately drew the cork with my penknife, and, each taking a moderate sup, felt the most indescribable comfort from the warmth, strength, and spirits with which it inspired us. We then carefully recorked the bottle, and, by means of a handkerchief, swung it in such a manner that there was no possibility of its getting broken.

Having rested awhile after this fortunate discovery, I again descended, and now recovered the chain, with which I instantly came up. I then fastened it on and went down for the third time, when I became fully satisfied that no exertions whatever, in that situation, would enable me to force open the door of the store-room. I therefore returned in despair.

There seemed now to be no longer any room for hope, and I could perceive in the countenances of my companions that they had made up their minds to perish. The wine had evidently produced in them a species of delirium, which, perhaps, I had been prevented from feeling by the immersion I had undergone since drinking it. They talked incoherently, and about matters unconnected with our condition, Peters repeatedly asking me questions about Nantucket. Augustus, too, I remember, approached me with a serious air, and requested me to lend him a pocket comb, as his hair was full of fish scales, and he wished to get them out before going on shore. Parker appeared somewhat less affected, and urged me to dive at random into the cabin, and bring up any article which might come to hand. To this I consented, and, in the first attempt, after staying under a full minute, brought up a small leather trunk belonging to Captain Barnard. This was immediately opened in the faint hope that it might contain something to eat or drink. We found nothing, however, except a box of razors and two linen shirts. I now went down again, and returned without any success. As my head came above water I heard a crash on deck, and, upon getting up, saw that my companions had ungratefully taken advantage of my absence to drink the remainder of the wine, having let the bottle fall in the endeavor to replace it before I saw them. I remonstrated with them on the heartlessness of their conduct, when Augustus burst into tears. The other two endeavored to laugh the matter off as a joke, but I hope never again to behold laughter of such a species: the distortion of countenance was absolutely frightful. Indeed, it was apparent that the stimulus, in the empty state of their stomachs, had taken instant and violent effect, and that they were all exceedingly intoxicated. With great difficulty I prevailed upon them to lie down, when they fell very soon into a heavy slumber, accompanied with loud stertorous breathing.

I now found myself, as it were, alone in the brig, and my reflections, to be sure, were of the most fearful and gloomy nature. No prospect offered itself to my view but a lingering death by famine, or, at the best, by being overwhelmed in the first gale which should spring up, for in our present exhausted condition we could have no hope of living through another.

The gnawing hunger which I now experienced was nearly insupportable, and I felt myself capable of going to any lengths in order to appease it. With my knife I cut off a small portion of the leather trunk, and endeavored to eat it, but found it utterly impossible to swallow a single morsel, although I fancied that some little alleviation of my suffering was obtained by chewing small pieces of it and spitting them out. Towards night my companions awoke, one by one, each in an indescribable state of weakness and horror, brought on by the wine, whose fumes had now evaporated. They shook as if with a violent ague, and uttered the most lamentable cries for water. Their condition affected me in the most lively degree, at the same time causing me to rejoice in the fortunate train of circumstances which had prevented me from indulging in the wine, and consequently from sharing their melancholy and most distressing sensations. Their conduct, however, gave me great uneasiness and alarm; for it was evident that, unless some favorable change took place, they could afford me no assistance in providing for our common safety. I had not yet abandoned all idea of being able to get up something from below; but the attempt could not possibly be resumed until some one of them was sufficiently master of himself to aid me by holding the end of the rope while I went down. Parker appeared to be somewhat more in possession of his senses than the others, and I endeavored, by every means in my power, to arouse him. Thinking that a plunge in the sea water might have a beneficial effect, I contrived to fasten the end of a rope around his body, and then, leading him to the companionway (he remaining quite passive all the while), pushed him in, and immediately drew him out. I had good reason to congratulate myself upon having made this experiment; for he appeared much revived and invigorated, and, upon getting out, asked me, in a rational manner, why I had so served him. Having explained my object, he expressed himself indebted to me, and said that he felt greatly better from the immersion, afterward conversing sensibly upon our situation. We then resolved to treat Augustus and Peters in the same way, which we immediately did, when they both experienced much benefit from the shock. This idea of sudden immersion had been suggested to me by reading in some medical work the good effect of the shower bath in a case where the patient was suffering from *mania a potu.*

Finding that I could now trust my companions to hold the end of the rope, I again made three or four plunges into the cabin, although it was now quite dark, and a gentle but long swell from the northward rendered the hulk somewhat unsteady. In the course of these attempts I succeeded in bringing up two case knives, a three-gallon jug, empty, and a blanket, but nothing which could serve us for food. I continued my efforts, after getting these articles, until I was completely exhausted, but brought up nothing else. During the night Parker and Peters occupied themselves by turns in the same manner; but nothing coming to hand, we now gave up this attempt in despair, concluding that we were exhausting ourselves in vain.

We passed the remainder of this night in a state of the most intense mental and bodily anguish that can possibly be imagined. The morning of the sixteenth at length dawned, and we looked eagerly around the horizon for relief, but to no purpose. The sea was still smooth, with only a long swell from the northward, as on yesterday. This was the sixth day since we had tasted either food or drink, with the exception of the bottle of port wine, and it was clear that we could hold out but a very little while longer unless something could be obtained. I never saw before, nor wish to see again, human beings so utterly emaciated as Peters and Augustus. Had I met them on shore in their present condition I should not have had the slightest suspicion that I had ever beheld them. Their countenances were totally changed in character, so that I could not bring myself to believe them really the same individuals with whom I had been in company but a few days before. Parker, although sadly reduced, and so feeble that he could not raise his head from his bosom, was not so far gone as the other two. He suffered with great patience, making no complaint, and endeavoring to inspire us with hope in every manner he could devise. For myself, although at the commencement of the voyage I had been in bad health, and was at all times of a delicate constitution, I suffered less than any of us, being much less reduced in frame, and retaining my powers of mind in a surprising degree, while the rest were completely prostrated in intellect, and seemed to be brought to a species of second childhood, generally simpering in their expressions, with idiotic smiles, and uttering the most absurd platitudes. At intervals, however, they would appear to revive suddenly, as if inspired all at once with a consciousness of their condition, when they would spring upon their feet in a momentary flash of vigor, and speak, for a short period, of their prospects, in a manner altogether rational, although full of the most intense despair. It is possible, however, that my companions may have entertained the same opinion of their own condition as I did of mine, and that I may have unwittingly been guilty of the same extravagances and imbecilities as themselves—this is a matter which cannot be determined.

About noon Parker declared that he saw land off the larboard quarter, and it was with the utmost difficulty I could restrain him from plunging into the sea with the view of swimming towards it. Peters and Augustus took little notice of what he said, being apparently wrapped up in moody contemplation. Upon looking in the direction pointed out, I could not perceive the faintest appearance of the shore—indeed, I was too well aware that we were far from any land to indulge in a hope of that nature. It was a long time, nevertheless, before I could convince Parker of his mistake. He then burst into a flood of tears, weeping like a child, with loud cries and sobs, for two or three hours, when, becoming exhausted, he fell asleep.

Peters and Augustus now made several ineffectual efforts to swallow portions of the leather. I advised them to chew it and spit it out; but they were too excessively debilitated to be able to follow my advice. I continued to chew pieces of it at intervals, and found some relief from so doing; my chief distress was for water, and I was only prevented from taking a draught from the sea by remembering the horrible consequences which thus have resulted to others who were similarly situated with ourselves.

The day wore on in this manner, when I suddenly discovered a sail to the eastward, and on our larboard bow. She appeared to be a large ship, and was coming nearly athwart us, being probably twelve or fifteen miles distant. None of my companions had as yet discovered her, and I forebore to tell them of her for the present, lest we might again be disappointed of relief. At length, upon her getting nearer, I saw distinctly that she was heading immediately for us, with her light sails filled. I could now contain myself no longer, and pointed her out to my fellow sufferers. They immediately sprang to their feet, again indulging in the most extravagant demonstrations of joy, weeping, laughing in an idiotic manner, jumping, stamping upon the deck, tearing their hair, and praying and cursing by turns. I was so affected by their conduct, as well as by what I now considered a sure prospect of deliverance, that I could not refrain from joining in with their madness, and gave way to the impulses of my gratitude and ecstasy by lying and rolling on the deck, clapping my hands, shouting, and other similar acts, until I was suddenly called to my recollection, and once more to the extreme of human misery and despair, by perceiving the ship all at once with her stern fully presented towards us, and steering in a direction nearly opposite to that in which I had at first perceived her.

It was some time before I could induce my poor companions to believe that this sad reverse in our prospects had actually taken place. They replied to all my assertions with a stare and a gesture implying that they were not to be deceived by such misrepresentations. The conduct of Augustus most sensibly affected me. In spite of all I could say or do to the contrary, he persisted in saying that the ship was rapidly nearing us, and in making preparations to go on board of her. Some seaweed floating by the brig, he maintained that it was the ship's boat, and endeavored to throw himself upon it, howling and shrieking in the most heart-rending manner, when I forcibly restrained him from thus casting himself into the sea.

Having become in some degree pacified, we continued to watch the ship until we finally lost sight of her, the weather becoming hazy, with a light breeze springing up. As soon as she was entirely gone, Parker turned suddenly towards me with an expression of countenance which made me shudder. There was about him an air of self-possession which I had not noticed in him until now, and before he opened his lips my heart told me what he would say. He proposed, in a few words, that one of us should die to preserve the existence of the others.

CHAPTER 12

I HAD, for some time past, dwelt upon the prospect of our being reduced to this last horrible extremity, and had secretly made up my mind to suffer death in any shape or under any circumstances rather than resort to such a course. Nor was this resolution in any degree weakened by the present intensity of hunger under which I labored. The proposition had not been heard by either Peters or Augustus. I therefore took Parker aside; and mentally praying to God for power to dissuade him from the horrible purpose he entertained, I expostulated with him for a long time, and in the most supplicating manner, begging him in the name of everything which he held sacred, and urging him by every species of argument which the extremity of the case suggested, to abandon the idea, and not to mention it to either of the other two.

He heard all I said without attempting to controvert any of my arguments, and I had begun to hope that he would be prevailed upon to do as I desired. But when I had ceased speaking, he said that he knew very well all I had said was true, and that to resort to such a course was the most horrible alternative which could enter into the mind of man; but that he had now held out as long as human nature could be sustained; that it was unnecessary for all to perish, when, by the death of one, it was possible, and even probable, that the rest might be finally preserved; adding that I might save myself the trouble of trying to turn him from his purpose, his mind having been thoroughly made up on the subject even before the appearance of the ship, and that only her heaving in sight had prevented him from mentioning his intention at an earlier period.

I now begged him, if he would not be prevailed upon to abandon his design, at least to defer it for another day, when some vessel might come to our relief; again reiterating every argument I could devise, and which I thought likely to have influence with one of his rough nature. He said, in reply, that he had not spoken until the very last possible moment; that he could exist no longer without sustenance of some kind; and that therefore in another day his suggestion would be too late, as regarded himself at least.

Finding that he was not to be moved by anything I could say in a mild tone, I now assumed a different demeanor, and told him that he must be aware I had suffered less than any of us from our calamities; that my health and strength, consequently, were at that moment far better than his own, or than that either of Peters or Augustus; in short, that I was in a condition to have my own way by force if I found it necessary; and that if he attempted in any manner to acquaint the others with his bloody and cannibal designs, I would not hesitate to throw him into the sea. Upon this he immediately seized me by the throat, and drawing a knife, made several ineffectual efforts to stab me in the stomach; an atrocity which his excessive debility alone prevented him from accomplishing. In the meantime, being roused to a high pitch of anger, I forced him to the vessel's side, with the full intention of throwing him overboard. He was saved from this fate, however, by the interference of Peters, who now approached and separated us, asking the cause of the disturbance. This Parker told before I could find means in any manner to prevent him.

The effect of his words was even more terrible than what I had anticipated. Both Augustus and Peters, who, it seems, had long secretly entertained the same fearful idea which Parker had been merely the first to broach, joined with him in his design and insisted upon its being immediately carried into effect. I had calculated that one at least of the two former would be found still possessed of sufficient strength of mind to side with myself in resisting any attempt to execute so dreadful a purpose; and, with the aid of either one of them, I had no fear of being able to prevent its accomplishment. Being disappointed in this expectation, it became absolutely necessary that I should attend to my own safety, as a further resistance on my part might possibly be

considered by men in their frightful condition a sufficient excuse
for refusing me fair play in the tragedy that I knew would speedily
be enacted.

I now told them I was willing to submit to the proposal, merely
requesting a delay of about one hour, in order that the fog which
had gathered around us might have an opportunity of lifting,
when it was possible that the ship we had seen might be again
in sight. After great difficulty I obtained from them a promise
to wait thus long; and, as I had anticipated (a breeze rapidly
coming in), the fog lifted before the hour had expired, when, no
vessel appearing in sight, we prepared to draw lots.

It is with extreme reluctance that I dwell upon the appalling
scene which ensued; a scene which, with its minutest details, no
afterevents have been able to efface in the slightest degree from
my memory, and whose stern recollection will embitter every
future moment of my existence. Let me run over this portion of
my narrative with as much haste as the nature of the events to be
spoken of will permit. The only method we could devise for the
terrific lottery, in which we were to take each a chance, was that
of drawing straws. Small splinters of wood were made to answer
our purpose, and it was agreed that I should be the holder. I
retired to one end of the hulk, while my poor companions silently
took up their station in the other with their backs turned towards
me. The bitterest anxiety which I endured at any period of this
fearful drama was while I occupied myself in the arrangement
of the lots. There are few conditions into which man can possibly fall where he will not feel a deep interest in the preservation
of his existence; an interest momentarily increasing with the frail-
ness of the tenure by which that existence may be held. But now
that the silent, definite, and stern nature of the business in which
I was engaged (so different from the tumultuous dangers of the
storm or the gradually approaching horrors of famine) allowed
me to reflect on the few chances I had of escaping the most
appalling of deaths—a death for the most appalling of purposes—
every particle of that energy which had so long buoyed me up
departed like feathers before the wind, leaving me a helpless prey

to the most abject and pitiable terror. I could not, at first, even summon up sufficient strength to tear and fit together the small splinters of wood, my fingers absolutely refusing their office, and my knees knocking violently against each other. My mind ran over rapidly a thousand absurd projects by which to avoid becoming a partner in the awful speculation. I thought of falling on my knees to my companions, and entreating them to let me escape this necessity; of suddenly rushing upon them, and, by putting one of them to death, of rendering the decision by lot useless—in short, of everything but of going through with the matter I had in hand. At last, after wasting a long time in this imbecile conduct, I was recalled to my senses by the voice of Parker, who urged me to relieve them at once from the terrible anxiety they were enduring. Even then I could not bring myself to arrange the splinters upon the spot, but thought over every species of finesse by which I could trick some one of my fellow sufferers to draw the short straw, as it had been agreed that whoever drew the shortest of four splinters from my hand was to die for the preservation of the rest. Before any one condemn me for this apparent heartlessness, let him be placed in a situation precisely similar to my own.

At length delay was no longer possible, and, with a heart almost bursting from my bosom, I advanced to the region of the forecastle, where my companions were awaiting me. I held out my hand with the splinters, and Peters immediately drew. He was free—*his*, at least, was not the shortest; and there was now another chance against my escape. I summoned up all my strength, and passed the lots to Augustus. He also drew immediately, and he also was free; and now, whether I should live or die, the chances were no more than precisely even. At this moment all the fierceness of the tiger possessed my bosom, and I felt towards my poor fellow creature, Parker, the most intense, the most diabolical hatred. But the feeling did not last; and, at length, with a convulsive shudder and closed eyes, I held out the two remaining splinters towards him. It was full five minutes before he could summon resolution to draw, during which period of heart-rending suspense I never once opened my eyes. Presently one of the two lots was quickly drawn from my hand. The decision was then over, yet I knew not whether it was for me or against me. No one spoke, and still I dared not satisfy myself by looking at the splinter I held. Peters at length took me by the hand, and I forced myself to look up, when I immediately saw by the countenance of Parker that I was safe, and that he it was who had been doomed to suffer. Gasping for breath, I fell senseless to the deck.

I recovered from my swoon in time to behold the consummation of the tragedy in the death of him who had been chiefly instrumental in bringing it about. He made no resistance whatever, and was stabbed in the back by Peters, when he fell instantly dead. I must not dwell upon the fearful repast which immediately ensued. Such things may be imagined, but words have no power to impress the mind with the exquisite horror of their reality. Let it suffice to say that, having in some measure appeased the raging thirst which consumed us by the blood of the victim, and having by common consent taken off the hands, feet, and head, throwing them together with the entrails, into the sea, we devoured the rest of the body, piecemeal, during the four ever memorable days of the seventeenth, eighteenth, nineteenth, and twentieth of the month.

On the nineteenth, there coming on a smart shower which lasted fifteen or twenty minutes, we contrived to catch some water by means of a sheet which had been fished up from the cabin by our drag just after the gale. The quantity we took in all did not amount to more than half a gallon; but even this scanty allowance supplied us with comparative strength and hope.

On the twenty-first we were again reduced to the last necessity. The weather still remained warm and pleasant, with occasional fogs and light breezes, most usually from N. to W.

On the twenty-second, as we were sitting close huddled together, gloomily revolving over our lamentable condition, there flashed through my mind all at once an idea which inspired me with a bright gleam of hope. I remembered that, when the foremast had been cut away, Peters, being in the windward chains, passed one of the axes into my hand, requesting me to put it, if possible, in a place of security, and that a few minutes before the last heavy sea struck the brig and filled her I had taken this ax into the forecastle and laid it in one of the larboard berths. I now thought it possible that, by getting at this ax, we might cut through the deck over the storeroom, and thus readily supply ourselves with provisions.

When I communicated this project to my companions, they uttered a feeble shout of joy, and we all proceeded forthwith to the forecastle. The difficulty of descending here was greater than that of going down in the cabin, the opening being much smaller, for it will be remembered that the whole framework about the cabin companion hatch had been carried away, whereas the fore-castleway, being a simple hatch of only about three feet square, had remained uninjured. I did not hesitate, however, to attempt the descent; and a rope being fastened round my body as before, I plunged boldly in, feet foremost, made my way quickly to the berth, and at the very first attempt brought up the ax. It was hailed with the most ecstatic joy and triumph, and the ease with which it had been obtained was regarded as an omen of our ultimate preservation.

We now commenced cutting at the deck with all the energy of rekindled hope, Peters and myself taking the ax by turns, Augustus' wounded arm not permitting him to aid us in any degree. As we were still so feeble as to be scarcely able to stand unsupported, and could consequently work but a minute or two without resting, it soon became evident that many long hours would be requisite to accomplish our task—that is, to cut an opening sufficiently large to admit of a free access to the storeroom. This consideration, however, did not discourage us; and, working all night by the light of the moon, we succeeded in effecting our purpose by daybreak on the morning of the twenty-third.

Peters now volunteered to go down; and, having made all arrangements as before, he descended, and soon returned, bringing up with him a small jar, which, to our great joy, proved to

be full of olives. Having shared these among us, and devoured
them with the greatest avidity, we proceeded to let him down
again. This time he succeeded beyond our utmost expectations,
returning instantly with a large ham and a bottle of Madeira wine.
Of the latter we each took a moderate sup, having learned by
experience the pernicious consequences of indulging too freely.
The ham, except about two pounds near the bone, was not in a
condition to be eaten, having been entirely spoiled by the salt
water. The sound part was divided among us. Peters and Augustus, not being able to restrain their appetite, swallowed theirs
upon the instant; but I was more cautious, and ate but a small
portion of mine, dreading the thirst which I knew would ensue.
We now rested awhile from our labors, which had been intoler-
ably severe.

By noon, feeling somewhat strengthened and refreshed, we
again renewed our attempt at getting up provision, Peters and
myself going down alternately, and always with more or less
success, until sundown. During this interval we had the good
fortune to bring up, altogether, four more small jars of olives,
another ham, a carboy containing nearly three gallons of excellent
Cape Madeira wine, and, what gave us still more delight, a small
tortoise of the Gallipago breed, several of which had been taken
on board by Captain Barnard, as the *Grampus* was leaving port,
from the schooner *Mary Pitts*, just returned from a sealing voyage
in the Pacific.

In a subsequent portion of this narrative I shall have frequent
occasion to mention this species of tortoise. It is found principally, as most of my readers may know, in the group of islands
called the Gallipagos, which, indeed, derive their name from the
animal—the Spanish word Gallipago meaning a fresh-water terra-
pin. From the peculiarity of their shape and action they have
been sometimes called elephant tortoise. They are frequently
found of an enormous size. I have myself seen several which
would weigh from twelve to fifteen hundred pounds, although
I do not remember that any navigator speaks of having seen them
weighing more than eight hundred. Their appearance is singular,

and even disgusting. Their steps are very slow, measured, and heavy, their bodies being carried about a foot from the ground. Their neck is long, and exceedingly slender; from eighteen inches to two feet is a very common length, and I killed one, where the distance from the shoulder to the extremity of the head was no less than three feet ten inches. The head has a striking resemblance to that of a serpent. They can exist without food for an almost incredible length of time, instances having been known where they have been thrown into the hold of a vessel and lain two years without nourishment of any kind—being as fat, and, in every respect, in as good order at the expiration of the time as when they were first put in. In one particular these extraordinary animals bear a resemblance to the dromedary, or camel of the desert. In a bag at the root of the neck they carry with them a constant supply of water. In some instances, upon killing them after a full year's deprivation of all nourishment, as much as three gallons of perfectly sweet and fresh water have been found in their bags. Their food is chiefly wild parsley and celery, with purslane, sea kelp, and prickly pears, upon which latter vegetable they thrive wonderfully, a great quantity of it being usually found on the hillsides near the shore wherever the animal itself is discovered. They are excellent and highly nutritious food, and have, no doubt, been the means of preserving the lives of thousands of seamen employed in the whale fishery and other pursuits in the Pacific.

The one which we had the good fortune to bring up from the storeroom was not of a large size, weighing probably sixty-five or seventy pounds. It was a female, and in excellent condition, being exceedingly fat, and having more than a quart of limpid and sweet water in its bag. This was indeed a treasure; and, falling on our knees with one accord, we returned fervent thanks to God for so seasonable a relief.

We had great difficulty in getting the animal up through the opening, as its struggles were fierce and its strength prodigious. It was upon the point of making its escape from Peters' grasp, and slipping back into the water, when Augustus, throwing a rope with a slipknot around its throat, held it up in this manner until I jumped into the hole by the side of Peters, and assisted him in lifting it out.

The water we drew carefully from the bay into the jug, which, it will be remembered, had been brought up before from the cabin. Having done this, we broke off the neck of a bottle so as to form, with the cork, a kind of glass, holding not quite half a gill. We then each drank one of these measures full, and resolved to limit ourselves to this quantity per day as long as it should hold out.

During the last two or three days, the weather having been dry and pleasant, the bedding we had obtained from the cabin, as well as our clothing, had become thoroughly dry, so that we passed this night (that of the twenty-third) in comparative comfort, enjoying a tranquil repose, after having supped plentifully on olives and ham, with a small allowance of the wine. Being afraid of losing some of our stores overboard during the night, in the event of a breeze springing up, we secured them as well as possible with cordage to the fragments of the windlass. Our tortoise, which we were anxious to preserve alive as long as we could, we threw on its back, and otherwise carefully fastened.

CHAPTER 13

JULY 24. This morning saw us wonderfully re-
cruited in spirits and strength. Notwithstanding the perilous situation in which we were still placed, ignorant of our position,
although certainly at a great distance from land, without more
food than would last us for a fortnight even with great care,
almost entirely without water, and floating about at the mercy of
every wind and wave on the merest wreck in the world, still the
infinitely more terrible distresses and dangers from which we
had so lately and so providentially been delivered caused us to
regard what we now endured as but little more than an ordinary
evil—so strictly comparative is either good or ill.

At sunrise we were preparing to renew our attempts at getting
up something from the storeroom, when, a smart shower coming
on, with some lightning, we turned our attention to the catching
of water by means of the sheet we had used before for this purpose. We had no other means of collecting the rain than by
holding the sheet spread out with one of the forechain plates in
the middle of it. The water, thus conducted to the center, was
drained through into our jug. We had nearly filled it in this
manner, when, a heavy squall coming on from the northward,
obliged us to desist, as the hulk began once more to roll so violently that we could no longer keep our feet. We now went
forward, and, lashing ourselves securely to the remnant of the
windlass as before, awaited the event with far more calmness
than could have been anticipated, or would have been imagined
possible under the circumstances. At noon the wind had freshened into a two-reef breeze, and by night into a stiff gale, accompanied with a tremendously heavy swell. Experience having
taught us, however, the best method of arranging our lashings,
we weathered this dreary night in tolerable security, although

thoroughly drenched at almost every instant by the sea, and in momentary dread of being washed off. Fortunately, the weather was so warm as to render the water rather grateful than otherwise.

July 25. This morning the gale had diminished to a mere ten-knot breeze, and the sea had gone down with it so considerably that we were able to keep ourselves dry upon the deck. To our great grief, however, we found that two jars of our olives, as well as the whole of our ham, had been washed overboard, in spite of the careful manner in which they had been fastened. We determined not to kill the tortoise as yet, and contented ourselves for the present with a breakfast on a few of the olives, and a measure of water each, which latter we mixed, half and half, with wine, finding great relief and strength from the mixture, without the distressing intoxication which had ensued upon drinking the Port. The sea was still far too rough for the renewal of our efforts at getting up provision from the storeroom. Several articles, of no importance to us in our present situation, floated up through the opening during the day, and were immediately washed overboard. We also now observed that the hulk lay more along than ever, so that we could not stand an instant without lashing ourselves. On this account we passed a gloomy and uncomfortable day. At noon the sun appeared to be nearly vertical, and we had no doubt that we had been driven down by the long succession of northward and northwesterly winds into the near vicinity of the equator. Towards evening saw several sharks, and were somewhat alarmed by the audacious manner in which an enormously large one approached us. At one time, a lurch throwing the deck very far beneath the water, the monster actually swam in upon us, floundering for some moments just over the companion hatch, and striking Peters violently with his tail. A heavy sea at length hurled him overboard, much to our relief. In moderate weather we might have easily captured him.

July 26. This morning, the wind having greatly abated, and the sea not being very rough, we determined to renew our exertions in the storeroom. After a great deal of hard labor during the whole day, we found that nothing further was to be expected from this quarter, the partitions of the room having been stove during the night, and its contents swept into the hold. This discovery, as may be supposed, filled us with despair.

July 27. The sea nearly smooth, with a light wind, and still from the northward and westward. The sun coming out hotly in the afternoon, we occupied ourselves in drying our clothes. Found great relief from thirst, and much comfort otherwise, by bathing in the sea; in this, however, we were forced to use great caution, being afraid of sharks, several of which were seen swimming around the brig during the day.

July 28. Good weather still. The brig now began to lie along so alarmingly that we feared she would eventually roll bottom up. Prepared ourselves as well as we could for this emergency, lashing our tortoise, water jug, and two remaining jars of olives as far as possible over to the windward, placing them outside the hull, below the main-chains. The sea very smooth all day, with little or no wind.

July 29. A continuance of the same weather. Augustus' wounded arm began to evince symptoms of mortification. He complained of drowsiness and excessive thirst, but no acute pain. Nothing could be done for his relief beyond rubbing his wounds with a little of the vinegar from the olives, and from this no benefit seemed to be experienced. We did everything in our power for his comfort, and trebled his allowance of water.

July 30. An excessively hot day, with no wind. An enormous shark kept close by the hulk during the whole of the forenoon. We made several unsuccessful attempts to capture him by means of a noose. Augustus much worse, and evidently sinking as much from want of proper nourishment as from the effect of his wounds. He constantly prayed to be released from his sufferings, wishing for nothing but death. This evening we ate the last of our olives, and found the water in our jug so putrid that we could not swallow it at all without the addition of wine. Determined to kill our tortoise in the morning.

July 31. After a night of excessive anxiety and fatigue, owing to the position of the hulk, we set about killing and cutting up our tortoise. It proved to be much smaller than we had supposed, although in good condition—the whole meat about it not amounting to more than ten pounds. With a view of preserving a portion of this as long as possible, we cut it into fine pieces, and filled with them our three remaining olive jars and the wine bottle (all of which had been kept), pouring in afterward the vinegar from the olives. In this manner we put away about three pounds of the tortoise, intending not to touch it until we had consumed the rest. We concluded to restrict ourselves to about four ounces of the meat per day; the whole would thus last us thirteen days. A brisk shower, with severe thunder and lightning, came on about dusk, but lasted so short a time that we only succeeded in catching about half a pint of water. The whole of this, by common consent, was given to Augustus, who now appeared to be in the last extremity. He drank the water from the sheet as we caught it (we holding it above him as he lay so as to let it run into his mouth), for we had now nothing left capable of holding water, unless we had chosen to empty out our wine from the carboy, or the stale water from the jug. Either of these expedients would have been resorted to had the shower lasted.

The sufferer seemed to derive but little benefit from the draught. His arm was completely black from the wrist to the shoulder, and his feet were like ice. We expected every moment to see him breathe his last. He was frightfully emaciated; so much so that, although he weighed a hundred and twenty-seven pounds upon his leaving Nantucket, he now did not weigh more than *forty or fifty at the farthest*. His eyes were sunk far in his head, being scarcely perceptible, and the skin of his cheeks hung so loosely as to prevent his masticating any food, or even swallowing any liquid, without great difficulty.

August 1. A continuance of the same calm weather, with an oppressively hot sun. Suffered exceedingly from thirst, the water in the jug being absolutely putrid and swarming with vermin. We contrived, nevertheless, to swallow a portion of it by mixing it with wine—our thirst, however, was but little abated. We found more relief by bathing in the sea, but could not avail ourselves of this expedient except at long intervals, on account of the continual presence of sharks. We now saw clearly that Augustus could not be saved; that he was evidently dying. We could do nothing to relieve his sufferings, which appeared to be great. About twelve o'clock he expired in strong convulsions, and without having spoken for several hours. His death filled us with the most gloomy forebodings, and had so great an effect upon our spirits that we sat motionless by the corpse during the whole day, and never addressed each other except in a whisper. It was not until some time after dark that we took courage to get up and throw the body overboard. It was then loathsome beyond expression, and so far decayed that, as Peters attempted to lift it, an entire leg came off in his grasp. As the mass of putrefaction slipped over the vessel's side into the water, the glare of phosphoric light with which it was surrounded plainly discovered to us seven or eight large sharks, the clashing of whose horrible teeth, as their prey was torn to pieces among them, might have been heard at the distance of a mile. We shrunk within ourselves in the extremity of horror at the sound.

August 2. The same fearfully calm and hot weather. The dawn found us in a state of pitiable dejection as well as bodily exhaustion. The water in the jug was now absolutely useless, being a thick gelatinous mass; nothing but frightful-looking worms mingled with slime. We threw it out, and washed the jug well in the sea, afterward pouring a little vinegar in it from our bottles of pickled tortoise. Our thirst could now scarcely be endured, and we tried in vain to relieve it by wine, which seemed only to add fuel to the flame, and excited us to a high degree of intoxication. We afterward endeavored to relieve our sufferings by mixing the wine with sea water; but this instantly brought about the most violent retchings, so that we never again attempted it. During the whole day we anxiously sought an opportunity of bathing, but to no purpose; for the hulk was now entirely besieged on all sides with sharks—no doubt the identical monsters who had devoured our poor companion on the evening before, and who were in momentary expectation of another similar feast. This circumstance occasioned us the most bitter regret, and filled us with the most depressing and melancholy forebodings. We had experienced indescribable relief in bathing, and to have this resource cut off in so frightful a manner was more than we could bear. Nor, indeed, were we altogether free from the apprehension of immediate danger, for the least slip or false movement would have thrown us at once within reach of these voracious fish, who frequently thrust themselves directly upon us, swimming up to leeward. No shouts or exertions on our part seemed to alarm them. Even when one of the largest was struck with an ax by Peters and much wounded, he persisted in his attempts to push in where we were. A cloud came up at dusk, but, to our extreme anguish, passed over without discharging itself. It is quite impossible to conceive our sufferings from thirst at this period. We passed a sleepless night, both on this account and through dread of the sharks.

August 3.   No prospect of relief, and the brig lying still more and more along, so that now we could not maintain a footing upon deck at all. Busied ourselves in securing our wine and tortoise-meat, so that we might not lose them in the event of our rolling over. Got out two stout spikes from the forechains, and, by means of the ax, drove them into the hull to windward within a couple of feet of the water; this not being very far from the keel, as we were nearly upon our beam-ends. To these spikes we now lashed our provisions, as being more secure than their former position beneath the chains. Suffered great agony from thirst during the whole day—no chance of bathing on account of the sharks, which never left us for a moment. Found it impossible to sleep.

August 4.   A little before daybreak we perceived that the hulk was heeling over, and aroused ourselves to prevent being thrown off by the movement. At first the roll was slow and gradual, and we contrived to clamber over to windward very well, having taken the precaution to leave ropes hanging from the spikes we had driven in for the provision. But we had not calculated sufficiently upon the acceleration of the impetus; for, presently the heel became too violent to allow of our keeping pace with it; and, before either of us knew what was to happen, we found ourselves hurled furiously into the sea, and struggling several fathoms beneath the surface, with the huge hull immediately above us.

In going under the water I had been obliged to let go my hold upon the rope; and finding that I was completely beneath the vessel, and my strength utterly exhausted, I scarcely made a struggle for life, and resigned myself, in a few seconds, to die. But here again I was deceived, not having taken into consideration the natural rebound of the hull to windward. The whirl of the water upward, which the vessel occasioned in rolling partially back, brought me to the surface still more violently than I had been plunged beneath. Upon coming up I found myself about twenty yards from the hulk, as near as I could judge. She was lying keel up, rocking furiously from side to side, and the sea in all directions around was much agitated, and full of strong whirlpools. I could see nothing of Peters. An oil cask was floating within a few feet of me, and various other articles from the brig were scattered about.

My principal terror was now on account of the sharks, which I knew to be in my vicinity. In order to deter these, if possible, from approaching me, I splashed the water vigorously with both hands and feet as I swam toward the hulk, creating a body of foam. I have no doubt that to this expedient, simple as it was, I was indebted for my preservation; for the sea all around the brig, just before her rolling over, was so crowded with these monsters, that I must have been, and really was, in actual contact with some of them during my progress. By great good fortune, however, I reached the side of the vessel in safety, although so utterly weakened by the violent exertion I had used that I should never have been able to get upon it but for the timely assistance of Peters, who now, to my great joy, made his appearance (having scrambled up to the keel from the opposite side of the hull), and threw me the end of a rope—one of those which had been attached to the spikes.

Having barely escaped this danger, our attention was now

directed to the dreadful imminency of another—that of absolute
starvation. Our whole stock of provision had been swept overboard in spite of all our care in securing it; and seeing no longer
the remotest possibility of obtaining more, we gave way both of
us to despair, weeping aloud like children, and neither of us attempting to offer consolation to the other. Such weakness can
scarcely be conceived, and to those who have never been similarly
situated will, no doubt, appear unnatural; but it must be remembered that our intellects were so entirely disordered by the long
course of privation and terror to which we had been subjected,
that we could not justly be considered, at that period, in the light
of rational beings. In subsequent perils, nearly as great, if not
greater, I bore up with fortitude against all the evils of my situation, and Peters, it will be seen, evinced a stoical philosophy
nearly as incredible as his present childlike supineness and im-
becility—the mental condition made the difference.

The overturning of the brig, even with the consequent loss of
the wine and turtle, would not, in fact, have rendered our situation more deplorable than before, except for the disappearance of
the bedclothes by which we had been hitherto enabled to catch
rain water, and of the jug in which we had kept it when caught;
for we found the whole bottom, from within two or three feet of
the bends as far as the keel, together with the keel itself, *thickly
covered with large barnacles, which proved to be excellent and
highly nutritious food.* Thus, in two important respects, the
accident we had so greatly dreaded proved a benefit rather than
an injury; it had opened to us a supply of provisions which we
could not have exhausted, using it moderately, in a month; and it
had greatly contributed to our comfort as regards position, we
being much more at our ease, and in infinitely less danger, than
before.

The difficulty, however, of now obtaining water blinded us to
all the benefits of the change in our condition. That we might
be ready to avail ourselves, as far as possible, of any shower which
might fall, we took off our shirts, to make use of them as we had
of the sheets—not hoping, of course, to get more in this way,

even under the most favorable circumstances, than half a gill at a time. No signs of a cloud appeared during the day, and the agonies of our thirst were nearly intolerable. At night, Peters obtained about an hour's disturbed sleep, but my intense sufferings would not permit me to close my eyes for a single moment.

August 5. Today, a gentle breeze springing up carried us through a vast quantity of seaweed, among which we were so fortunate as to find eleven small crabs, which afforded us several delicious meals. Their shells being quite soft, we ate them entire, and found that they irritated our thirst far less than the barnacles. Seeing no trace of sharks among the seaweed, we also ventured to bathe, and remained in the water for four or five hours, during which we experienced a very sensible diminution of our thirst. Were greatly refreshed, and spent the night somewhat more comfortably than before, both of us snatching a little sleep.

August 6. This day we were blessed by a brisk and continual rain, lasting from about noon until after dark. Bitterly did we now regret the loss of our jug and carboy; for, in spite of the little means we had of catching the water, we might have filled one, if not both of them. As it was, we contrived to satisfy the cravings of thirst by suffering the shirts to become saturated, and then wringing them so as to let the grateful fluid trickle into our mouths. In this occupation we passed the entire day.

August 7. Just at daybreak we both at the same instant descried a sail to the eastward, and *evidently coming towards us!* We hailed the glorious sight with a long, although feeble shout of rapture; and began instantly to make every signal in our power, by flaring the shirts in the air, leaping as high as our weak condition would permit, and even by hallooing with all the strength of our lungs, although the vessel could not have been less than fifteen miles distant. However, she still continued to near our hulk, and we felt that, if she but held her present course, she must eventually come so close as to perceive us. In about an hour after we first discovered her, we could clearly see the people on her decks. She was a long, low, and rakish-looking topsail schooner, with a black ball in her fore-topsail, and had, apparently, a full crew. We now became alarmed, for we could hardly imagine it possible that she did not observe us, and were apprehensive that she meant to leave us to perish as we were— an act of fiendish barbarity, which, however incredible it may appear, has been repeatedly perpetrated at sea, under circumstances very nearly similar, and by beings who were regarded as belonging to the human species.* In this instance, however, by the mercy of God, we were destined to be most happily deceived; for, presently we were aware of a sudden commotion on the deck of the stranger, who immediately afterward ran up a British flag, and, hauling her wind, bore up directly upon us. In half an hour more we found ourselves in her cabin. She proved to be the *Jane Guy*, of Liverpool, Captain Guy, bound on a sealing and trading voyage to the South Seas and Pacific.

* The case of the brig *Polly*, of Boston, is one so much in point, and her fate, in many respects, so remarkably similar to our own, that I cannot forbear alluding to it here. This vessel, of one hundred and thirty tons burden, sailed from Boston, with a cargo of lumber and provisions, for Santa Croix, on the 12th of December, 1811, under the command of Captain Casneau. There were eight souls on board besides the captain—the mate, four seamen, and the cook, together with a Mr. Hunt, and a Negro girl belonging to him. On the fifteenth, having cleared the shoal of Georges, she sprung a leak in a gale of wind from the southeast, and was finally capsized; but, the mast going by the board, she afterward righted. They remained in this situation, without fire, and with very little provision, for the period of *one hundred and ninety-one days* (from December the fifteenth to June the twentieth), when Captain Casneau and Samuel Badger, the only survivors, were taken off the wreck by the *Fame*, of Hull, Captain Featherstone, bound home from Rio Janeiro. When picked up, they were in latitude 28° N., longitude 13° W., *having drifted above two thousand miles!* On the ninth of July, the *Fame* fell in with the brig *Dromeo*, Captain Perkins, who landed the two sufferers in Kennebeck. The narrative from which we gather these details ends in the following words:

"It is natural to inquire how they could float such a vast distance, upon the most frequented part of the Atlantic and not be discovered all this time. *They were passed by more than a dozen sail, one of which came so nigh them that they could distinctly see the people on deck and on the rigging looking at them; but, to the inexpressible disappointment of the starving and freezing men, they stifled the dictates of compassion, hoisted sail, and cruelly abandoned them to their fate.*" (Poe's note.)

CHAPTER 14

THE *Jane Guy* was a fine-looking topsail schooner of a hundred and eighty tons burden. She was unusually sharp in the bows, and on a wind, in moderate weather, the fastest sailer I have ever seen. Her qualities, however, as a rough sea boat, were not so good, and her draught of water was by far too great for the trade to which she was destined. For this peculiar service, a larger vessel, and one of a light proportionate draught, is desirable —say a vessel of from three to three hundred and fifty tons. She should be bark-rigged, and in other respects of a different construction from the usual South Sea ships. It is absolutely necessary that she should be well armed. She should have, say ten or twelve twelve-pound carronades, and two or three long twelves, with brass blunderbusses, and watertight arm-chests for each top. Her anchors and cables should be of far greater strength than is required for any other species of trade, and, above all, her crew should be numerous and efficient; not less, for such a vessel as I have described, than fifty or sixty able-bodied men. The *Jane Guy* had a crew of thirty-five, all able seamen, besides the captain and mate, but she was not altogether as well armed or otherwise equipped, as a navigator acquainted with the difficulties and dangers of the trade could have desired.

Captain Guy was a gentleman of great urbanity of manner, and of considerable experience in the southern traffic, to which he had devoted a great portion of his life. He was deficient, however, in energy, and consequently, in that spirit of enterprise which is here so absolutely requisite. He was part owner of the vessel in which he sailed, and was invested with discretionary powers to cruise in the South Seas for any cargo which might come most readily to hand. He had on board, as usual in such voyages, beads, looking glasses, tinderworks, axes, hatchets, saws,

119

adzes, planes, chisels, gouges, gimlets, files, spokeshaves, rasps, hammers, nails, knives, scissors, razors, needles, thread, crockery-ware, calico, trinkets, and other similar articles.

The schooner sailed from Liverpool on the tenth of July, crossed the Tropic of Cancer on the twenty-fifth, in longitude twenty degrees west, and reached Sal, one of the Cape Verd Islands, on the twenty-ninth, where she took in salt and other necessaries for the voyage. On the third of August, she left the Cape Verds and steered southwest, stretching over towards the coast of Brazil, so as to cross the equator between the meridians of twenty-eight and thirty degrees west longitude. This is the course usually taken by vessels bound from Europe to the Cape of Good Hope, or by that route to the East Indies. By proceeding thus they avoid the calms and strong contrary currents which continually prevail on the coast of Guinea, while in the end, it is found to be the shortest track, as westerly winds are never wanting afterward by which to reach the Cape. It was Captain Guy's intention to make his first stoppage at Kerguelen's Land—I hardly know for what reason. On the day we were picked up the schooner was off Cape St. Roque, in longitude thirty-one W.; so that, when found, we had drifted probably, from north to south, *not less than five-and-twenty degrees!*

On board the *Jane Guy* we were treated with all the kindness our distressed situation demanded. In about a fortnight, during which time we continued steering to the southeast, with gentle breezes and fine weather, both Peters and myself recovered entirely from the effects of our late privation and dreadful suffering, and we began to remember what had passed rather as a frightful dream from which we had been happily awakened, than as events which had taken place in sober and naked reality. I have since found that this species of partial oblivion is usually brought about by sudden transition, whether from joy to sorrow or from sorrow to joy—the degree of forgetfulness being proportioned to the degree of difference in the exchange. Thus, in my own case, I now feel it impossible to realize the full extent of the misery which I endured during the days spent upon the hulk. The incidents are remembered, but not the feelings which the incidents elicited at the time of their occurrence. I only know, that when they did occur, I *then* thought human nature could sustain nothing more of agony.

We continued our voyage for some weeks without any incidents of greater moment than the occasional meeting with whalingships, and more frequently with the black or right whale, so called in contradistinction to the spermaceti. These, however, were chiefly found south of the twenty-fifth parallel. On the sixteenth of September, being in the vicinity of the Cape of Good Hope, the schooner encountered her first gale of any violence since leaving Liverpool. In this neighborhood, but more frequently to the south and east of the promontory (we were to the westward), navigators have often to contend with storms from the northward which rage with great fury. They always b ing with them a heavy sea, and one of their most dangerous features is the instantaneous chopping round of the wind, an occurrence almost certain to take place during the greatest force of the gale. A perfect hurricane will be blowing at one moment from the northward or northeast, and in the next not a breath of wind will be felt in that direction, while from the southwest it will come out all at once with a violence almost inconceivable. A bright spot to the southward is the sure forerunner of the change, and vessels are thus enabled to take the proper precautions.

It was about six in the morning when the blow came on with a white squall, and, as usual, from the northward. By eight it had increased very much, and brought down upon us one of the most tremendous seas I had then ever beheld. Everything had been made as snug as possible, but the schooner labored excessively, and gave evidence of her bad qualities as a sea boat, pitching her forecastle under at every plunge, and with the greatest difficulty struggling up from one wave before she was buried in another. Just before sunset the bright spot for which we had been on the lookout made its appearance in the southwest, and in an hour afterward we perceived the little headsail we carried flapping listlessly against the mast. In two minutes more, in spite of every preparation, we were hurled on our beam-ends as if by magic, and a perfect wilderness of foam made a clear breach over us as we lay. The blow from the southwest, however, luckily proved to be nothing more than a squall, and we had the good fortune to right the vessel without the loss of a spar. A heavy cross sea gave us great trouble for a few hours after this, but towards morning we found ourselves in nearly as good condition as before the gale. Captain Guy considered that he had made an escape little less than miraculous.

On the thirteenth of October we came in sight of Prince Edward's Island, in latitude 46° 53′ S., longitude 37° 46′ E. Two days afterward we found ourselves near Possession Island, and presently passed the islands of Crozet, in latitude 42° 59′ S., longitude 48° E. On the eighteenth we made Kerguelen's or Desolation Island, in the Southern Indian Ocean, and came to anchor in Christmas Harbor, having four fathoms of water.

This island, or rather group of islands, bears southeast from the Cape of Good Hope, and is distant therefrom nearly eight hundred leagues. It was first discovered in 1772, by the Baron de Kergulen, or Kerguelen, a Frenchman, who, thinking the land to form a portion of an extensive southern continent, carried home information to that effect, which produced much excitement at the time. The government, taking the matter up, sent the baron back in the following year for the purpose of giving his new discovery a critical examination, when the mistake was discovered. In 1777, Captain Cook fell in with the same group, and gave to the principal one the name of Desolation Island, a title which it certainly well deserves. Upon approaching the land, however, the navigator might be induced to suppose otherwise, as the sides of most of the hills, from September to March, are clothed with very brilliant verdure. This deceitful appearance is caused by a small plant resembling saxifrage, which is abundant, growing in large patches on a species of crumbling moss. Besides this plant there is scarcely a sign of vegetation on the island, if we except some coarse rank grass near the harbor, some lichen, and a shrub which bears resemblance to a cabbage shooting into seed, and which has a bitter and acrid taste.

The face of the country is hilly, although none of the hills can be called lofty. Their tops are perpetually covered with snow. There are several harbors, of which Christmas Harbor is the most convenient. It is the first to be met with on the northeast side of the island after passing Cape François, which forms the northern shore, and, by its peculiar shape, serves to distinguish the harbor. Its projecting point terminates in a high rock, through which is a large hole, forming a natural arch. The entrance is in latitude 48° 40′ S., longitude 69° 6′ E. Passing in here, good anchorage may be found under the shelter of several small islands, which form a sufficient protection from all easterly winds. Proceeding on eastwardly from this anchorage you come to Wasp Bay, at the head of the harbor. This is a small basin, completely landlocked, into which you can go with four fathoms, and find anchorage in from ten to three, hard clay bottom. A ship might lie here with her best bower ahead all the year round without risk. To the westward, at the head of Wasp Bay, is a small stream of excellent water, easily procured.

Some seal of the fur and hair species are still to be found on Kerguelen's Island, and sea elephants abound. The feathered tribes are discovered in great numbers. Penguins are very plenty, and of these there are four different kinds. The royal penguin, so called from its size and beautiful plumage, is the largest. The upper part of the body is usually gray, sometimes of a lilac tint; the under portion of the purest white imaginable. The head is of a glossy and most brilliant black, the feet also. The chief beauty of the plumage, however, consists in two broad stripes of a gold color, which pass along from the head to the breast. The bill is long, and either pink or bright scarlet. These birds walk erect, with a stately carriage. They carry their heads high with their wings drooping like two arms, and as their tails project from their body in a line with the legs, the resemblance to a human figure is very striking, and would be apt to deceive the spectator at a casual glance or in the gloom of the evening. The royal penguins which we met with on Kerguelen's Land were rather larger than a goose. The other kinds are the macaroni, the jackass, and the rookery penguin. These are much smaller, less beautiful in plumage, and different in other respects.

Besides the penguin many other birds are here to be found, among which may be mentioned sea hens, blue petrels, teal, ducks, Port Egmont hens, shags, Cape pigeons, the nelly, sea swallows, terns, sea gulls, Mother Carey's chickens, Mother Carey's geese, or the great petrel, and, lastly, the albatross.

The great petrel is as large as the common albatross, and is carnivorous. It is frequently called the breakbones, or osprey petrel. They are not at all shy, and, when properly cooked, are palatable food. In flying they sometimes sail very close to the surface of the water, with the wings expanded, without appearing to move them in the least degree, or make any exertion with them whatever.

The albatross is one of the largest and fiercest of the South Sea birds. It is of the gull species, and takes its prey on the wing, never coming on land except for the purpose of breeding. Between this bird and the penguin the most singular friendship exists. Their nests are constructed with great uniformity upon a plan concerted between the two species—that of the albatross being placed in the center of a little square formed by the nests of four penguins. Navigators have agreed in calling an assemblage of such encampments *a rookery*. These rookeries have been often described, but as my readers may not all have seen these descriptions, and as I shall have occasion hereafter to speak of the penguin and albatross, it will not be amiss to say something here of their mode of building and living.

When the season for incubation arrives, the birds assemble in vast numbers, and for some days appear to be deliberating upon the proper course to be pursued. At length they proceed to action. A level piece of ground is selected, of suitable extent, usually comprising three or four acres, and situated as near the sea as possible, being still beyond its reach. The spot is chosen with reference to its evenness of surface, and that is preferred which is the least encumbered with stones. This matter being arranged, the birds proceed, with one accord, and actuated apparently by one mind, to trace out, with mathematical accuracy, either a square or other parallelogram, as may best suit the nature of the ground, and of just sufficient size to accommodate easily all the birds assembled, and no more—in this particular seeming determined upon preventing the access of future stragglers who have not participated in the labor of the encampment. One side of the place thus marked out runs parallel with the water's edge, and is left open for ingress or egress.

Having defined the limits of the rookery, the colony now begin to clear it of every species of rubbish, picking up stone by stone, and carrying them outside of the lines, and close by them, so as to form a wall on the three inland sides. Just within this wall a perfectly level and smooth walk is formed, from six to eight feet wide, and extending around the encampment—thus serving the purpose of a general promenade.

The next process is to partition out the whole area into small squares exactly equal in size. This is done by forming narrow paths, very smooth, and crossing each other at right angles throughout the entire extent of the rookery. At each intersection of these paths the nest of an albatross is constructed, and a penguin's nest in the center of each square—thus every penguin is surrounded by four albatrosses, and each albatross by a like number of penguins. The penguin's nest consists of a hole in the earth, very shallow, being only just of sufficient depth to keep her single egg from rolling. The albatross is somewhat less simple in her arrangements, erecting a hillock about a foot high and two in diameter. This is made of earth, seaweed, and shells. On its summit she builds her nest.

The birds take especial care never to leave their nests unoccupied for an instant during the period of incubation, or, indeed, until the young progeny are sufficiently strong to take care of themselves. While the male is absent at sea in search of food, the female remains on duty, and it is only upon the return of her

partner that she ventures abroad. The eggs are never left uncov-
ered at all—while one bird leaves the nest, the other nestling in
by its side. This precaution is rendered necessary by the thievish
propensities prevalent in the rookery, the inhabitants making no
scruple to purloin each other's eggs at every good opportunity.

Although there are some rookeries in which the penguin and
albatross are the sole population, yet in most of them a variety of
oceanic birds are to be met with, enjoying all the privileges of
citizenship, and scattering their nests here and there, wherever
they can find room, never interfering, however, with the stations
of the larger species. The appearance of such encampments,
when seen from a distance, is exceedingly singular. The whole
atmosphere just above the settlement is darkened with the immense number of albatrosses (mingled with the smaller tribes)
which are continually hovering over it, either going to the ocean
or returning home. At the same time a crowd of penguins are to
be observed, some passing to and fro in the narrow alleys, and
some marching with the military strut so peculiar to them, around
the general promenade ground which encircles the rookery. In
short, survey it as we will, nothing can be more astonishing than
the spirit of reflection evinced by these feathered beings, and
nothing surely can be better calculated to elicit reflection in every
well-regulated human intellect.

On the morning after our arrival in Christmas Harbor the
chief mate, Mr. Patterson, took the boats, and (although it was
somewhat early in the season) went in search of seal, leaving the
captain and a young relation of his on a point of barren land to
the westward, they having some business, whose nature I could
not ascertain, to transact in the interior of the island. Captain Guy
took with him a bottle, in which was a sealed letter, and made
his way from the point on which he was set on shore towards
one of the highest peaks in the place. It is probable that his design
was to leave the letter on that height for some vessel which he
expected to come after him. As soon as we lost sight of him we
proceeded (Peters and myself being in the mate's boat) on our
cruise around the coast, looking for seal. In this business we were

occupied about three weeks, examining with great care every nook and corner, not only of Kerguelen's Land, but of the several small islands in the vicinity. Our labors, however, were not crowned with any important success. We saw a great many fur seal, but they were exceedingly shy, and with the greatest exertions, we could only procure three hundred and fifty skins in all. Sea elephants were abundant, especially on the western coast of the mainland, but of these we killed only twenty, and this with great difficulty. On the smaller islands we discovered a good many of the hair seal, but did not molest them. We returned to the schooner on the eleventh, where we found Captain Guy and his nephew, who gave a very bad account of the interior, representing it as one of the most dreary and utterly barren countries in the world. They had remained two nights on the island, owing to some misunderstanding, on the part of the second mate, in regard to the sending a jolly boat from the schooner to take them off.

CHAPTER 15

ON THE TWELFTH we made sail from Christmas Harbor, retracing our way to the westward, and leaving Marion's Island, one of Crozet's group, on the larboard. We afterward passed Prince Edward's Island, leaving it also on our left; then, steering more to the northward, made, in fifteen days, the islands of Tristan d'Acunha, in latitude 37° 8′ S., longitude 12° 8′ W.

This group, now so well known, and which consists of three circular islands, was first discovered by the Portuguese, and was visited afterward by the Dutch in 1643, and by the French in 1767. The three islands together form a triangle, and are distant from each other about ten miles, there being fine open passages between. The land in all of them is very high, especially in Tristan d'Acunha, properly so called. This is the largest of the group, being fifteen miles in circumference, and so elevated that it can be seen in clear weather at the distance of eighty or ninety miles. A part of the land towards the north rises more than a thousand feet perpendicularly from the sea. A tableland at this height extends back nearly to the center of the island, and from this tableland arises a lofty cone like that of Teneriffe. The lower half of this cone is clothed with trees of good size, but the upper region is barren rock, usually hidden among the clouds, and covered with snow during the greater part of the year. There are no shoals or other dangers about the island, the shores being remarkably bold and the water deep. On the northwestern coast is a bay, with a beach of black sand, where a landing with boats can be easily effected, provided there be a southerly wind. Plenty of excellent water may here be readily procured; also cod, and other fish, may be taken with hook and line.

The next island in point of size, and the most westwardly of the group, is that called the Inaccessible. Its precise situation is 37° 17′ S. latitude, longitude 12° 24′ W. It is seven or eight miles in circumference, and on all sides presents a forbidding and precipitous aspect. Its top is perfectly flat, and the whole region is sterile, nothing growing upon it except a few stunted shrubs.

Nightingale Island, the smallest and most southerly, is in latitude 37° 26′ S., longitude 12° 12′ W. Off its southern extremity is a high ledge of rocky islets; a few also of a similar appearance are seen to the northeast. The ground is irregular and sterile, and a deep valley partially separates it.

The shores of these islands abound, in the proper season, with sea lions, sea elephants, the hair and fur seal, together with a great variety of oceanic birds. Whales are also plenty in their vicinity. Owing to the ease with which these various animals were here formerly taken, the group has been much visited since its discovery. The Dutch and French frequented it at a very early period. In 1790, Captain Patten, of the ship *Industry*, of Philadelphia, made Tristan d'Acunha, where he remained seven months (from August, 1790, to April, 1791) for the purpose of collecting sealskins. In this time he gathered no less than five thousand six hundred, and says that he would have had no difficulty in loading a large ship with oil in three weeks. Upon his arrival he found no quadrupeds, with the exception of a few wild goats—the island now abounds with all our most valuable domestic animals, which have been introduced by subsequent navigators.

I believe it was not long after Captain Patten's visit that Captain Colquhoun, of the American brig *Betsey*, touched at the largest of the islands for the purpose of refreshment. He planted onions, potatoes, cabbages, and a great many other vegetables, an abundance of all which are now to be met with.

In 1811, a Captain Heywood, in the *Nereus*, visited Tristan. He found there three Americans, who were residing upon the island to prepare sealskins and oil. One of these men was named Jonathan Lambert, and he called himself the sovereign of the country. He had cleared and cultivated about sixty acres of land,

and turned his attention to raising the coffee plant and sugar cane, with which he had been furnished by the American Minister at Rio Janeiro. This settlement, however, was finally abandoned, and in 1817 the islands were taken possession of by the British government, who sent a detachment for that purpose from the Cape of Good Hope. They did not, however, retain them long; but, upon the evacuation of the country as a British possession, two or three English families took up their residence there independently of the government. On the twenty-fifth of March, 1824, the *Berwick*, Captain Jeffrey, from London to Van Diemen's Land, arrived at the place, where they found an Englishman of the name of Glass, formerly a corporal in the British artillery. He claimed to be supreme governor of the islands, and had under his control twenty-one men and three women. He gave a very favorable account of the salubrity of the climate and of the productiveness of the soil. The population occupied themselves chiefly in collecting sealskins and sea elephant oil, with which they traded to the Cape of Good Hope, Glass owning a small schooner. At the period of our arrival the governor was still a resident, but his little community had multiplied, there being fifty-six persons upon Tristan, besides a smaller settlement of seven on Nightingale Island. We had no difficulty in procuring almost every kind of refreshment which we required—sheep, hogs, bullocks, rabbits, poultry, goats, fish in great variety, and vegetables were abundant. Having come to anchor close in with the large island, in eighteen fathoms, we took all we wanted on board very conveniently. Captain Guy also purchased of Glass five hundred sealskins and some ivory. We remained here a week, during which the prevailing winds were from the northward and westward, and the weather somewhat hazy. On the fifth of November we made sail to the southward and westward, with the intention of having a thorough search for a group of islands called the Auroras, respecting whose existence a great diversity of opinion has existed.

These islands are said to have been discovered as early as 1762, by the commander of the ship *Aurora.* In 1790, Captain Manuel

de Oyarvido, in the ship *Princess*, belonging to the Royal Philip-
pine Company, sailed, as he asserts, directly among them. In
1794, the Spanish corvette *Atrevida* went with the determination
of ascertaining their precise situation, and, in a paper published
by the Royal Hydrographical Society of Madrid in the year 1809,
the following language is used respecting this expedition: "The
corvette *Atrevida* practised, in their immediate vicinity, from
the twenty-first to the twenty-seventh of January, all the necessary observations, and measured by chronometers the difference
of longitude between these islands and the port of Soledad in
the Malninas. The islands are three; they are very nearly in the
same meridian; the centre one is rather low, and the other two
may be seen at nine leagues distance." The observations made
on board the *Atrevida* give the following results as the precise
situation of each island. The most northern is in latitude 52° 37'
24" S., longitude 47° 43' 15" W.; the middle one in latitude
53° 2' 40" S., longitude 47° 55' 15" W.; and the most southern
in latitude 53° 15' 22" S., longitude 47° 57' 15" W.

On the twenty-seventh of January, 1820, Captain James
Weddell, of the British navy, sailed from Staten Island also in
search of the Auroras. He reports that, having made the most
diligent search and passed not only immediately over the spots
indicated by the commander of the *Atrevida*, but in every direction throughout the vicinity of these spots, he could discover
no indication of land. These conflicting statements have induced
other navigators to look out for the islands; and, strange to say,
while some have sailed through every inch of sea where they are
supposed to lie without finding them, there have been not a few
who declare positively that they have seen them, and even been
close in with their shores. It was Captain Guy's intention to
make every exertion within his power to settle the question so
oddly in dispute.*

We kept on our course, between the south and west, with vari-
able weather, until the twentieth of the month, when we found
ourselves on the debated ground, being in latitude 53° 15' S.,
longitude 47° 58' W.—that is to say, very nearly upon the spot

indicated as the situation of the most southern of the group. Not perceiving any sign of land, we continued to the westward in the parallel of fifty-three degrees south, as far as the meridian of fifty degrees west. We then stood to the north as far as the parallel of fifty-two degrees south, when we turned to the eastward, and kept our parallel by double altitudes, morning and evening, and meridian altitudes of the planets and moon. Having thus gone eastwardly to the meridian of the western coast of Georgia, we kept that meridian until we were in the latitude from which we set out. We then took diagonal courses throughout the entire extent of sea circumscribed, keeping a lookout constantly at the masthead, and repeating our examination with the greatest care for a period of three weeks, during which the weather was remarkably pleasant and fair, with no haze whatsoever. Of course we were thoroughly satisfied that, whatever islands might have existed in this vicinity at any former period, no vestige of them remained at the present day. Since my return home I find that the same ground was traced over, with equal care, in 1822, by Captain Johnson, of the American schooner *Henry,* and by Captain Morrell, in the American schooner *Wasp*—in both cases with the same result as in our own.

* Among the vessels which at various times have professed to meet with the Auroras may be mentioned the ship *San Miguel,* in 1769; the ship *Aurora,* in 1774; the brig *Pearl,* in 1779; and the ship *Dolores,* in 1790. They all agree in giving the mean latitude fifty-three degrees south. (Poe's note.)

CHAPTER 16

IT HAD BEEN Captain Guy's original intention, after satisfying himself about the Auroras, to proceed through the Strait of Magellan, and up along the western coast of Patagonia; but information received at Tristan d'Acunha induced him to steer to the southward, in the hope of falling in with some small islands said to lie about the parallel of 60° S., longitude 41° 20′ W. In the event of his not discovering these lands, he designed, should the season prove favorable, to push on toward the pole. Accordingly, on the twelfth of December, we made sail in that direction. On the eighteenth we found ourselves about the station indicated by Glass, and cruised for three days in that neighborhood without finding any traces of the islands he had mentioned. On the twenty-first, the weather being unusually pleasant, we again made sail to the southward, with the resolution of penetrating in that course as far as possible. Before entering upon this portion of my narrative, it may be as well, for the information of those readers who have paid little attention to the progress of discovery in these regions, to give some brief account of the very few attempts at reaching the southern pole which have hitherto been made.

That of Captain Cook was the first of which we have any distinct account. In 1772 he sailed to the south in the *Resolution*, accompanied by Lieutenant Furneaux in the *Adventure*. In December he found himself as far as the fifty-eighth parallel of south latitude, and in longitude 26° 57′ E. Here he met with narrow fields of ice, about eight or ten inches thick, and running northwest and southeast. This ice was in large cakes, and usually it was packed so closely that the vessels had great difficulty in forcing a passage. At this period Captain Cook supposed, from the vast number of birds to be seen, and from other indications, that he was in the near vicinity of land. He kept on to the southward, the weather being exceedingly cold, until he reached the sixty-fourth parallel, in longitude 38° 14′ E. Here he had mild weather, with gentle breezes, for five days, the thermometer being at thirty-six. In January, 1773, the vessels crossed the Antarctic circle, but did not succeed in penetrating much farther; for, upon reaching latitude 67° 15′, they found all farther progress impeded by an immense body of ice, extending all along the southern horizon as far as the eye could reach. This ice was of every variety—and some large floes of it, miles in extent, formed a compact mass, rising eighteen or twenty feet above the water. It being late in the season, and no hope entertained of rounding these obstructions, Captain Cook now reluctantly turned to the northward.

In the November following he renewed his search in the Antarctic. In latitude 59° 40′ he met with a strong current setting to the southward. In December, when the vessels were in latitude 67° 31′, longitude 142° 54′ W., the cold was excessive, with heavy gales and fog. Here also birds were abundant: the albatross, the penguin, and the petrel especially. In latitude 70° 23′ some large islands of ice were encountered, and shortly afterward the clouds to the southward were observed to be of a snowy whiteness, indicating the vicinity of field ice. In latitude 71° 10′, longitude 106° 54′ W., the navigators were stopped, as before, by an immense frozen expanse, which filled the whole area of the southern horizon. The northern edge of this expanse was ragged and broken, so firmly wedged together as to be utterly impassable, and extending about a mile to the southward. Behind it the frozen surface was comparatively smooth for some distance, until terminated in the extreme background by gigantic ranges of ice mountains, the one towering above the other. Captain Cook concluded that this vast field reached the southern pole or was joined to a continent. Mr. J. N. Reynolds, whose great exertions and perseverance have at length succeeded in getting set on foot a national expedition, partly for the purpose of exploring these regions, thus speaks of the attempt of the *Resolution*: "We are not surprised that Captain Cook was unable to go beyond 71° 10′, but we are astonished that he did attain that point on the meridian of 106° 54′ west longitude. Palmer's Land lies south of the Shetland, latitude sixty-four degrees, and tends to the southward and westward farther than any navigator has yet penetrated. Cook was standing for this land when his progress was arrested by the ice; which, we apprehend, must always be the case in that point, and so early in the season as the sixth of January—and we should not be surprised if a portion of the icy mountains described was attached to the main body of Palmer's Land, or to some other portions of land lying farther to the southward and westward.'

In 1803, Captains Kreutzenstern and Lisiausky were dispatched by Alexander of Russia for the purpose of circumnavigating the globe. In endeavoring to get south, they made no farther than 59° 58′, in longitude 70° 15′ W. They here met with strong currents setting eastwardly. Whales were abundant, but they saw no ice. In regard to this voyage, Mr. Reynolds observes that, if Kreutzenstern had arrived where he did earlier in the season, he must have encountered ice—it was March when he reached the latitude specified. The winds prevailing, as they do, from the southward and westward, had carried the floes, aided by currents, into that icy region bounded on the north by Georgia, east by Sandwich Land and the South Orkneys, and west by the South Shetland islands.

In 1822, Captain James Weddell, of the British navy, with two very small vessels, penetrated farther to the south than any previous navigator, and this too, without encountering extraordinary difficulties. He states that although he was frequently hemmed in by ice *before* reaching the seventy-second parallel, yet, upon attaining it, not a particle was to be discovered, and that, upon arriving at the latitude of 74° 15′, no fields, and only three islands of ice were visible. It is somewhat remarkable that, although vast flocks of birds were seen, and other usual indications of land, and although, south of the Shetlands, unknown coasts were observed from the masthead tending southwardly, Weddell discourages the idea of land existing in the polar regions of the south.

On the eleventh of January, 1823, Captain Benjamin Morrell, of the American schooner *Wasp*, sailed from Kerguelen's Land with a view of penetrating as far south as possible. On the first of February he found himself in latitude 64° 52′ S., longitude 118° 27′ E. The following passage is extracted from his journal of that date: "The wind soon freshened to an eleven-knot breeze, and we embraced this opportunity of making to the west; being however convinced that the farther we went south beyond latitude sixty-four degrees, the less ice was to be apprehended, we steered a little to the southward, until we crossed the Antarctic circle, and were in latitude 69° 15′ E. In this latitude there was no *field ice*, and very few ice islands in sight."

Under the date of March fourteenth I find also this entry: "The sea was now entirely free of field ice, and there were not more than a dozen ice islands in sight. At the same time the temperature of the air and water was at least thirteen degrees higher (more mild) than we had ever found it between the parallels of sixty and sixty-two south. We were now in latitude 70° 14′ S., and the temperature of the air was forty-seven, and that of the water forty-four. In this situation I found the variation to be 14° 27′ easterly, per azimuth. . . . I have several times passed within the Antarctic circle, on different meridians, and have uniformly found the temperature, both of the air and water, to become more and more mild the farther I advanced beyond the sixty-fifth degree of south latitude, and that the variation decreases in the same proportion. While north of this latitude, say between sixty and sixty-five south, we frequently had great difficulty in finding a passage for the vessel between the immense and almost innumerable ice islands, some of which were from one to two miles in circumference, and more than five hundred feet above the surface of the water."

Being nearly destitute of fuel and water, and without proper instruments, it being also late in the season, Captain Morrell was now obliged to put back, without attempting any farther progress to the southward, although an entirely open sea lay before him. He expresses the opinion that, had not these overruling considerations obliged him to retreat, he could have penetrated, if not to the pole itself, at least to the eighty-fifth parallel. I have given his ideas respecting these matters somewhat at length, that the reader may have an opportunity of seeing how far they were borne out by my own subsequent experience.

In 1831, Captain Briscoe, in the employ of the Messieurs Enderby, whaleship owners of London, sailed in the brig *Lively* for the South Seas, accompanied by the cutter *Tula*. On the twenty-eighth of February, being in latitude 66° 30′ S., longitude 47° 31′ E., he descried land, and "clearly discovered through the snow the black peaks of a range of mountains running E. S. E." He remained in this neighborhood during the whole of the following month, but was unable to approach the coast nearer than within ten leagues, owing to the boisterous state of the weather. Finding it impossible to make farther discovery during this season, he returned northward to winter in Van Diemen's Land.

In the beginning of 1832 he again proceeded southwardly, and on the fourth of February land was seen to the southeast in latitude 67° 15′, longitude 69° 29′ W. This was soon found to be an island near the headland of the country he had first discovered. On the twenty-first of the month he succeeded in landing on the latter, and took possession of it in the name of William IV., calling it Adelaide's Island, in honor of the English queen. These particulars being made known to the Royal Geographical Society of London, the conclusion was drawn by that body "that there is a continuous tract of land extending from 47° 30′ E. to 69° 29′ W. longitude, running the parallel of from sixty-six to sixty-seven degrees south latitude." In respect to this conclusion Mr. Reynolds observes, "In the correctness of it we by no means concur; nor do the discoveries of Briscoe warrant any such inference. It was within these limits that Weddell proceeded south on a meridian to the east of Georgia, Sandwich Land, and the South Orkney and Shetland Islands." My own experience will be found to testify most directly to the falsity of the conclusion arrived at by the society.

These are the principal attempts which have been made at penetrating to a high southern latitude, and it will now be seen that there remained, previous to the voyage of the *Jane*, nearly three hundred degrees of longitude in which the Antarctic circle had not been crossed at all. Of course a wide field lay before us for discovery, and it was with feelings of most intense interest that I heard Captain Guy express his resolution of pushing boldly to the southward.

CHAPTER 17

WE KEPT our course southwardly for four days after giving up the search for Glass's Islands, without meeting with any ice at all. On the twenty-sixth, at noon, we were in latitude 63° 23′ S., longitude 41° 25′ W. We now saw several large ice islands, and a floe of field ice, not, however, of any great extent. The winds generally blew from the southeast, or the northeast, but were very light. Whenever we had a westerly wind, which was seldom, it was invariably attended with a rain squall. Every day we had more or less snow. The thermometer, on the twenty-seventh, stood at thirty-five.

January 1, 1828. This day we found ourselves completely hemmed in by the ice, and our prospects looked cheerless indeed. A strong gale blew, during the whole forenoon, from the northeast, and drove large cakes of the drift against the rudder and counter with such violence that we all trembled for the consequences. Towards evening, the gale still blowing with fury, a large field in front separated, and we were enabled, by carrying a press of sail, to force a passage through the smaller flakes into some open water beyond. As we approached this space we took in sail by degrees, and having at length got clear, lay to under a single reefed foresail.

January 2. We had now tolerably pleasant weather. At noon we found ourselves in latitude 69° 10′ S., longitude 42° 20′ W., having crossed the Antarctic circle. Very little ice was to be seen to the southward, although large fields of it lay behind us. This day we rigged some sounding gear, using a large iron pot capable of holding twenty gallons, and a line of two hundred fathoms. We found the current setting to the north, about a quarter of a mile per hour. The temperature of the air was now about thirty-three. Here we found the variation to be 14° 28′ easterly, per azimuth.

January 5. We had still held on to the southward without any very great impediments. On this morning, however, being in latitude 73° 15′ E., longitude 42° 10′ W., we were again brought to a stand by an immense expanse of firm ice. We saw, nevertheless, much open water to the southward, and felt no doubt of being able to reach it eventually. Standing to the eastward along the edge of the floe, we at length came to a passage of about a mile in width, through which we warped our way by sundown. The sea in which we now were was thickly covered with ice islands, but had no field ice, and we pushed on boldly as before. The cold did not seem to increase, although we had snow very frequently, and now and then hail squalls of great violence. Immense flocks of the albatross flew over the schooner this day, going from southeast to northwest.

January 7. The sea still remained pretty well open, so that we had no difficulty in holding on our course. To the westward we saw some icebergs of incredible size, and in the afternoon passed very near one whose summit could not have been less than four hundred fathoms from the surface of the ocean. Its girth was probably, at the base, three quarters of a league, and several streams of water were running from crevices in its sides. We remained in sight of this island two days, and then only lost it in a fog.

January 10. Early this morning we had the misfortune to lose a man overboard. He was an American, named Peter Vredenburgh, a native of New York, and was one of the most valuable hands on board the schooner. In going over the bows his foot slipped, and he fell between two cakes of ice, never rising again. At noon of this day we were in latitude 78° 30′, longitude 40° 15′ W. The cold was now excessive, and we had hail squalls continually from the northward and eastward. In this direction also we saw several more immense icebergs, and the whole horizon to the eastward appeared to be blocked up with field ice, rising in tiers, one mass above the other. Some driftwood floated by during the evening, and a great quantity of birds flew over, among which were nellies, petrels, albatrosses, and a large bird of a brilliant blue plumage. The variation here, per azimuth, was less than it had been previously to our passing the Antarctic circle.

January 12. Our passage to the south again looked doubtful, as nothing was to be seen in the direction of the pole but one apparently limitless floe, backed by absolute mountains of ragged ice, one precipice of which arose frowningly above the other. We stood to the westward until the fourteenth, in the hope of finding an entrance.

January 14. This morning we reached the western extremity of the field which had impeded us, and, weathering it, came to an open sea, without a particle of ice. Upon sounding with two hundred fathoms, we here found a current setting southwardly at the rate of half a mile per hour. The temperature of the air was forty-seven, that of the water thirty-four. We now sailed to the southward without meeting any interruption of moment until the sixteenth, when, at noon, we were in latitude 81° 21', longitude 42° W. We here again sounded, and found a current setting still southwardly, and at the rate of three quarters of a mile per hour. The variation per azimuth had diminished, and the temperature of the air was mild and pleasant, the thermometer being as high as fifty-one. At this period not a particle of ice was to be discovered. All hands on board now felt certain of attaining the pole.

January 17. This day was full of incident. Innumerable flights of birds flew over us from the southward, and several were shot from the deck; one of them, a species of pelican, proved to be excellent eating. About midday a small floe of ice was seen from the masthead off the larboard bow, and upon it there appeared to be some large animal. As the weather was good and nearly calm, Captain Guy ordered out two of the boats to see what it was. Dirk Peters and myself accompanied the mate in the larger boat. Upon coming up with the floe, we perceived that it was in possession of a gigantic creature of the race of the Arctic bear, but far exceeding in size the largest of these animals. Being well armed, we made no scruple of attacking it at once. Several shots were fired in quick succession, the most of which took effect, apparently, in the head and body. Nothing discouraged, however, the monster threw himself from the ice, and swam, with open jaws, to the boat in which were Peters and myself. Owing to the confusion which ensued among us at this unexpected turn of the adventure, no person was ready immediately with a second shot, and the bear had actually succeeded in getting half his vast bulk across our gunwale, and seizing one of the men by the small of his back, before any efficient means were taken to repel him. In this extremity nothing but the promptness and agility of Peters saved us from destruction. Leaping upon the back of the huge beast, he plunged the blade of a knife behind the neck, reaching the spinal marrow at a blow. The brute tumbled into the sea lifeless, and without a struggle, rolling over Peters as he fell. The latter soon recovered himself, and a rope being thrown him, he secured the carcass before entering the boat. We then returned in triumph to the schooner, towing our trophy behind us. This bear, upon admeasurement, proved to be full fifteen feet in his greatest length. His wool was perfectly white, and very coarse, curling tightly. The eyes were of a blood red, and larger than those of the Arctic bear—the snout also more rounded, rather resembling the snout of the bulldog. The meat was tender, but excessively rank and fishy, although the men devoured it with avidity, and declared it excellent eating.

Scarcely had we got our prize alongside, when the man at the masthead gave the joyful shout of *"land on the starboard bow!"* All hands were now upon the alert, and, a breeze springing up very opportunely from the northward and eastward, we were soon close in with the coast. It proved to be a low rocky islet, of about a league in circumference, and altogether destitute of vegetation, if we except a species of prickly pear. In approaching it from the northward, a singular ledge of rock is seen projecting into the sea, and bearing a strong resemblance to corded bales of cotton. Around this ledge to the westward is a small bay, at the bottom of which our boats effected a convenient landing.

It did not take us long to explore every portion of the island, but, with one exception, we found nothing worthy of observation. In the southern extremity, we picked up near the shore, half buried in a pile of loose stones, a piece of wood, which seemed to have formed the prow of a canoe. There had been evidently some attempt at carving upon it, and Captain Guy fancied that he made out the figure of a tortoise, but the resemblance did not strike me very forcibly. Besides this prow, if such it were, we found no other token that any living creature had ever been here before. Around the coast we discovered occasional small floes of ice—but these were very few. The exact situation of this islet (to which Captain Guy gave the name of Bennet's Islet, in honor of his partner in the ownership of the schooner) is 82° 50′ S. latitude, 42° 20′ W. longitude.

We had now advanced to the southward more than eight degrees farther than any previous navigators, and the sea still lay perfectly open before us. We found, too, that the variation uniformly decreased as we proceeded, and, what was still more surprising, that the temperature of the air, and latterly of the water, became milder. The weather might even be called pleasant, and we had a steady but very gentle breeze always from some northern point of the compass. The sky was usually clear, with now and then a slight appearance of thin vapor in the southern horizon—this, however, was invariably of brief duration. Two difficulties alone presented themselves to our view; we were getting short of fuel, and symptoms of scurvy had occurred among several of the crew. These considerations began to impress upon Captain Guy the necessity of returning, and he spoke of it frequently. For my own part, confident as I was of soon arriving at land of some description upon the course we were pursuing, and having every reason to believe, from present appearances, that we should not find it the sterile soil met with in the higher Arctic latitudes, I warmly pressed upon him the expediency of persevering, at least for a few days longer, in the direction we were now holding. So tempting an opportunity of solving the great problem in regard to an Antarctic continent had never yet been afforded to man, and I confess that I felt myself bursting with indignation at the timid and ill-timed suggestions of our commander. I believe, indeed, that what I could not refrain from saying to him on this head had the effect of inducing him to push on. While, therefore, I cannot but lament the most unfortunate and bloody events which immediately arose from my advice, I must still be allowed to feel some degree of gratification at having been instrumental, however remotely, in opening to the eye of science one of the most intensely exciting secrets which has ever engrossed its attention.

CHAPTER 18

JANUARY 18. This morning* we continued to the southward, with the same pleasant weather as before. The sea was entirely smooth, the air tolerably warm and from the northeast, the temperature of the water fifty-three. We now again got our sounding gear in order, and, with a hundred and fifty fathoms of line, found the current setting towards the pole at the rate of a mile an hour. This constant tendency to the southward, both in the wind and current, caused some degree of speculation, and even of alarm, in different quarters of the schooner, and I saw distinctly that no little impression had been made upon the mind of Captain Guy. He was exceedingly sensitive to ridicule, however, and I finally succeeded in laughing him out of his apprehensions. The variation was now very trivial. In the course of the day we saw several large whales of the right species, and innumerable flights of the albatross passed over the vessel. We also picked up a bush, full of red berries, like those of the hawthorn, and the carcass of a singular-looking land animal. It was three feet in length, and but six inches in height, with four very short legs, the feet armed with long claws of a brilliant scarlet, and resembling coral in substance. The body was covered with a straight silky hair, perfectly white. The tail was peaked like that of a rat, and about a foot and a half long. The head

* The terms *morning* and *evening*, which I have made use of to avoid confusion in my narrative, as far as possible, must not, of course, be taken in their ordinary sense. For a long time past we had had no night at all, the daylight being continual. The dates throughout are according to nautical time, and the bearings must be understood as per compass. I would also remark, in this place, that I cannot, in the first portion of what is here written, pretend to strict accuracy in respect to dates, or latitudes and longitudes, having kept no regular journal until after the period of which this first portion treats. In many instances I have relied altogether upon memory. (Poe's note.)

resembled a cat's with the exception of the ears—these were flapped like the ears of a dog. The *teeth* were of the same brilliant scarlet as the claws.

January 19. Today, being in latitude 83° 20′, longitude 43° 5′ W. (the sea being of an extraordinarily dark color), we again saw land from the masthead, and, upon a closer scrutiny, found it to be one of a group of very large islands. The shore was precipitous, and the interior seemed to be well wooded, a circumstance which occasioned us great joy. In about four hours from our first discovering the land we came to anchor in ten fathoms, sandy bottom, a league from the coast, as a high surf, with strong ripples here and there, rendered a nearer approach of doubtful expediency. The two largest boats were now ordered out, and a party, well armed (among whom were Peters and myself), proceeded to look for an opening in the reef which appeared to encircle the island. After searching about for some time, we discovered an inlet, which we were entering, when we saw four large canoes put off from the shore, filled with men who seemed to be well armed. We waited for them to come up, and as they moved with great rapidity, they were soon within hail. Captain Guy now held up a white handkerchief on the blade of an oar, when the strangers made a full stop, and commenced a loud jabbering all at once, intermingled with occasional shouts, in which we could distinguish the words *Anamoo-moo!* and *Lama-Lama!* They continued this for at least half an hour, during which we had a good opportunity of observing their appearance.

In the four canoes, which might have been fifty feet long and five broad, there were a hundred and ten savages in all. They were about the ordinary stature of Europeans, but of a more muscular and brawny frame. Their complexion [was] a jet black, with thick and long woolly hair. They were clothed in skins of an unknown black animal, shaggy and silky, and made to fit the body with some degree of skill, the hair being inside, except where turned out about the neck, wrists, and ankles. Their arms consisted principally of clubs, of a dark, and apparently very heavy wood. Some spears, however, were observed among them, headed with flint, and a few slings. The bottoms of the canoes were full of black stones about the size of a large egg.

When they had concluded their harangue (for it was clear they intended their jabbering for such), one of them who seemed to be the chief stood up in the prow of his canoe, and made signs for us to bring our boats alongside of him. This hint we pretended not to understand, thinking it the wiser plan to maintain, if possible, the interval between us, as their number more than quadrupled our own. Finding this to be the case, the chief ordered the three other canoes to hold back, while he advanced towards us with his own. As soon as he came up with us he leaped on board the largest of our boats, and seated himself by the side of Captain Guy, pointing at the same time to the schooner, and repeating the words *Anamoo-moo!* and *Lama-Lama!* We now put back to the vessel, the four canoes following at a little distance.

Upon getting alongside the chief evinced symptoms of extreme surprise and delight, clapping his hands, slapping his thighs and breast, and laughing obstreperously. His followers behind joined in his merriment, and for some minutes the din was so excessive as to be absolutely deafening. Quiet being at length restored, Captain Guy ordered the boats to be hoisted up, as a necessary precaution, and gave the chief (whose name we soon found to be *Too-wit*) to understand that we could admit no more than twenty of his men on deck at one time. With this arrangement he appeared perfectly satisfied, and gave some directions to the canoes, when one of them approached, the rest remaining about fifty yards off. Twenty of the savages now got on board, and proceeded to ramble over every part of the deck, and scramble about among the rigging, making themselves much at home, and examining every article with great inquisitiveness.

It was quite evident that they had never before seen any of the white race—from whose complexion, indeed, they appeared to recoil. They believed the *Jane* to be a living creature, and seemed to be afraid of hurting it with the points of their spears, carefully turning them up. Our crew were much amused with the conduct of Too-wit in one instance. The cook was splitting some wood near the galley, and, by accident, struck his ax into the deck, making a gash of considerable depth. The chief immediately ran up, and pushing the cook on one side rather roughly, commenced a half whine, half howl, strongly indicative of sympathy in what he considered the sufferings of the schooner, patting and smoothing the gash with his hand, and washing it from a bucket of sea water which stood by. This was a degree of ignorance for which we were not prepared, and for my part I could not help thinking some of it affected.

When the visitors had satisfied, as well as they could, their curiosity in regard to our upper works, they were admitted below, when their amazement exceeded all bounds. Their astonishment now appeared to be far too deep for words, for they roamed about in silence, broken only by low ejaculations. The arms afforded them much food for speculation, and they were suffered to handle and examine them at leisure. I do not believe that they had the least suspicion of their actual use, but rather took them for idols, seeing the care we had of them, and the attention with which we watched their movements while handling them. At the great guns their wonder was redoubled. They approached them with every mark of the profoundest reverence and awe, but forbore to examine them minutely. There were two large mirrors in the cabin, and here was the acme of their amazement. Too-wit was the first to approach them, and he had got in the middle of the cabin, with his face to one and his back to the other, before he fairly perceived them. Upon raising his eyes and seeing his reflected self in the glass, I thought the savage would go mad; but, upon turning short round to make a retreat, and beholding himself a second time in the opposite direction, I was afraid he would expire upon the spot. No persuasions could prevail upon him to take another look; but, throwing himself upon the floor, with his face buried in his hands, he remained thus until we were obliged to drag him upon deck.

The whole of the savages were admitted on board in this manner, twenty at a time, Too-wit being suffered to remain

during the entire period. We saw no disposition to thievery
among them, nor did we miss a single article after their departure. Throughout the whole of their visit they evinced the
most friendly manner. There were, however, some points in their
demeanor which we found it impossible to understand: for example, we could not get them to approach several very harmless
objects—such as the schooner's sails, an egg, an open book, or a
pan of flour. We endeavored to ascertain if they had among
them any articles which might be turned to account in the way
of traffic, but found great difficulty in being comprehended. We
made out, nevertheless, what greatly astonished us, that the
islands abounded in the large tortoise of the Gallipagos, one of
which we saw in the canoe of Too-wit. We saw also some *biche
de mer* in the hands of one of the savages, who was greedily de-
vouring it in its natural state. These anomalies, for they were
such when considered in regard to the latitude, induced Captain
Guy to wish for a thorough investigation of the country, in the
hope of making a profitable speculation in his discovery. For
my own part, anxious as I was to know something more of these
islands, I was still more earnestly bent on prosecuting the voyage
to the southward without delay. We had now fine weather, but
there was no telling how long it would last; and being already
in the eighty-fourth parallel, with an open sea before us, a current
setting strongly to the southward, and the wind fair, I could not
listen with any patience to a proposition of stopping longer than
was absolutely necessary for the health of the crew and the taking
on board a proper supply of fuel and fresh provisions. I represented to the captain that we might easily make this group on
our return, and winter here in the event of being blocked up by
the ice. He at length came into my views (for in some way,
hardly known to myself, I had acquired much influence over
him), and it was finally resolved that, even in the event of our
finding *biche de mer*, we should only stay here a week to recruit,
and then push on to the southward while we might. Accordingly we made every necessary preparation, and under the guidance of Too-wit, got the *Jane* through the reef in safety, coming

to anchor about a mile from the shore, in an excellent bay, completely landlocked, on the southeastern coast of the main island, and in ten fathoms of water, black sandy bottom. At the head of this bay there were three fine springs (we were told) of good water, and we saw abundance of wood in the vicinity. The four canoes followed us in, keeping, however, at a respectful distance. Too-wit himself remained on board, and, upon our dropping anchor, invited us to accompany him on shore, and visit his village in the interior. To this Captain Guy consented; and ten savages being left on board as hostages, a party of us, twelve in all, got in readiness to attend the chief. We took care to be well armed, yet without evincing any distrust. The schooner had her guns run out, her boarding nettings up, and every other proper precaution was taken to guard against surprise. Directions were left with the chief mate to admit no person on board during our absence, and, in the event of our not appearing in twelve hours, to send the cutter, with a swivel, around the island in search of us.

At every step we took inland the conviction forced itself upon us that we were in a country differing essentially from any hitherto visited by civilized men. We saw nothing with which we had been formerly conversant. The trees resembled no growth of either the torrid, the temperate, or the northern frigid zones, and were altogether unlike those of the lower southern latitudes we had already traversed. The very rocks were novel in their mass, their color, and their stratification; and the streams themselves utterly incredible as it may appear, had so little in common with those of other climates, that we were scrupulous of tasting them, and, indeed, had difficulty in bringing ourselves to believe that their qualities were purely those of nature. At a small brook which crossed our path (the first we had reached) Too-wit and his attendants halted to drink. On account of the singular character of the water, we refused to taste it, supposing it to be polluted; and it was not until some time afterward we came to understand that such was the appearance of the streams throughout the whole group. I am at a loss to give a distinct idea of the nature of this liquid, and cannot do so without many words. Although it flowed with rapidity in all declivities where common water would do so, yet never, except when falling in a cascade, had it the customary appearance of *limpidity*. It was, nevertheless, in point of fact, as perfectly limpid as any limestone water in existence, the difference being only in appearance. At first sight, and especially in cases where little declivity was found, it bore resemblance, as regards consistency, to a thick infusion of gum Arabic in common water. But this was only the least remarkable of its extraordinary qualities. It was *not* colorless, nor was it of any one uniform color—presenting to the eye, as it flowed, every possible shade of purple, like the hues of a changeable silk. This variation in shade was produced in a manner which excited as profound astonishment in the minds of our party as the mirror had done in the case of Too-wit. Upon collecting a basinful, and allowing it to settle thoroughly, we perceived that the whole mass of liquid was made up of a number of distinct veins, each of a distinct hue; that these veins did not commingle; and that their cohesion was perfect in regard to their own particles among themselves, and imperfect in regard to neighboring veins. Upon passing the blade of a knife athwart the veins, the water closed over it immediately, as with us, and also, in withdrawing it, all traces of the passage of the knife were instantly obliterated. If, however, the blade was passed down accurately between the two veins, a perfect separation was effected, which the power of cohesion did not immediately rectify. The phenomena of this water formed the first definite link in that vast chain of apparent miracles with which I was destined to be at length encircled.

CHAPTER 19

We were nearly three hours in reaching the village, it being more than nine miles in the interior, and the path lying through a rugged country. As we passed along, the party of Too-wit (the whole hundred and ten savages of the canoes) was momentarily strengthened by smaller detachments, of from two to six or seven, which joined us, as if by accident, at different turns in the road. There appeared so much of system in this that I could not help feeling distrust, and I spoke to Captain Guy of my apprehensions. It was now too late, however, to recede, and we concluded that our best security lay in evincing a perfect confidence in the good faith of Too-wit. We accordingly went on, keeping a wary eye upon the maneuvers of the savages, and not permitting them to divide our numbers by pushing in between. In this way, passing through a precipitous ravine, we at length reached what we were told was the only collection of habitations upon the island. As we came in sight of them, the chief set up a shout, and frequently repeated the word *Klock-Klock;* which we supposed to be the name of the village, or perhaps the generic name for villages.

The dwellings were of the most miserable description imaginable, and, unlike those of even the lowest of the savage races with which mankind are acquainted, were of no uniform plan. Some of them (and these we found belonged to the *Wampoos* or *Yampoos*, the great men of the land) consisted of a tree cut down at about four feet from the root, with a large black skin thrown over it, and hanging in loose folds upon the ground. Under this the savage nestled. Others were formed by means of rough limbs of trees, with the withered foliage upon them, made to recline, at an angle of forty-five degrees, against a bank of clay, heaped up, without regular form, to the height of five or six feet. Others, again, were mere holes dug in the earth perpendicularly, and covered over with similar branches, these being removed when the tenant was about to enter, and pulled on again when he had entered. A few were built among the forked limbs of trees as they stood, the upper limbs being partially cut through, so as to bend over upon the lower, thus forming thicker shelter from the weather. The greater number, however, consisted of small shallow caverns, apparently scratched in the face of a precipitous ledge of dark stone, resembling fuller's earth, with which three sides of the village were bounded. At the door of each of these primitive caverns was a small rock, which the tenant carefully placed before the entrance upon leaving his residence, for what purpose I could not ascertain, as the stone itself was never of sufficient size to close up more than a third of the opening.

This village, if it were worthy of the name, lay in a valley of some depth, and could only be approached from the southward, the precipitous ledge of which I have already spoken cutting off all access in other directions. Through the middle of the valley ran a brawling stream of the same magical-looking water which has been described. We saw several strange animals about the dwellings, all appearing to be thoroughly domesticated. The largest of these creatures resembled our common hog in the structure of the body and snout; the tail, however, was bushy, and the legs slender as those of the antelope. Its motion was exceedingly awkward and indecisive, and we never saw it attempt to run. We noticed also several animals very similar in appearance, but of a greater length of body, and covered with a black wool. There were a great variety of tame fowls running about, and these seemed to constitute the chief food of the natives. To our astonishment we saw black albatross among these birds in a state of entire domestication, going to sea periodically for food, but always returning to the village as a home, and using the southern shore in the vicinity as a place of incubation. There they were joined by their friends the pelicans as usual, but these latter never followed them to the dwellings of the savages.

Among the other kinds of tame fowls were ducks, differing very little from the canvasback of our own country, black gannets, and a large bird not unlike the buzzard in appearance, but not carnivorous. Of fish there seemed to be a great abundance. We saw, during our visit, a quantity of dried salmon, rock cod, blue dolphins, mackerel, blackfish, skate, conger eels, elephant fish, mullets, soles, parrot fish, leatherjackets, gurnards, hake, flounders, paracutas, and innumerable other varieties. We noticed, too, that most of them were similar to the fish about the group of the Lord Auckland islands, in a latitude as low as fifty-one degrees south. The Gallipago tortoise was also very plentiful. We saw but few wild animals, and none of a large size, or of a species with which we were familiar. One or two serpents of a formidable aspect crossed our path, but the natives paid them little attention, and we concluded that they were not venomous.

As we approached the village with Too-wit and his party, a vast crowd of the people rushed out to meet us, with loud shouts, among which we could only distinguish the everlasting *Anamoo-moo!* and *Lama-Lama!* We were much surprised at perceiving that, with one or two exceptions, these newcomers were entirely naked, the skins being used only by the men of the canoes. All the weapons of the country seemed also to be in the possession of the latter, for there was no appearance of any among the villagers. There were a great many women and children, the former not altogether wanting in what might be termed personal beauty. They were straight, tall, and well formed, with a grace and freedom of carriage not to be found in civilized society. Their lips, however, like those of the men, were thick and clumsy, so that, even when laughing, the teeth were never disclosed. Their hair was of a finer texture than that of the males. Among these naked villagers there might have been ten or twelve who were clothed, like the party of Too-wit, in dresses of black skin, and armed with lances and heavy clubs. These appeared to have great influence among the rest, and were always addressed by the title *Wampoo*. These, too, were the tenants of the black skin palaces. That of Too-wit was situated in the center of the village, and was much larger and somewhat better constructed than others of its kind. The tree which formed its support was cut off at a distance of twelve feet or thereabout from the root, and there were several branches left just below the cut, these serving to extend the covering, and in this way prevent its flapping about the trunk. The covering, too, which consisted of four very large skins fastened together with wooden skewers, was secured at the bottom with pegs driven through it and into the ground. The floor was strewed with a quantity of dry leaves by way of carpet.

To this hut we were conducted with great solemnity, and as many of the natives crowded in after us as possible. Too-wit seated himself on the leaves, and made signs that we should follow his example. This we did, and presently found ourselves in a situation peculiarly uncomfortable, if not indeed critical. We were on the ground, twelve in number, with the savages, as many as forty, sitting on their hams so closely around us that, if any disturbance had arisen, we should have found it impossible to make use of our arms, or indeed to have risen on our feet. The pressure was not only inside the tent, but outside, where probably was every individual on the whole island, the crowd being prevented from trampling us to death only by the incessant exertions and vociferations of Too-wit. Our chief security lay, however, in the presence of Too-wit himself among us, and we resolved to stick by him closely, as the best chance of extricating ourselves from the dilemma, sacrificing him immediately upon the first appearance of hostile design.

After some trouble a certain degree of quiet was restored, when the chief addressed us in a spech of great length, and very nearly resembling the one delivered in the canoes, with the exception that the *Anamoo-moos!* were now somewhat more strenuously insisted upon than the *Lama-Lamas!* We listened in profound silence until the conclusion of his harangue, when Captain Guy replied by assuring the chief of his eternal friendship and good will, concluding what he had to say by a present of several strings of blue beads and a knife. At the former the monarch, much to our surprise, turned up his nose with some expression of contempt; but the knife gave him the most unlimited satisfaction, and he immediately ordered dinner. This was handed into the tent over the heads of the attendants, and consisted of the palpitating entrails of a species of unknown animal, probably one of the slim-legged hogs which we had observed in our approach to the village. Seeing us at a loss how to proceed, he began, by way of setting us an example, to devour yard after yard of the enticing food, until we could positively stand it no longer, and evinced such manifest symptoms of rebellion of stomach as inspired his majesty with a degree of astonishment only inferior to that brought about by the looking glasses. We declined, however, partaking of the delicacies before us, and endeavored to make him understand that we had no appetite whatever, having just finished a hearty *déjeuner*.

When the monarch had made an end of his meal, we commenced a series of cross-questioning in every ingenious manner we could devise, with a view of discovering what were the chief productions of the country, and whether any of them might be turned to profit. At length he seemed to have some idea of our meaning, and offered to accompany us to a part of the coast where he assured us the *biche de mer* (pointing to a specimen of that animal) was to be found in great abundance. We were glad of this early opportunity of escaping from the oppression of the crowd, and signified our eagerness to proceed. We now left the tent, and, accompanied by the whole population of the village, followed the chief to the southeastern extremity of the island, not far from the bay where our vessel lay at anchor. We waited here for about an hour, until the four canoes were brought round by some of the savages to our station. The whole of our party then getting into one of them, we were paddled along the edge of the reef before mentioned, and of another still farther out, where we saw a far greater quantity of *biche de mer* than the oldest seaman among us had ever seen in those groups of the lower latitudes most celebrated for this article of commerce. We stayed near these reefs only long enough to satisfy ourselves that we could easily load a dozen vessels with the animal if necessary, when we were taken alongside the schooner, and parted with Too-wit, after obtaining from him a promise that he would bring us, in the course of twenty-four hours, as many of the canvasback ducks and Gallipago tortoises as his canoes would hold. In the whole of this adventure we saw nothing in the demeanor of the natives calculated to create suspicion, with the single exception of the systematic manner in which their party was strengthened during our route from the schooner to the village.

CHAPTER 20

THE CHIEF was as good as his word, and we were soon plentifully supplied with fresh provision. We found the tortoises as fine as we had ever seen, and the ducks surpassed our best species of wild fowl, being exceedingly tender, juicy, and well flavored. Besides these, the savages brought us upon our making them comprehend our wishes, a vast quantity of brown celery and scurvy grass, with a canoeload of fresh fish and some dried. The celery was a treat indeed, and the scurvy grass proved of incalculable benefit in restoring those of our men who had shown symptoms of disease. In a very short time we had not a single person on the sick list. We had also plenty of other kinds of fresh provision, among which may be mentioned a species of shellfish resembling the mussel in shape, but with the taste of an oyster. Shrimps, too, and prawns were abundant, and albatross and other birds' eggs with dark shells. We took in, too, a plentiful stock of the flesh of the hog which I have mentioned before. Most of the men found it a palatable food, but I thought it fishy and otherwise disagreeable. In return for these good things we presented the natives with blue beads, brass trinkets, nails, knives, and pieces of red cloth, they being fully delighted in the exchange. We established a regular market on shore, just under the guns of the schooner, where our barterings were carried on with every appearance of good faith, and a degree of order which their conduct at the village of *Klock-Klock* had not led us to expect from the savages.

Matters went on thus very amicably for several days, during which parties of the natives were frequently on board the schooner, and parties of our men frequently on shore, making long excursions into the interior, and receiving no molestation whatever. Finding the ease with which the vessel might be loaded with *biche de mer*, owing to the friendly disposition of the islanders, and the readiness with which they would render us assistance in collecting it, Captain Guy resolved to enter into negotiation with Too-wit for the erection of suitable houses in which to cure the article, and for the services of himself and tribe in gathering as much as possible, while he himself took advantage of the fine weather to prosecute his voyage to the southward. Upon mentioning this project to the chief he seemed very willing to enter into an agreement. A bargain was accordingly struck, perfectly satisfactory to both parties, by which it was arranged that, after making the necessary preparations, such as laying off the proper grounds, erecting a portion of the buildings, and doing some other work in which the whole of our crew would be required, the schooner should proceed on her route, leaving three of her men on the island to superintend the fulfillment of the project, and instruct the natives in drying the *biche de mer*. In regard to terms, these were made to depend upon the exertions of the savages in our absence. They were to receive a stipulated quantity of blue beads, knives, red cloth, and so forth, for every certain number of piculs of the *biche de mer* which should be ready on our return.

A description of the nature of this important article of commerce, and the method of preparing it, may prove of some interest to my readers, and I can find no more suitable place than this for introducing an account of it. The following comprehensive notice of the substance is taken from a modern history of a voyage to the South Seas.

"It is that *mollusca* from the Indian Seas which is known in commerce by the French name *bouche de mer* (a nice morsel from the sea). If I am not much mistaken, the celebrated Cuvier calls it *gasteropoda pulmonifera*. It is abundantly gathered in the coasts of the Pacific islands, and gathered especially for the Chinese market, where it commands a great price, perhaps as much as their much-talked-of edible bird's nests, which are probably made up of the gelatinous matter picked up by a species of swallow from the body of these molluscae. They have no shell, no legs, nor any prominent part, except an *absorbing* and an *excretory*, opposite organs; but, by their elastic wings, like caterpillars or worms, they creep in shallow waters, in which, when low, they can be seen by a kind of swallow, the sharp bill of which, inserted in the soft animal, draws a gummy and filamentous substance, which, by drying, can be wrought into the solid walls of their nest. Hence the name of *gasteropoda pulmonifera.*

"This mollusca is oblong, and of different sizes, from three to eighteen inches in length; and I have seen a few that were not less than two feet long. They were nearly round, a little flattish on one side, which lies next to the bottom of the sea; and they are from one to eight inches thick. They crawl up into shallow water at particular seasons of the year, probably for the purpose of gendering, as we often find them in pairs. It is when the sun has the most power on the water, rendering it tepid, that they approach the shore; and they often go up into places so shallow that, on the tide's receding, they are left dry, exposed to the heat of the sun. But they do not bring forth their young in shallow water, as we never see any of their progeny, and the full-grown ones are always observed coming in from deep water. They feed principally on that class of zoöphites which produce the coral.

"The *biche de mer* is generally taken in three or four feet of water; after which they are brought on shore, and split at one end with a knife, the incision being one inch or more, according to the size of the mollusca. Through this opening the entrails are forced out by pressure, and they are much like those of any other small tenant of the deep. The article is then washed, and afterward boiled to a certain degree, which must not be too much or too little. They are then buried in the ground for four hours, then boiled again for a short time, after which they are dried, either by the fire or the sun. Those cured by the sun are worth the most; but where one picul (133⅓ lbs.) can be cured that way, I can cure thirty piculs by the fire. When once properly cured, they can be kept in a dry place for two or three years without any risk; but they should be examined once in every few months, say four times a year, to see if any dampness is likely to affect them.

"The Chinese, as before stated, consider *biche de mer* a very great luxury, believing that it wonderfully strengthens and nourishes the system, and renews the exhausted system of the immoderate voluptuary. The first quality commands a high price in Canton, being worth ninety dollars a picul; the second quality, seventy-five dollars; the third, fifty dollars; the fourth, thirty dollars; the fifth, twenty dollars; the sixth, twelve dollars; the seventh, eight dollars; and the eighth, four dollars; small cargoes, however, will often bring more in Manila, Singapore, and Batavia."

An agreement having been thus entered into, we proceeded immediately to land everything necessary for preparing the buildings and clearing the ground. A large flat space near the eastern shore of the bay was selected, where there was plenty both of wood and water, and within a convenient distance of the principal reefs on which the *biche de mer* was to be procured. We now all set to work in good earnest, and soon, to the great astonishment of the savages, had felled a sufficient number of trees for our purpose, getting them quickly in order for the framework of the houses, which in two or three days were so far under way that we could safely trust the rest of the work to the three men whom we intended to leave behind. These were John Carson, Alfred Harris, and —— Peterson (all natives of London, I believe), who volunteered their services in this respect.

By the last of the month we had everything in readiness for departure. We had agreed, however, to pay a formal visit of leavestaking to the village, and Too-wit insisted so pertinaciously upon our keeping the promise, that we did not think it advisable to run the risk of offending him by a final refusal. I believe that not one of us had at this time the slightest suspicion of the good faith of the savages. They had uniformly behaved with the greatest decorum, aiding us with alacrity in our work, offering us their commodities frequently without price, and never, in any instance, pilfering a single article, although the high value they set upon the goods we had with us was evident by the extravagant demonstrations of joy always manifested upon our making them a present. The women especially were most obliging in every respect, and, upon the whole, we should have been the most suspicious of human beings had we entertained a single thought of perfidy on the part of a people who treated us so well. A very short while sufficed to prove that this apparent kindness of disposition was only the result of a deeply laid plan for our destruction, and that the islanders for whom we entertained such inordinate feelings of esteem, were among the most barbarous, subtle, and bloodthirsty wretches that ever contaminated the face of the globe.

It was on the first of February that we went on shore for the purpose of visiting the village. Although, as said before, we entertained not the slightest suspicion, still no proper precaution was neglected. Six men were left in the schooner with instructions to permit none of the savages to approach the vessel during our absence, under any pretence whatever, and to remain constantly on deck. The boarding nettings were up, the guns double-shotted with grape and canister, and the swivels loaded with canisters of musket balls. She lay, with her anchor apeak, about a mile from the shore, and no canoe could approach her in any direction without being distinctly seen and exposed to the full fire of our swivels immediately.

The six men being left on board, our shore party consisted of thirty-two persons in all. We were armed to the teeth, having with us muskets, pistols, and cutlasses, besides each had a long kind of seaman's knife, somewhat resembling the Bowie knife now so much used throughout our western and southern country. A hundred of the blackskin warriors met us at the landing for the purpose of accompanying us on our way. We noticed, however, with some surprise, that they were now entirely without arms; and, upon questioning Too-wit in relation to this circumstance, he merely answered that *Mattee non we pa pa si*—meaning that there was no need of arms where all were brothers. We took this in good part, and proceeded.

We had passed the spring and rivulet of which I before spoke, and were now entering upon a narrow gorge leading through the chain of soapstone hills among which the village was situated. This gorge was very rocky and uneven, so much so that it was with no little difficulty we scrambled through it on our first visit to Klock-klock. The whole length of the ravine might have been a mile and a half, or probably two miles. It wound in every possible direction through the hills (having apparently formed, at some remote period, the bed of a torrent), in no instance proceeding more than twenty yards without an abrupt turn. The sides of this dell would have averaged, I am sure, seventy or eighty feet in perpendicular altitude throughout the whole of their extent, and in some portions they arose to an astonishing height, overshadowing the pass so completely that but little of the light of day could penetrate. The general width was about forty feet, and occasionally it diminished so as not to allow the passage of more than five or six persons abreast. In short, there could be no place in the world better adapted for the consummation of an ambuscade, and it was no more than natural that we should look carefully to our arms as we entered upon it. When I now think of our egregious folly, the chief subject of astonishment seems to be, that we should have ever ventured, under any circumstances, so completely into the power of unknown savages as to permit them to march both before and behind us in our progress through this ravine. Yet such was the order we blindly took up, trusting foolishly to the force of our party, the unarmed condition of Too-wit and his men, the certain efficacy of our firearms (whose effect was yet a secret to the natives), and, more than all, to the long-sustained pretension of friendship kept up by these infamous wretches. Five or six of them went on before, as if to lead the way, ostentatiously busying themselves in removing the larger stones and rubbish from the path. Next came our own party. We walked closely together, taking care only to prevent separation. Behind followed the main body of the savages, observing unusual order and decorum.

Dirk Peters, a man named Wilson Allen, and myself were on the right of our companions, examining, as we went along, the singular stratification of the precipice which overhung us. A fissure in the soft rock attracted our attention. It was about wide enough for one person to enter without squeezing, and extended back into the hill some eighteen or twenty feet in a straight course, sloping afterward to the left. The height of the opening, as far as we could see into it from the main gorge, was perhaps sixty or seventy feet. There were one or two stunted shrubs growing from the crevices, bearing a species of filbert which I felt some curiosity to examine, and pushed in briskly for that purpose, gathering five or six of the nuts at a grasp, and then hastily retreating. As I turned, I found that Peters and Allen had followed me. I desired them to go back, as there was not room for two persons to pass, saying they should have some of my nuts. They accordingly turned, and were scrambling back, Allen being close to the mouth of the fissure, when I was suddenly aware of a concussion resembling nothing I had ever before experienced, and which impressed me with a vague conception, if indeed I then thought of anything, that the whole foundations of the solid globe were suddenly rent asunder, and that the day of universal dissolution was at hand.

CHAPTER 21

As soon as I could collect my scattered senses, I found myself nearly suffocated, and groveling in utter darkness among a quantity of loose earth, which was also falling upon me heavily in every direction, threatening to bury me entirely. Horribly alarmed at this idea, I struggled to gain my feet, and at last succeeded. I then remained motionless for some moments, endeavoring to conceive what had happened to me, and where I was. Presently I heard a deep groan just at my ear, and afterward the smothered voice of Peters calling to me for aid in the name of God. I scrambled one or two paces forward, when I fell directly over the head and shoulders of my companion, who, I soon discovered, was buried in a loose mass of earth as far as his middle, and struggling desperately to free himself from the pressure. I tore the dirt from around him with all the energy I could command, and at length succeeded in getting him out.

As soon as we sufficiently recovered from our fright and surprise to be capable of conversing rationally, we both came to the conclusion that the walls of the fissure in which we had ventured had, by some convulsion of nature, or probably from their own weight, caved in overhead, and that we were consequently lost forever, being thus entombed alive. For a long time we gave up supinely to the most intense agony and despair, such as cannot be adequately imagined by those who have never been in a similar situation. I firmly believed that no incident ever occurring in the course of human events is more adapted to inspire the supremeness of mental and bodily distress than a case like our own, of living inhumation. The blackness of darkness which envelops the victim, the terrific oppression of lungs, the stifling fumes from the damp earth, unite with the ghastly considerations that we are beyond the remotest confines of hope, and that such is the allotted portion of *the dead,* to carry into the human heart a degree of appalling awe and horror not to be tolerated—never to be conceived.

At length Peters proposed that we should endeavor to ascertain precisely the extent of our calamity, and grope about our prison; it being barely possible, he observed, that some opening might yet be left us for escape. I caught eagerly at this hope, and, arousing myself to exertion, attempted to force my way through the loose earth. Hardly had I advanced a single step before a glimmer of light became perceptible, enough to convince me that, at all events, we should not immediately perish for want of air. We now took some degree of heart, and encouraged each other to hope for the best. Having scrambled over a bank of rubbish which impeded our farther progress in the direction of the light, we found less difficulty in advancing, and also experienced some relief from the excessive oppression of lungs which had tormented us. Presently we were enabled to obtain a glimpse of the objects around, and discovered that we were near the extremity of the straight portion of the fissure, where it made a turn to the left. A few struggles more, and we reached the bend, when, to our inexpressible joy, there appeared a long seam or crack extending upward a vast distance, generally at an angle of about forty-five degrees, although sometimes much more precipitous. We could not see through the whole extent of this opening; but, as a good deal of light came down it, we had little doubt of finding at the top of it (if we could by any means reach the top) a clear passage into the open air.

I now called to mind that three of us had entered the fissure from the main gorge, and that our companion, Allen, was still missing; we determined at once to retrace our steps and look for him. After a long search, and much danger from the farther caving in of the earth above us, Peters at length cried out to me that he had hold of our companion's foot, and that his whole body was deeply buried beneath the rubbish beyond the possibility of extricating him. I soon found that what he said was too true, and that, of course, life had been long extinct. With

sorrowful hearts, therefore, we left the corpse to its fate, and
again made our way to the bend.

The breadth of the seam was barely sufficient to admit us, and,
after one or two ineffectual efforts at getting up, we began once
more to despair. I have before said that the chain of hills through
which ran the main gorge was composed of a species of soft rock
resembling soapstone. The sides of the cleft we were now attempting to ascend were of the same material, and so excessively
slippery, being wet, that we could get but little foothold upon
them even in their least precipitous parts; in some places, where
the ascent was nearly perpendicular, the difficulty was, of course,
much aggravated; and, indeed, for some time we thought in-
surmountable. We took courage, however, from despair; and
what, by dint of cutting steps in the soft stone with our Bowie
knives, and swinging, at the risk of our lives, to small projecting
points of a harder species of slaty rock which now and then pro-
truded from the general mass, we at length reached a natural
platform, from which was perceptible a patch of blue sky, at the
extremity of a thickly wooded ravine. Looking back now, with
somewhat more leisure, at the passage through which we had thus
far proceeded, we clearly saw, from the appearance of its sides,
that it was of late formation, and we concluded that the concussion, whatever it was, which had so unexpectedly overwhelmed
us, had also, at the same moment, laid open this path for escape.
Being quite exhausted with exertion, and, indeed, so weak that we
were scarcely able to stand or articulate, Peters now proposed
that we should endeavor to bring our companions to the rescue
by firing the pistols which still remained in our girdles—the
muskets as well as cutlasses had been lost among the loose earth
at the bottom of the chasm. Subsequent events proved that, had
we fired, we should have sorely repented it; but luckily a half
suspicion of foul play had by this time arisen in my mind, and
we forbore to let the savages know of our whereabouts.

After having reposed for about an hour, we pushed on slowly
up the ravine, and had gone no great way before we heard a succession of tremendous yells. At length we reached what might

be called the surface of the ground; for our path hitherto, since leaving the platform, had lain beneath an archway of high rock and foliage, at a vast distance overhead. With great caution we stole to a narrow opening, through which we had a clear sight of the surrounding country, when the whole dreadful secret of the concussion broke upon us in one moment and at one view.

The spot from which we looked was not far from the summit of the highest peak in the range of the soapstone hills. The gorge in which our party of thirty-two had entered ran within fifty feet to the left of us. But, for at least one hundred yards, the channel or bed of this gorge was entirely filled up with the chaotic ruins of more than a million tons of earth and stone that had been artificially tumbled within it. The means by which the vast mass had been precipitated were not more simple than evident, for sure traces of the murderous work were yet remaining. In several spots along the top of the eastern side of the gorge (we were now on the western) might be seen stakes of wood driven into the earth. In these spots the earth had not given way; but throughout the whole extent of the face of the precipice from which the mass *had* fallen, it was clear, from marks left in the soil resembling those made by the drill of the rock blaster, that stakes similar to those we saw standing had been inserted, at not more than a yard apart, for the length of perhaps three hundred feet, and ranging at about ten feet back from the edge of the gulf. Strong cords of grapevine were attached to the stakes still remaining on the hill, and it was evident that such cords had also been attached to each of the other stakes. I have already spoken of the singular stratification of these soapstone hills; and the description just given of the narrow and deep fissure through which we effected our escape from inhumation will afford a further conception of its nature. This was such that almost every natural convulsion would be sure to split the soil into perpendicular layers or ridges running parallel with one another; and a very moderate exertion of art would be sufficient for effecting the same purpose. Of this stratification the savages had availed themselves to accomplish their treacherous ends. There can be no doubt that, by the continuous line of stakes, a partial rupture of the soil had been brought about, probably to the depth of one or two feet, when, by means of a savage pulling at the end of each of the cords (these cords being attached to the tops of the stakes, and extending back from the edge of the cliff), a vast leverage power was obtained, capable of hurling the whole face of the hill, upon a given signal, into the bosom of the abyss below. The fate of our poor companions was no longer a matter of uncertainty. We alone had escaped from the tempest of that overwhelming destruction. We were the only living white men upon the island.

CHAPTER 22

OUR SITUATION, as it now appeared, was scarcely less dreadful than when we had conceived ourselves entombed forever. We saw before us no prospect but that of being put to death by the savages, or of dragging out a miserable existence in captivity among them. We might, to be sure, conceal ourselves for a time from their observation among the fastnesses of the hills, and, as a final resort, in the chasm from which we had just issued; but we must either perish in the long Polar winter through cold and famine, or be ultimately discovered in our efforts to obtain relief.

The whole country around us seemed to be swarming with savages, crowds of whom, we now perceived, had come over from the islands to the southward on flat rafts, doubtless with a view of lending their aid in the capture and plunder of the *Jane*. The vessel still lay calmly at anchor in the bay, those on board being apparently quite unconscious of any danger awaiting them. How we longed at that moment to be with them! either to aid in effecting their escape, or to perish with them in attempting a defense. We saw no chance even of warning them of their danger without bringing immediate destruction upon our own heads, with but a remote hope of benefit to them. A pistol fired might suffice to apprise them that something wrong had occurred; but the report could not possibly inform them that their only prospect of safety lay in getting out of the harbor forthwith—it could not tell them that no principles of honor now bound them to remain, that their companions were no longer among the living. Upon hearing the discharge they could not be more thoroughly prepared to meet the foe, who were now getting ready to attack, than they already were, and always had been. No good, therefore, and infinite harm, would result from our firing, and, after mature deliberation, we forbore.

Our next thought was to attempt to rush toward the vessel, to seize one of the four canoes which lay at the head of the bay, and endeavor to force a passage on board. But the utter impossibility of succeeding in this desperate task soon became evident. The country, as I said before, was literally swarming with the natives, skulking among the bushes and recesses of the hills, so as not to be observed from the schooner. In our immediate vicinity especially, and blockading the sole path by which we could hope to attain the shore in the proper point, were stationed the whole party of the blackskin warriors, with Too-wit at their head, and apparently only waiting for some re-enforcement to commence his onset upon the *Jane*. The canoes, too, which lay at the head of the bay, were manned with savages, unarmed, it is true, but who undoubtedly had arms within reach. We were forced, therefore, however unwillingly, to remain in our place of concealment, mere spectators of the conflict which presently ensued.

In about half an hour we saw some sixty or seventy rafts, or flatboats, with outriggers, filled with savages, and coming round the southern bight of the harbor. They appeared to have no arms except short clubs, and stones which lay in the bottom of the rafts. Immediately afterward another detachment, still larger, approached in an opposite direction, and with similar weapons. The four canoes, too, were now quickly filled with natives, starting up from the bushes at the head of the bay, and put off swiftly to join the other parties. Thus, in less time than I have taken to tell it, and as if by magic, the *Jane* saw herself surrounded by an immense multitude of desperadoes evidently bent upon capturing her at all hazards.

That they would succeed in so doing could not be doubted for an instant. The six men left in the vessel, however resolutely they might engage in her defense, were altogether unequal to the proper management of the guns, or in any manner to sustain a contest at such odds. I could hardly imagine that they would make resistance at all, but in this was deceived; for presently I saw them get springs upon the cable, and bring the vessel's starboard broadside to bear upon the canoes, which by this time were within pistol range, the rafts being nearly a quarter of a mile to windward. Owing to some cause unknown, but most probably to the agitation of our poor friends at seeing themselves in so hopeless a situation, the discharge was an entire failure. Not a canoe was hit or a single savage injured, the shot striking short and *ricocheting* over their heads. The only effect produced upon them was astonishment at the unexpected report and smoke, which was so excessive that for some moments I almost thought they would abandon their design entirely, and return to the shore. And this they would most likely have done had our men followed up their broadside by a discharge of small arms, in which, as the canoes were now so near at hand, they could not have failed in doing some execution, sufficient, at least, to deter this party from a farther advance, until they could have given the rafts also a broadside. But, in place of this, they left the canoe party to recover from their panic, and, by looking about them, to see that no injury had been sustained, while they flew to the larboard to get ready for the rafts.

The discharge to larboard produced the most terrible effect. The star and double-headed shot of the large guns cut seven or eight of the rafts completely asunder, and killed, perhaps, thirty or forty of the savages outright, while a hundred of them, at least, were thrown into the water, the most of them dreadfully wounded. The remainder, frightened out of their senses, commenced at once a precipitate retreat, not even waiting to pick up their maimed companions, who were swimming about in every direction, screaming and yelling for aid. This great success, however, came too late for the salvation of our devoted people. The canoe party were already on board the schooner to the number of more than a hundred and fifty, the most of them having succeeded in scrambling up the chains and over the boarding nettings even before the matches had been applied to the larboard guns. Nothing now could withstand their brute rage. Our men were borne down at once, overwhelmed, trodden under foot, and absolutely torn to pieces in an instant.

Seeing this, the savages on the rafts got the better of their fears, and came up in shoals to the plunder. In five minutes the *Jane* was a pitiable scene indeed of havoc and tumultuous outrage. The decks were split open and ripped up; the cordage, sails, and everything movable on deck demolished as if by magic; while, by dint of pushing at the stern, towing with the canoes, and hauling at the sides, as they swam in thousands around the vessel, the wretches finally forced her on shore (the cable having been slipped), and delivered her over to the good offices of Too-wit, who, during the whole of the engagement, had remained, like a skillful general, his post of security and reconnoissance among the hills, but, now that the victory was completed to his satisfaction, condescended to scamper down with his warriors of the black skin, and become a partaker in the spoils.

Too-wit's descent left us at liberty to quit our hiding place and reconnoiter the hill in the vicinity of the chasm. At about fifty yards from the mouth of it we saw a small spring of water, at which we slaked the burning thirst that now consumed us. Not far from the spring we discovered several of the filbert bushes which I mentioned before. Upon tasting the nuts we found them palatable, and very nearly resembling in flavor the common English filbert. We collected our hats full immediately, deposited them within the ravine, and returned for more. While we were busily employed in gathering these, a rustling in the bushes alarmed us, and we were upon the point of stealing back to our covert, when a large black bird of the bittern species strugglingly and slowly arose above the shrubs. I was so much startled that I could do nothing, but Peters had sufficient presence of mind to run up to it before it could make its escape, and seize it by the neck. Its struggles and screams were tremendous, and we had thoughts of letting it go, lest the noise should alarm some of the savages who might be still lurking in the neighborhood. A stab with a Bowie knife, however, at length brought it to the ground, and we dragged it into the ravine, congratulating ourselves that, at all events, we had thus obtained a supply of food enough to last us for a week.

We now went out again to look about us, and ventured a considerable distance down the southern declivity of the hill, but met with nothing else which could serve us for food. We therefore collected a quantity of dry wood and returned, seeing one or two large parties of the natives on their way to the village, laden with the plunder of the vessel, and who, we were apprehensive, might discover us in passing beneath the hill.

Our next care was to render our place of concealment as secure as possible, and with this object, we arranged some brushwood over the aperture which I have before spoken of as the one through which we saw the patch of blue sky, on reaching the platform from the interior of the chasm. We left only a very small opening, just wide enough to admit of our seeing the bay, without the risk of being discovered from below. Having done this, we congratulated ourselves upon the security of the position; for we were now completely excluded from observation, as long as we chose to remain within the ravine itself, and not venture out upon the hill. We could perceive no traces of the savages having ever been within this hollow; but, indeed, when we came to reflect upon the probability that the fissure through which we attained it had been only just now created by the fall of the cliff opposite, and that no other way of attaining it could be perceived, we were not so much rejoiced at the thought of being secure from molestation as fearful lest there should be absolutely no means left us for descent. We resolved to explore the summit of the hill thoroughly, when a good opportunity should offer. In the meantime we watched the motions of the savages through our loophole.

They had already made a complete wreck of the vessel, and were now preparing to set her on fire. In a little while we saw the smoke ascending in huge volumes from her main hatchway, and, shortly afterward, a dense mass of flame burst up from the forecastle. The rigging, masts, and what remained of the sails caught immediately, and the fire spread rapidly along the decks.

Still a great many of the savages retained their stations about her, hammering with large stones, axes, and cannon balls at the bolts and other copper and ironwork. On the beach, and in canoes and rafts, there were not less, altogether, in the immediate vicinity of the schooner, than ten thousand natives, besides the shoals of them who, laden with booty, were making their way inland and over to the neighboring islands. We now anticipated a catastrophe, and were not disappointed. First of all there came a smart shock (which we felt as distinctly where we were as if we had been slightly galvanized), but unattended with any visible signs of an explosion. The savages were evidently startled, and paused for an instant from their labors and yellings. They were upon the point of recommencing, when suddenly a mass of smoke puffed up from the decks, resembling a black and heavy thundercloud—then, as if from its bowels, arose a tall stream of vivid fire to the height, apparently, of a quarter of a mile—then there came a sudden circular expansion of the flame—then the whole atmosphere was magically crowded, in a single instant, with a wild chaos of wood, and metal, and human limbs—and, lastly, came the concussion in its fullest fury, which hurled us impetuously from our feet, while the hills echoed and re-echoed the tumult, and a dense shower of the minutest fragments of the ruins tumbled headlong in every direction around us.

The havoc among the savages far exceeded our utmost expectation, and they had now, indeed, reaped the full and perfect fruits of their treachery. Perhaps a thousand perished by the explosion, while at least an equal number were desperately mangled. The whole surface of the bay was literally strewn with the struggling and drowning wretches, and on shore matters were even worse. They seemed utterly appalled by the suddenness and completeness of their discomfiture, and made no efforts at assisting one another. At length we observed a total change in their demeanor. From absolute stupor, they appeared to be, all at once, aroused to the highest pitch of excitement, and rushed wildly about, going to and from a certain point on the beach, with the strangest expressions of mingled horror, rage, and intense curiosity depicted on their countenances, and shouting, at the top of their voices, *Tekeli-li! Tekeli-li!*

Presently we saw a large body go off into the hills, whence they returned in a short time, carrying stakes of wood. These they brought to the station where the crowd was the thickest, which now separated so as to afford us a view of the object of all this excitement. We perceived something white lying upon the ground, but could not immediately make out what it was. At length we saw that it was the carcass of the strange animal with the scarlet teeth and claws which the schooner had picked up at sea on the eighteenth of January. Captain Guy had had the body preserved for the purpose of stuffing the skin and taking it to England. I remember he had given some directions about it just before our making the island, and it had been brought into the cabin and stowed away in one of the lockers. It had now been thrown on shore by the explosion; but why it had occasioned so much concern among the savages was more than we could comprehend. Although they crowded around the carcass at a little distance, none of them seemed willing to approach it closely. By-and-by the men with the stakes drove them in a circle around it, and, no sooner was this arrangement completed, than the whole of the vast assemblage rushed into the interior of the islands, with loud screams of *Tekeli-li! Tekeli-li!*

CHAPTER 23

DURING the six or seven days immediately following we remained in our hiding place upon the hill, going out only occasionally, and then with the greatest precaution, for water and filberts. We had made a kind of penthouse on the platform, furnishing it with a bed of dry leaves, and placing in it three large flat stones, which served us for both fireplace and table. We kindled a fire without difficulty by rubbing two pieces of dry wood together, the one soft, the other hard. The bird we had taken in such good season proved excellent eating, although somewhat tough. It was not an oceanic fowl, but a species of bittern, with jet black and grizzly plumage, and diminutive wings in proportion to its bulk. We afterward saw three of the same kind in the vicinity of the ravine, apparently seeking for the one we had captured; but, as they never alighted, we had no opportunity of catching them.

As long as this fowl lasted we suffered nothing from our situation, but it was now entirely consumed, and it became absolutely necessary that we should look out for provision. The filberts would not satisfy the cravings of hunger, afflicting us, too, with severe gripings of the bowels, and, if freely indulged in, with violent headache. We had seen several large tortoises near the seashore to the eastward of the hill, and perceived they might be easily taken, if we could get at them without the observation of the natives. It was resolved, therefore, to make an attempt at descending.

We commenced by going down the southern declivity, which seemed to offer the fewest difficulties, but had not proceeded a hundred yards before (as we had anticipated from appearances on the hilltop) our progress was entirely arrested by a branch of the gorge in which our companions had perished. We now passed along the edge of this for about a quarter of a mile, when we were again stopped by a precipice of immense depth, and, not being able to make our way along the brink of it, we were forced to retrace our steps by the main ravine.

We now pushed over to the eastward, but with precisely similar fortune. After an hour's scramble, at the risk of breaking our necks, we discovered that we had merely descended into a vast pit of black granite, with fine dust at the bottom, and whence the only egress was by the rugged path in which we had come down. Toiling again up this path, we now tried the northern edge of the hill. Here we were obliged to use the greatest possible caution in our maneuvers, as the least indiscretion would expose us to the full view of the savages in the village. We crawled along, therefore, on our hands and knees, and, occasionally, were even forced to throw ourselves at full length, dragging our bodies along by means of the shrubbery. In this careful manner we had proceeded but a little way, when we arrived at a chasm far deeper than any we had yet seen, and leading directly into the main gorge. Thus our fears were fully confirmed, and we found ourselves cut off entirely from access to the world below. Thoroughly exhausted by our exertions, we made the best of our way back to the platform, and, throwing ourselves upon the bed of leaves, slept sweetly and soundly for some hours.

For several days after this fruitless search we were occupied in exploring every part of the summit of the hill, in order to inform ourselves of its actual resources. We found that it would afford us no food, with the exception of the unwholesome filberts, and a rank species of scurvy grass, which grew in a little patch of not more than four rods square, and would be soon exhausted. On the fifteenth of February, as near as I can remember, there was not a blade of this left, and the nuts were growing scarce; our situation, therefore, could hardly be more lamentable.* On the sixteenth we again went round the walls of our prison, in hope of finding some avenue of escape, but to no purpose. We also

* This day was rendered remarkable by our observing in the south several huge wreaths of the grayish vapor I have before spoken of. (Poe's note.)

descended the chasm in which we had been overwhelmed, with the faint expectation of discovering, through this channel, some opening to the main ravine. Here, too, we were disappointed, although we found and brought up with us a musket.

On the seventeenth we set out with the determination of examining more thoroughly the chasm of black granite into which we had made our way in the first search. We remembered that one of the fissures in the sides of this pit had been but partially looked into, and we were anxious to explore it, although with no expectation of discovering here any opening.

We found no great difficulty in reaching the bottom of the hollow as before, and were now sufficiently calm to survey it with some attention. It was, indeed, one of the most singular looking places imaginable, and we could scarcely bring ourselves to believe it altogether the work of nature. The pit, from its eastern to its western extremity, was about five hundred yards in length, when all its windings were threaded; the distance from east to west in a straight line not being more (I should suppose, having no means of accurate examination) than forty or fifty yards. Upon first descending into the chasm, that is to say, for a hundred feet downward from the summit of the hill, the sides of the abyss bore little resemblance to each other, and, apparently, had at no time been connected, the one surface being of the soapstone, and the other of marl, granulated with some metallic matter. The average breadth, or interval between the two cliffs, was probably here sixty feet, but there seemed to be no regularity of formation. Passing down, however, beyond the limit spoken of, the interval rapidly contracted, and the sides began to run parallel, although for some distance farther, they were still dissimilar in their material and form of surface. Upon arriving within fifty feet of the bottom, a perfect regularity commenced. The sides were now entirely uniform in substance, in color, and in lateral direction, the material being a very black and shining granite, and the distance between the two sides, at all points facing each other, exactly twenty yards. The precise formation of the chasm will be best understood by means of a delineation taken upon the spot; for I had luckily with me a pocketbook and pencil, which I preserved with great care through a long series of subsequent adventure, and to which I am indebted for memoranda of many subjects which would otherwise have been crowded from my remembrance.

This figure (see Figure 1) gives the general outlines of the chasm, without the minor cavities in the sides, of which there were several, each cavity having a corresponding protuberance opposite. The bottom of the gulf was covered to the depth of three or four inches with a powder almost impalpable, beneath

FIGURE 1

which we found a continuation of the black granite. To the right, at the lower extremity, will be noticed the appearance of a small opening; this is the fissure alluded to above, and to examine which more minutely than before was the object of our second visit. We now pushed into it with vigor, cutting away a quantity of brambles which impeded us, and removing a vast heap of sharp flints somewhat resembling arrowheads in shape. We were encouraged to persevere, however, by perceiving some little light proceeding from the farther end. We at length squeezed our way for about thirty feet, and found that the aperture was a low and regularly formed arch, having a bottom of the same impalpable powder as that in the main chasm. A strong light now broke upon us, and, turning a short bend, we found ourselves in another lofty chamber, similar to the one we had left in every respect but longitudinal form. Its general figure is here given. (See Figure 2.)

FIGURE 2

The total length of this chasm, commencing at the opening *a* and proceeding round the curve *b* to the extremity *d*, is five hundred and fifty yards. At *c* we discovered a small aperture similar to the one through which we had issued from the other chasm, and this was choked up in the same manner with brambles and a quantity of the white arrowhead flints. We forced our way through it, finding it about forty feet long, and emerged into a third chasm. This, too, was precisely like the first, except in its longitudinal shape, which was thus. (See Figure 3.)

FIGURE 3   FIGURE 5

We found the entire length of the third chasm three hundred and twenty yards. At the point *a* was an opening about six feet wide, and extending fifteen feet into the rock, where it terminated in a bed of marl, there being no other chasm beyond, as we had expected. We were about leaving this fissure, into which very little light was admitted, when Peters called my attention to a range of singular looking indentures in the surface of the marl forming the termination of the cul-de-sac. With a very slight exertion of the imagination, the left, or most northerly of these indentures might have been taken for the intentional, although rude, representation of a human figure standing erect, with outstretched arm. The rest of them bore also some little resemblance to alphabetical characters, and Peters was willing, at all events, to adopt the idle opinion that they were really such. I convinced him of his error, finally, by directing his attention to the floor of the fissure, where, among the powder, we picked up, piece by piece, several large flakes of the marl, which had evidently been broken off by some convulsion from the surface where the indentures were found, and which had projecting points exactly fitting the indentures; thus proving them to have been the work of nature. Figure 4 presents an accurate copy of the whole.

FIGURE 4

After satisfying ourselves that these singular caverns afforded us no means of escape from our prison, we made our way back, dejected and dispirited, to the summit of the hill. Nothing worth mentioning occurred during the next twenty-four hours, except that, in examining the ground to the eastward of the third chasm, we found two triangular holes of great depth, and also with black granite sides. Into these holes we did not think it worth-while to attempt descending, as they had the appearance of mere natural wells, without outlet. They were each about twenty yards in circumference, and their shape, as well as relative position in regard to the third chasm, is shown in Figure 5 on page 185.

CHAPTER 24

ON THE TWENTIETH of the month, finding it altogether impossible to subsist any longer upon the filberts, the use of which occasioned us the most excruciating torment, we resolved to make a desperate attempt at descending the southern declivity of the hill. The face of the precipice was here of the softest species of soapstone, although nearly perpendicular throughout its whole extent (a depth of a hundred and fifty feet at the least), and in many places even overarching. After a long search we discovered a narrow ledge about twenty feet below the brink of the gulf; upon this Peters contrived to leap, with what assistance I could render him by means of our pocket handkerchiefs tied together. With somewhat more difficulty I also got down; and we then saw the possibility of descending the whole way by the process in which we had clambered up from the chasm when we had been buried by the fall of the hill—that is, by cutting steps in the face of the soapstone with our knives. The extreme hazard of the attempt can scarcely be conceived; but, as there was no other resource, we determined to undertake it.

Upon the ledge where we stood there grew some filbert bushes; and to one of these we made fast an end of our rope of handkerchiefs. The other end being tied round Peters' waist, I lowered him down over the edge of the precipice until the handkerchiefs were stretched tight. He now proceeded to dig a deep hole in the soapstone (as far in as eight or ten inches), sloping away the rock above to the height of a foot, or thereabout, so as to allow of his driving, with the butt of a pistol, a tolerably strong peg into the leveled surface. I then drew him up for about four feet, when he made a hole similar to the one below, driving in a peg as before, and having thus a resting place for both feet and

hands. I now unfastened the handkerchiefs from the bush, throwing him the end, which he tied to the peg in the uppermost hole,
letting himself down gently to a station about three feet lower
than he had yet been—that is, to the full extent of the handkerchiefs. Here he dug another hole, and drove another peg. He
then drew himself up, so as to rest his feet in the hole just cut,
taking hold with his hands upon the peg in the one above. It was
now necessary to untie the handkerchiefs from the topmost peg,
with the view of fastening them to the second; and here he found
that an error had been committed in cutting the holes at so great
a distance apart. However, after one or two unsuccessful and
dangerous attempts at reaching the knot (having to hold on with
his left hand while he labored to undo the fastening with his
right), he at length cut the string, leaving six inches of it affixed
to the peg. Tying the handkerchiefs now to the second peg,
he descended to a station below the third, taking care not to go
too far down. By these means (means which I should never have
conceived of myself, and for which we were indebted altogether
to Peters' ingenuity and resolution) my companion finally succeeded, with the occasional aid of projections in the cliff, in
reaching the bottom without accident.

It was some time before I could summon sufficient resolution
to follow him; but I did at length attempt it. Peters had taken
off his shirt before descending, and this, with my own, formed
the rope necessary for the adventure. After throwing down the
musket found in the chasm, I fastened this rope to the bushes,
and let myself down rapidly, striving, by the vigor of my movements, to banish the trepidation which I could overcome in no
other manner. This answered sufficiently well for the first four or
five steps; but presently I found my imagination growing terribly
excited by thoughts of the vast depth yet to be descended, and
the precarious nature of the pegs and soapstone holes which were
my only support. It was in vain I endeavored to banish these
reflections, and to keep my eyes steadily bent upon the flat
surface of the cliff before me. The more earnestly I struggled
not to think, the more intensely vivid became my conceptions,

and the more horribly distinct. At length arrived that crisis of fancy, so fearful in all similar cases, the crisis in which we begin to anticipate the feelings with which we *shall* fall—to picture to ourselves the sickness, and dizziness, and the last struggle, and the half swoon, and the final bitterness of the rushing and headlong descent. And now I found these fancies creating their own realities, and all imagined horrors crowding upon me in fact. I felt my knees strike violently together, while my fingers were gradually yet certainly relaxing their grasp. There was a ringing in my ears, and I said, "This is my knell of death!" And now I was consumed with the irrepressible desire of looking below. I could not, I would not, confine my glances to the cliff; and, with a wild, indefinable emotion, half of horror, half of a relieved oppression, I threw my vision far down into the abyss. For one moment my fingers clutched convulsively upon their hold, while, with the movement, the faintest possible idea of ultimate escape wandered, like a shadow, through my mind—in the next my whole soul was pervaded with *a longing to fall;* a desire, a yearning, a passion utterly uncontrollable. I let go at once my grasp upon the peg, and, turning half round from the precipice, remained tottering for an instant against its naked face. But now there came a spinning of the brain; a shrill-sounding and phantom voice screamed within my ears; a dusky, fiendish, and filmy figure stood immediately beneath me; and, sighing, I sunk down with a bursting heart, and plunged within its arms.

I had swooned, and Peters had caught me as I fell. He had observed my proceedings from his station at the bottom of the cliff; and perceiving my imminent danger, had endeavored to inspire me with courage by every suggestion he could devise; although my confusion of mind had been so great as to prevent my hearing what he said, or being conscious that he had even spoken to me at all. At length, seeing me totter, he hastened to ascend to my rescue, and arrived just in time for my preservation. Had I fallen with my full weight, the rope of linen would inevitably have snapped, and I should have been precipitated into the abyss; as it was, he contrived to let me down gently, so as to remain suspended without danger until animation returned. This was in about fifteen minutes. On recovery, my trepidation had entirely vanished; I felt a new being, and, with some little further aid from my companion, reached the bottom also in safety.

We now found ourselves not far from the ravine which had proved the tomb of our friends, and to the southward of the spot where the hill had fallen. The place was one of singular wildness, and its aspect brought to my mind the descriptions given by travelers of those dreary regions marking the site of degraded Babylon. Not to speak of the ruins of the disruptured cliff, which formed a chaotic barrier in the vista to the northward, the surface of the ground in every other direction was strewn with huge tumuli, apparently the wreck of some gigantic structures of art; although, in detail, no semblance of art could be detected. Scoriae were abundant, and large shapeless blocks of the black granite, intermingled with others of marl,* and both granulated with metal. Of vegetation there were no traces whatsoever throughout the whole of the desolate area within sight. Several immense scorpions were seen, and various reptiles not elsewhere to be found in the high latitudes.

As food was our most immediate object, we resolved to make our way to the seacoast, distant not more than half a mile, with a view of catching turtle, several of which we had observed from our place of concealment on the hill. We had proceeded some hundred yards, threading our route cautiously between the huge rocks and tumuli, when, upon turning a corner, five savages sprung upon us from a small cavern, felling Peters to the ground with a blow from a club. As he fell the whole party rushed upon him to secure their victim, leaving me time to recover from my astonishment. I still had the musket, but the barrel had received so much injury in being thrown from the precipice that I cast it aside as useless, preferring to trust my pistols, which had been carefully preserved in order. With these I advanced upon the assailants, firing one after the other in quick succession. Two

---

* The marl was also black; indeed, we noticed no light-colored substances of any kind upon the island. (Poe's note.)

savages fell, and one, who was in the act of thrusting a spear
into Peters, sprung to his feet without accomplishing his purpose.
My companion being thus released, we had no further difficulty.
He had his pistols also, but prudently declined using them,
confiding in his great personal strength, which far exceeded that
of any person I have ever known. Seizing a club from one of
the savages who had fallen, he dashed out the brains of the three
who remained, killing each instantaneously with a single blow
of the weapon, and leaving us completely masters of the field.

So rapidly had these events passed, that we could scarcely
believe in their reality, and were standing over the bodies of the
dead in a species of stupid contemplation, when we were
brought to recollection by the sound of shouts in the distance.
It was clear that the savages had been alarmed by the firing, and
that we had little chance of avoiding discovery. To regain the
cliff, it would be necessary to proceed in the direction of the
shouts; and even should we succeed in arriving at its base, we
should never be able to ascend it without being seen. Our situation was one of the greatest peril, and we were hesitating in
which path to commence a flight, when one of the savages whom
I had shot, and supposed dead, sprang briskly to his feet, and
attempted to make his escape. We overtook him, however, before
he had advanced many paces, and were about to put him to
death, when Peters suggested that we might derive some benefit
from forcing him to accompany us in our attempt at escape. We
therefore dragged him with us, making him understand that we
would shoot him if he offered resistance. In a few minutes he was
perfectly submissive, and ran by our sides as we pushed in among
the rocks, making for the seashore.

So far, the irregularities of the ground we had been traversing
hid the sea, except at intervals, from our sight, and, when we
first had it fairly in view, it was, perhaps, two hundred yards
distant. As we emerged into the open beach we saw, to our great
dismay, an immense crowd of the natives pouring from the
village, and from all visible quarters of the island, making
towards us with gesticulations of extreme fury, and howling like

wild beasts. We were upon the point of turning upon our steps, and trying to secure a retreat among the fastnesses of the rougher ground, when I discovered the bows of two canoes projecting from behind a large rock which ran out into the water. Towards these we now ran with all speed, and, reaching them, found them unguarded, and without any other freight than three of the large Gallipago turtles and the usual supply of paddles for sixty rowers. We instantly took possession of one of them, and, forcing our captive on board, pushed out to sea with all the strength we could command.

We had not made, however, more than fifty yards from the shore before we became sufficiently calm to perceive the great oversight of which we had been guilty in leaving the other canoe in the power of the savages, who, by this time, were not more than twice as far from the beach as ourselves, and were rapidly advancing to the pursuit. No time was now to be lost. Our hope was, at best, a forlorn one, but we had none other. It was very doubtful whether, with the utmost exertion, we could get back in time to anticipate them in taking possession of the canoe; but yet there was a chance that we could. We might save ourselves if we succeeded, while not to make the attempt was to resign ourselves to inevitable butchery.

The canoe was modeled with the bow and stern alike, and, in place of turning it round, we merely changed our position in paddling. As soon as the savages perceived this they redoubled their yells, as well as their speed, and approached with inconceivable rapidity. We pulled, however, with all the energy of desperation, and arrived at the contested point before more than one of the natives had attained it. This man paid dearly for his superior agility, Peters shooting him through the head with a pistol as he approached the shore. The foremost among the rest of his party were probably some twenty or thirty paces distant as we seized upon the canoe. We at first endeavored to pull her into the deep water, beyond the reach of the savages, but, finding her too firmly aground, and there being no time to spare, Peters, with one or two heavy strokes from the butt of the musket, succeeded in dashing out a large portion of the bow and of one side. We then pushed off. Two of the natives by this time had got hold of our boat, obstinately refusing to let go, until we were forced to dispatch them with our knives. We were now clear off, and making great way out to sea. The main body of the savages, upon reaching the broken canoe, set up the most tremendous yell of rage and disappointment conceivable. In truth, from everything I could see of these wretches, they appeared to be the most wicked, hypocritical, vindictive, bloodthirsty, and altogether fiendish race of men upon the face of the globe. It is clear we should have had no mercy had we fallen into their hands. They made a mad attempt at following us in the fractured canoe, but, finding it useless, again vented their rage in a series of hideous vociferations, and rushed up into the hills.

We were thus relieved from immediate danger, but our situation was still sufficiently gloomy. We knew that four canoes of the kind we had were at one time in the possession of the savages, and were not aware of the fact (afterward ascertained from our captive) that two of these had been blown to pieces in the explosion of the *Jane Guy*. We calculated, therefore, upon being yet pursued, as soon as our enemies could get round to the bay (distant about three miles) where the boats were usually laid up. Fearing this, we made every exertion to leave the island behind us, and went rapidly through the water, forcing the prisoner to take a paddle. In about half an hour, when we had gained, probably, five or six miles to the southward, a large fleet of the flat-bottomed canoes or rafts were seen to emerge from the bay, evidently with the design of pursuit. Presently they put back, despairing to overtake us.

CHAPTER 25

WE NOW FOUND ourselves in the wide and desolate Antarctic Ocean, in a latitude exceeding eighty-four degrees, in a frail canoe, and with no provision but the three turtles. The long Polar winter, too, could not be considered as far distant, and it became necessary that we should deliberate well upon the course to be pursued. There were six or seven islands in sight belonging to the same group, and distant from each other about five or six leagues; but upon neither of these had we any intention to venture. In coming from the northward in the *Jane Guy* we had been gradually leaving behind us the severest regions of ice —this, however little it may be in accordance with the generally received notions respecting the Antarctic, was a fact experience would not permit us to deny. To attempt, therefore, getting back, would be folly—especially at so late a period of the season. Only one course seemed to be left open for hope. We resolved to steer boldly to the southward, where there was at least a probability of discovering other lands, and more than a probability of finding a still milder climate.

So far we had found the Antarctic, like the Arctic Ocean, peculiarly free from violent storms or immoderately rough water; but our canoe was, at best, of frail structure, although large, and we set busily to work with a view of rendering her as safe as the limited means in our possession would admit. The body of the boat was of no better material than bark—the bark of a tree unknown. The ribs were of a tough osier, well adapted to the purpose for which it was used. We had fifty feet room from stem to stern, from four to six in breadth, and in depth throughout four feet and a half—the boats thus differing vastly in shape from those of any other inhabitants of the Southern Ocean with whom civilized nations are acquainted. We never did believe them the workmanship of the ignorant islanders who owned them; and some days after this period discovered, by questioning our captive, that they were in fact made by the natives of a group to the southwest of the country where we found them, having fallen accidentally into the hands of our barbarians. What we could do for the security of our boat was very little indeed. Several wide rents were discovered near both ends, and these we contrived to patch up with pieces of woollen jacket. With the help of the superfluous paddles, of which there were a great many, we erected a kind of framework about the bow, so as to break the force of any seas which might threaten to fill us in that quarter. We also set up two paddle blades for masts, placing them opposite each other, one by each gunwale, thus saving the necessity of a yard. To these masts we attached a sail made of our shirts—doing this with some difficulty, as here we could get no assistance from our prisoner whatever, although he had been willing enough to labor in all the other operations. The sight of the linen seemed to affect him in a very singular manner. He could not be prevailed upon to touch it or go near it, shuddering when we attempted to force him, and shrieking out, *Tekeli-li.*

Having completed our arrangements in regard to the security of the canoe, we now set sail to the south-southeast for the present, with the view of weathering the most southerly of the group in sight. This being done, we turned the bow full to the southward. The weather could by no means be considered disagreeable. We had a prevailing and very gentle wind from the northward, a smooth sea, and continual daylight. No ice whatever was to be seen; *nor did I ever see one particle of this after leaving the parallel of Bennett's Islet.* Indeed, the temperature of the water was here far too warm for its existence in any quantity. Having killed the largest of our tortoises, and obtained from him not only food but a copious supply of water, we continued on our course, without any incident of moment, for perhaps seven or eight days, during which period we must have proceeded a vast distance to the southward, as the wind blew constantly with us, and a very strong current set continually in the direction we were pursuing.

March 1.* Many unusual phenomena now indicated that we were entering upon a region of novelty and wonder. A high range of light gray vapor appeared constantly in the southern horizon, flaring up occasionally in lofty streaks, now darting from east to west, now from west to east, and again presenting a level and uniform summit—in short, having all the wild variations of the Aurora Borealis. The average height of this vapor, as apparent from our station, was about twenty-five degrees. The temperature of the sea seemed to be increasing momentarily, and there was a very perceptible alteration in its color.

March 2. Today, by repeated questioning of our captive, we came to the knowledge of many particulars in regard to the island of the massacre, its inhabitants, and customs—but with these how can I *now* detain the reader? I may say, however, that we learned there were eight islands in the group—that they were governed by a common king, named *Tsalemon* or *Psalemoun,* who resided in one of the smallest of the islands—that the black skins forming the dress of the warriors came from an animal of huge size to be found only in a valley near the court of the king— that the inhabitants of the group fabricated no other boats than the flat-bottomed rafts—the four canoes being all of the kind in their possession, and these having been obtained, by mere accident, from some large island in the southwest—that his own name was Nu-Nu—that he had no knowledge of Bennett's Islet—and that the appellation of the island we had left was *Tsalal.* The commencement of the words *Tsalemon* and *Tsalal* was given with a prolonged hissing sound, which we found it impossible to imitate, even after repeated endeavors, and which was precisely the same with the note of the black bittern we had eaten upon the summit of the hill.

March 3. The heat of the water was now truly remarkable,

---

* For obvious reasons I cannot pretend to strict accuracy in these dates. They are given principally with a view to perspicuity of narration, and as set down in my pencil memoranda. (Poe's note.)

and its color was undergoing a rapid change, being no longer transparent, but of a milky consistency and hue. In our immediate vicinity it was usually smooth, never so rough as to endanger the canoe—but we were frequently surprised at perceiving, to our right and left, at different distances, sudden and extensive agitations of the surface—these, we at length noticed, were always preceded by wild flickerings in the region of the vapor to the southward.

March 4. Today, with the view of widening our sail, the breeze from the northward dying away perceptibly, I took from my coat pocket a white handkerchief. Nu-Nu was seated at my elbow, and the linen accidentally flaring in his face, he became violently affected with convulsions. These were succeeded by drowsiness and stupor, and low murmurings of *Tekeli-li! Tekeli-li!*

March 5. The wind had entirely ceased, but it was evident that we were still hurrying on to the southward, under the influence of a powerful current. And now, indeed, it would seem reasonable that we should experience some alarm at the turn events were taking—but we felt none. The countenance of Peters indicated nothing of this nature, although it wore at times an expression I could not fathom. The Polar winter appeared to be coming on—but coming without its terrors. I felt a *numbness* of body and mind—a dreaminess of sensation—but this was all.

March 6. The gray vapor had now arisen many more degrees above the horizon, and was gradually losing its grayness of tint. The heat of the water was extreme, even unpleasant to the touch, and its milky hue was more evident than ever. Today a violent agitation of the water occurred very close to the canoe. It was attended, as usual, with a wild flaring up of the vapor at its summit, and a momentary division at its base. A fine white powder, resembling ashes—but certainly not such— fell over the canoe and over a large surface of the water, as the flickering died away among the vapor and the commotion subsided in the sea. Nu-Nu now threw himself on his face in the bottom of the boat, and no persuasions could induce him to arise.

March 7. This day we questioned Nu-Nu concerning the motives of his countrymen in destroying our companions; but he appeared to be too utterly overcome by terror to afford us any rational reply. He still obstinately lay in the bottom of the boat; and, upon our reiterating the questions as to the motive made use only of idiotic gesticulations, such as raising with his forefinger the upper lip, and displaying the teeth which lay beneath it. These were black. We had never before seen the teeth of an inhabitant of Tsalal.

March 8. Today there floated by us one of the white animals whose appearance upon the beach at Tsalal had occasioned so wild a commotion among the savages. I would have picked it up, but there came over me a sudden listlessness, and I forbore. The heat of the water still increased, and the hand could no longer be endured within it. Peters spoke little, and I knew not what to think of his apathy. Nu-Nu breathed, and no more.

March 9. The white ashy material fell now continually around us, and in vast quantities. The range of vapor to the southward had arisen prodigiously in the horizon, and began to assume more distinctness of form. I can liken it to nothing but a limitless cataract, rolling silently into the sea from some immense and far-distant rampart in the heaven. The gigantic curtain ranged along the whole extent of the southern horizon. It emitted no sound.

March 21. A sullen darkness now hovered above us—but from out the milky depths of the ocean a luminous glare arose, and stole up along the bulwarks of the boat. We were nearly overwhelmed by the white ashy shower which settled upon us and upon the canoe, but melted into the water as it fell. The summit of the cataract was utterly lost in the dimness and the distance. Yet we were evidently approaching it with a hideous velocity. At intervals there were visible in it wide, yawning, but momentary rents, and from out these rents, within which was a chaos of flitting and indistinct images, there came rushing and mighty, but soundless winds, tearing up the enkindled ocean in their course.

March 22. The darkness had materially increased, relieved only by the glare of the water thrown back from the white curtain before us. Many gigantic and pallidly white birds flew continuously now from beyond the veil, and their scream was the eternal *Tekeli-li!* as they retreated from our vision. Here-upon Nu-Nu stirred in the bottom of the boat; but upon touching him, we found his spirit departed. And now we rushed into the embraces of the cataract, where a chasm threw itself open to receive us. But there arose in our pathway a shrouded human figure, very far larger in its proportions than any dweller among men. And the hue of the skin of the figure was of the perfect whiteness of the snow.

NOTE

THE CIRCUMSTANCES connected with the late sudden and distressing death of Mr. Pym are already well known to the public through the medium of the daily press. It is feared that the few remaining chapters which were to have completed his narrative, and which were retained by him, while the above were in type, for the purpose of revision, have been irrecoverably lost through the accident by which he perished himself. This, however, may prove not to be the case, and the papers, if ultimately found, will be given to the public.

No means have been left untried to remedy the deficiency. The gentleman whose name is mentioned in the preface, and who, from the statement there made, might be supposed able to fill the vacuum, has declined the task—this, for satisfactory reasons connected with the general inaccuracy of the details afforded him, and his disbelief in the entire truth of the latter portions of the narration. Peters, from whom some information might be expected, is still alive, and a resident of Illinois, but cannot be met with at present. He may hereafter be found, and will, no doubt, afford material for a conclusion of Mr. Pym's account.

The loss of two or three final chapters (for there were but two or three) is the more deeply to be regretted, as, it cannot be doubted, they contained matter relative to the Pole itself, or at least to regions in its very near proximity; and as, too, the statements of the author in relation to these regions may shortly be verified or contradicted by means of the governmental expedition now preparing for the Southern Ocean.

On one point in the narrative some remarks may be well offered; and it would afford the writer of this appendix much pleasure if what he may here observe should have a tendency to throw credit, in any degree, upon the very singular pages now published. We allude to the chasms found in the island of Tsalal, and to the whole of the figures upon pages 184-186.

Mr. Pym has given the figures of the chasms without comment, and speaks decidedly of the *indentures* found at the extremity of the most easterly of these chasms as having but a fanciful resemblance to alphabetical characters, and, in short, as being positively *not such.* This assertion is made in a manner so simple, and sustained by a species of demonstrations so conclusive, viz. (the fitting of the projections of the fragments found among the dust into the indentures upon the wall), that we are forced to believe the writer in earnest; and no reasonable reader should suppose otherwise. But as the facts in relation to *all* the figures are most singular (especially when taken in connection with statements made in the body of the narrative), it may be as well to say a word or two concerning them all—this, too, the more especially as the facts in question have, beyond doubt, escaped the attention of Mr. Poe.

Figure 1, then, Figure 2, Figure 3, and Figure 5, when conjoined with one another in the precise order which the chasms themselves presented, and when deprived of the small lateral branches or arches (which, it will be remembered, served only as a means of communication between the main chambers, and were of totally distinct character), constitute an Ethiopian verbal root—the root ${\Omega}$ "To be shady"—whence all the inflections of shadow or darkness.

In regard to the "left or most northwardly" of the indentures in Figure 4, it is more than probable that the opinion of Peters was correct, and that the hieroglyphical appearance was really the work of art, and intended as the representation of a human form. The delineation is before the reader, and he may, or may not, perceive the resemblance suggested; but the rest of the indentures afford strong confirmation of Peters' idea. The upper range is evidently the Arabic verbal root "To be white," whence all the inflections of brilliancy and whiteness. The lower range is not so immediately perspicuous. The characters are somewhat broken and disjointed; nevertheless, it cannot be doubted that, in their perfect state, they formed the full Egyptian word, ⊓&℧Ƴ𝖯𝖧𝖢, "The region of the south." It should be observed that these interpretations confirm the opinion of Peters in regard to the "most northwardly" of the figures. The arm is outstretched towards the south.

Conclusions such as these open a wide field for speculation and exciting conjecture. They should be regarded, perhaps, in connection with some of the most faintly detailed incidents of the narrative; although in no visible manner is this chain of connection complete. *Tekeli-li!* was the cry of the affrighted natives of Tsalal upon discovering the carcass of the *white* animal picked up at sea. This also was the shuddering exclamation of the captive Tsalalian upon encountering the *white* materials in possession of Mr. Pym. This also was the shriek of the swift-flying, *white*, and gigantic birds which issued from the vapory *white* curtain of the South. Nothing *white* was to be found at Tsalal, and nothing otherwise in the subsequent voyage to the region beyond. It is not impossible that "Tsalal," the appellation of the island of the chasms, may be found, upon minute philological scrutiny, to betray either some alliance with the chasms themselves, or some reference to the Ethiopian characters so mysteriously written in their windings.

"I have graven it within the hills, and my vengeance upon the dust within the rock."